'Can you not think of someone you might recommend, Andrew? Will you not save me from taking the next fortune-hunter that crosses my path?'

'Are you playing a game with me?' Andrew stopped walking, turning to look into her eyes. 'If this is your idea of amusement we may banter and then forget it—but if you are in earnest I shall give the matter some serious thought. However, I think you must give yourself a little more time.'

Mariah pouted. 'Must I? Very well. I am prepared to wait a few months longer, if I must, but please take me seriously. If you cannot help me I may have to decide for myself—and then I might make a mistake. How would you feel with that on your conscience? I am a lonely widow at the mercy of unscrupulous men—and I am asking you for help. Ignore me at your peril.'

'My hands are tied for the moment. Come, can you truly not wait a little longer to find a husband who will love and care for you?'

'If he was the right man I would wait for ever,' Mariah said, and for once she was not laughing. Her heart raced. Surely he must know what was in her mind? She could not have been plainer...

SECRETS AND SCANDALS

Nothing stays secret for long
in Regency Society!

The truth threatens to reveal a scandal
for all three couples in this
exciting new trilogy from

Anne Herries

THE DISAPPEARING DUCHESS—
February 2012

THE MYSTERIOUS LORD MARLOWE—
March 2012

THE SCANDALOUS LORD LANCHESTER—
April 2012

You can also find these as ebooks
at www.millsandboon.co.uk

THE SCANDALOUS LORD LANCHESTER

Anne Herries

First published in Great Britain 2012
by Mills & Boon, an imprint of Harlequin (UK) Limited.
Harlequin (UK) Limited, Eton House, 18-24 Paradise Road,
Richmond, Surrey TW9 1SR

© Anne Herries 2012

ISBN: 978 0 263 22907 3

Harlequin (UK) policy is to use papers that are natural, renewable and recyclable products and made from wood grown in sustainable forests. The logging and manufacturing process conform to the legal environmental regulations of the country of origin.

Printed and bound in Great Britain
by CPI Antony Rowe, Chippenham, Wiltshire

Anne Herries lives in Cambridgeshire, where she is fond of watching wildlife, and spoils the birds and squirrels that are frequent visitors to her garden. Anne loves to write about the beauty of nature, and sometimes puts a little into her books—although they are mostly about love and romance. She writes for her own enjoyment, and to give pleasure to her readers. She is a winner of the Romantic Novelists' Association Romance Prize. She invites readers to contact her on her website: www.lindasole.co.uk

Previous novels by the same author:

THE RAKE'S REBELLIOUS LADY
A COUNTRY MISS IN HANOVER SQUARE*
AN INNOCENT DEBUTANTE IN
  HANOVER SQUARE*
THE MISTRESS OF HANOVER SQUARE*
FORBIDDEN LADY†
THE LORD'S FORCED BRIDE†
THE PIRATE'S WILLING CAPTIVE†
HER DARK AND DANGEROUS LORD†
BOUGHT FOR THE HAREM
HOSTAGE BRIDE
THE DISAPPEARING DUCHESS**
THE MYSTERIOUS LORD MARLOWE**

A Season in Town trilogy
†*The Melford Dynasty*
***Secrets and Scandals*

And in the Regency series
The Steepwood Scandal:

LORD RAVENSDEN'S MARRIAGE
COUNTERFEIT EARL

And in *The Hellfire Mysteries*:

AN IMPROPER COMPANION
A WEALTHY WIDOW
A WORTHY GENTLEMAN

Prologue

See Naples and die. Those romantic words could be taken two ways. Andrew, Lord Lanchester, smiled wryly as he looked at the rundown hovels along the waterfront and knew them to be the haunt of knaves, cutthroats and thieves. Was he truly likely to find the man he sought in those rundown hovels? Looking about him at the peeling paint and trying not to gag on the stench of the gutters, Andrew frowned. The man he was searching for was a rogue and a thief and *his* journey would in all probability be a wasted one. Yet he had no choice if he wanted to clear his own name of the shadow that hung over it.

For the moment his commanding officer had promised to keep silent about the letter accusing Andrew of stealing regimental silver worth more than ten thousand pounds.

'You know I would take your word above anyone's, Lanchester, but the fact remains that the silver was stolen at a time when you were in charge of its safe-keeping—and this letter accuses you of taking it.'

'I swear to you, Harrison, that I am innocent of the crime. Yes, at the time I was a little short of funds for a while. It was difficult, I shall not deny it, but I solved my problem. Of what possible use would the silver be to me? If it was melted down, the metal would be worth only a fraction of its true worth and it must be impossible to sell.'

'Unless it was taken abroad somewhere.'

'Even so…' Andrew felt a spurt of anger. 'You think that my visit to Italy at about that time might have been for such a purpose?'

'I have not said I suspect you, Lanchester. Curb your pride, man. If I wished, I could take this to headquarters and have you brought to a court-martial—but I am as certain as it is possible to be that whoever took the silver meant to implicate you. My opinion is that you have an enemy. Think carefully, Andrew—who hates you enough to want you brought down?'

'I have no idea. As far as I know I have no enemies—at least none that would go to such lengths to ruin me.'

'There must be someone…what about Lieutenant Gordon? Did you not have him disciplined for cheating at cards and general behaviour unworthy of a gentleman and officer?'

'William Gordon?' Andrew wrinkled his brow. 'Good grief, I had forgotten that—it was so long ago. He offered his resignation and disappeared a few months later. Wasn't there some scandal over another officer's wife?'

'Yes. The officer wanted it hushed up, but Gordon was asked to resign. The last I heard he inherited a small estate, gambled most of it away in a few weeks and disappeared abroad. I believe he was in Italy for a time, though I've heard nothing for ages. He might even be dead.'

'Lieutenant Gordon…' Andrew was thoughtful. 'It is possible, of course, though I do not see why he should hate me that much.'

'I do not say it is Gordon, but someone wants you discredited. Are you in someone's way? Who would benefit if you were socially ruined—or dead?' Andrew raised his brows, but Major Harrison looked grim. 'You wouldn't be the first man to take his own life because he couldn't stand the stigma of social disgrace. Even a whisper might spoil your chances of a good marriage, for instance. Someone might hope for more than your ruin.'

'Yes, I see that…the devil of it is that I had been thinking I might make a certain lady an offer. This changes things. Obviously, I cannot even consider marriage until I've cleared my name.'

Chapter One

Mariah, widow and spoiled darling of the late Lord Winston Fanshawe, stood at the window of her bedchamber and surveyed the scene before her. The lakes were undoubtedly beautiful. On this cloudless day of warm sunshine the water lay glistening, sparkling like blue diamonds, and the surrounding countryside was glorious. She thought she actually preferred the lakes to the other parts of Italy they had visited these past few months. Mariah and her travelling companions, Lord and Lady Hubert, were staying in a villa overlooking Lake Como. Only a short distance from Milan, it was more secluded than some of the other lakes and the woods were delightful. Her friends had spoiled her throughout the trip, deferring to her needs and preferences, going out of their way to make her happy.

Why, then, did her throat catch and her eyes fill too easily with tears? Why did she feel so alone, even when in the midst of friends? Surely it was not because of her recent unpleasant experiences at the hands of Captain Blake? He had kidnapped her and kept her drugged when she refused to give him what he wanted, which was her hand in marriage and her fortune.

Such an ordeal might have broken another woman, but Mariah had recovered swiftly. No, it was not that painful episode that had brought on this feeling of loneliness, but something more personal.

She sighed, feeling restless, already considering where she would go next. Nowhere was home to her, despite the fact that she had several properties left to her by her late husband. Since his death she had wandered from place to place, never feeling settled for more than a few days. Even when staying with her long-time friend, Justin, Duke of Avonlea, and his lovely wife Lucinda, she had felt alone—empty inside.

Just what was she searching for?

'Mariah, dearest. We have a visitor—will you come down?'

Turning, she looked at Sylvia, Lady Hubert, the friend who had done so much to help her forget her troubles these past months. She had needed to get away from England after her abduction and Sylvia had suggested she join them on this trip.

Mariah did not recall much of her ordeal. The men who had kidnapped her had subdued her with some kind of a foul drug. She thought a cloth soaked in a strong-smelling solution had been placed over her nose and mouth in the carriage as she tried to assist Jane. Her brave, impetuous friend Jane, who had pretended to be her in the hope that they would let Mariah go. She was so fond of the girl she'd known for most of her life—and of Jane's brother, Andrew.

Thoughts of Andrew Lanchester made Mariah's hands clench at her sides. She refused to break her heart for the foolish man! He was probably still mooning over Lucinda Avonlea. Surely he must know that Justin's wife was deeply in love with her husband? Mariah tossed her head. If she allowed herself to think of him, she would be a fool indeed.

'You ought to come down, dearest.' Sylvia's words broke into her thoughts. 'It will seem odd if you do not.'

'Must I?' she asked in answer to Sylvia's question. They had so many visitors that it sometimes seemed she could never be quiet. 'Who is it this morning?'

'Someone you will be pleased to see, I think. He brings you letters from home—and claims to be a friend.'

Mariah's breath caught in her throat and her heart started to thump madly. 'Is it…Lord Lanchester?' she asked, trying to keep the excitement from her voice. 'He did say he might visit…'

'Do you know the gentleman?'

'Yes. He is Justin's neighbour and perfectly respectable.'

'I did not doubt it.' Lady Hubert smiled. 'Well, shall you come?'

'Yes, of course.' Mariah smiled. 'Give me a moment to tidy my hair. I shall not be long.'

As her friend departed, she glanced at herself in the mirror, patting her heavy dark blonde hair, which she wore caught up in a knot at the nape of her neck, and tweaking a few tendrils about her face. Despite walking in the sunshine most days, her skin still had that perfect English-rose colouring that was so much admired.

Her pulses raced as she left her room and walked down the wide marble staircase. The villa, set in amongst trees, which clung to the hillsides surrounding the lake, was a rather magnificent one and belonged to Count Paolo. He was a particular friend of Lord Hubert and had lent it to them for two months, while he was away in Venice on business.

Mariah's feeling of ennui had fled, her nerves tingling with excitement. What would Andrew have to say to her? A few months ago she had thought he was on the verge of making her an offer, then he had seemed to draw back. What had she done to make him change his mind? Could she have mistaken the signs? So many men went out of their way to flatter and court her, but Andrew Lanchester was different. She had hoped for a time that he had come to admire and appreciate her for what she was—a woman of spirit with a mind of her own.

Entering the salon where the company was gathered, she saw Sylvia and Lord Hubert laughing at something their visitor had just said and her heart caught. When Andrew Lanchester was smiling he was such a handsome man, his dark hair and his expressive eyes giving him an air of distinction. He was a man of integrity, a little stern at times, but good company. As Andrew turned to look at her she drew a deep breath, feeling slightly shaky.

'Lady Fanshawe—Mariah,' he said, coming towards her, his hand outstretched. 'How are you? I trust your tour of Italy has improved your health?'

Mariah laughed. 'I was not ill, Andrew,' she said, giving him a challenging look. He had not been so formal when she stayed at his home the previous year. 'I am not such a goose that a little thing like abduction would cause me to go into a decline. No, no, I needed a change, that is all—and my good friends look after me very well.'

'I am glad to hear it,' Andrew said, but a frown creased his brow. 'Jane and Lucinda send their love. I have some letters for you—one from Justin concerning some business, I believe. He did not wish to entrust it to the post and so gave it to me.'

'Thank you for giving up your time to bring it to me.' Mariah said, keeping her emotions under strict control. 'I believe Jane is to be congratulated? Her letter reached us after much delay. I should have liked to see her married, but had no idea of her intention before we left. I shall visit her when we return to England—and I must buy her a gift.'

'I am sure she will be pleased to see you,' Andrew said. 'How are you enjoying your visit? I know this is not the first time you have visited Italy—but have you been to the lakes before?'

'Winston brought me here on our honeymoon,' Mariah said, her throat catching. 'We spent most of our time visiting the lakes and then Venice. It was after we left Venice to return to Milan that Winston's illness worsened. That was the first time I realised that my husband would not live long.'

Mariah's voice was husky with remembered grief. The knowledge that her kind and loving husband would soon die had almost broken her. It was only then that she understood how much she truly loved her husband. She had wed him out of pique—after Justin Avonlea had proposed to her from a sense of duty—and the desire to be spoiled, to be rich and indulged, admired and envied wherever she went. However, his care of her and his generous spirit had made her love him and she had been devastated by the thought of losing him.

'My husband did not wish to return to England to die. He loved the sunshine and it made him happy to spend his last days here.'

'I did not realise that,' Andrew said, his gaze narrowed.

'I do not normally speak of that time because it upsets me.'

Mariah turned away, blinking back the foolish tears that had unaccountably come to her eyes. Surely she was over her husband's death by now, so what had brought this mood on? Was it seeing Andrew again after having given up all hope of him?

Her silence had caused a moment of awkwardness, swiftly covered by Sylvia. 'It is so pleasant to see acquaintances from home,' she said. 'I do hope you will dine with us this evening, Lord Lanchester. I am giving a little dinner party for friends and would be delighted if you could join us.'

'I should be honoured to make one of your party,' Andrew said. 'Mariah, I have some messages from Lucinda. She was quite close to her confinement when I left England. Would you give me a few minutes of your time—perhaps a walk in the gardens?'

'Yes, why not?' Mariah took the arm he offered, smiling as she bid her heart to behave. 'I should like to hear how she goes on. Had she not been in a delicate situation when we left, I think she would have liked to accompany us to Italy.'

'I am perfectly certain she would,' Andrew replied, drawing her out into the garden. 'She spoke of visiting you if you were still here next spring. The babe will be old enough to travel with her nurse by then.'

'Poor Andrew,' Mariah said softly. 'I think you like Lucinda very well, do you not?'

'I am fond of them both. Justin is a good friend,' Andrew said and hesitated, then, 'But tell me, Mariah, are you truly over that unpleasant business of last year?'

'It does not keep me awake at night,' she replied. 'I must accept that my fortune attracts the wrong sort of suitor, Andrew. I had hoped that I might receive an offer from a gentleman I could trust, but unfortunately I have not met anyone I think would make me a comfortable husband.'

'You will not want a gambler, of course,' Andrew said and looked thoughtful. 'What are your requirements?'

'Oh, someone with good manners, a man I can respect and rely on to care for me and any children we may have.'

'That is a very modest list.' Andrew arched his right brow. 'I would have expected more—a sense of humour at the very least, good looks and a fortune to match your own.'

'I think it would be foolish to set my standards too high. I might have sought love once, but now I think I would settle for liking and respect. What I do not want is a man who thinks only of my fortune.'

'I see…' He was silent, thoughtful, then, 'Would you like me to investigate some of your suitors—discover whether or not they are desperate for money or perhaps more respectable than you might imagine?'

'Would you?' Mariah avoided his eyes. If she revealed too much, she might give herself away and that might lead to humiliation. 'If you were to escort me while you stay here, Andrew, it might scare the fortune hunters away.' She braced herself, turning to smile at him. 'Now tell me what Lucinda had to say that she did not write in her letters…'

After the visitors had gone, Mariah draped a stole over her arms and went for a walk to the top of the hill. Sylvia had chattered on about the visitors until she was driven by the need to be alone for a short time.

Her emotions were at breaking point, and she was torn by a mixture of despair and anger.

How could Andrew be so blind? To offer to vet her suitors for her was so frustrating that it had taken all Mariah's strength of will not to scream at him.

As a young girl living at Avonlea, Mariah had had a crush on their handsome neighbour, but Andrew hadn't noticed her. His manner had been that of a brother and he had treated her either with indifference or with a lofty scorn that had often driven her to tears in those years of growing into a young woman. He'd gone to London on a visit and come back a different man; then, all of a sudden, she'd learned that he'd joined the army. His leaving had broken her heart, but Mariah had forgotten him as the years passed and she grew into a beautiful young woman with a string of admirers and friends—but somehow she hadn't fallen in love with anyone.

'Oh, damn it,' Mariah said aloud. 'Winston, why did you have to leave me?' She was so alone and at times felt desperate. Must she live like this for the rest of her life, relying on friends for company, never having someone special of her own?

She turned away from the edge of the cliff and began to walk blindly through the woods, holding back her tears. She was angry with life and with herself for not having more sense and saw nothing until she heard an exclamation of alarm and then a pair of strong hands reached out and grabbed her arm.

'Forgive me,' an English voice said. 'If you continue to walk in that direction, you may fall over the edge. There is a steep trail just beyond those trees and at one place there has been a recent fall of rock. It ought to be fenced off to save the unwary from accident.'

'Oh…thank you,' Mariah said and looked into the face of a man she could only describe as handsome in a dark, rather forbidding way. 'Forgive me. I almost walked into you. My mind was wandering.'

'I am glad to have been of service,' he said and inclined his head to her. 'My name is Peter Grainger—Lieutenant Grainger—and I have recently arrived in the district. My aunt and uncle have rented a villa at the other side of the lake and I was out on a walk when I discovered the fall. Are you staying near by, ma'am? Forgive me, I do not know your name.'

'Mariah Fanshawe,' she replied, a faint blush in her cheeks as she saw how intently he was staring at her. 'I am staying with Lord and Lady Hubert—we are farther down the hill, nearer the lake. I walked up here to enjoy the view, but I am a little out of my way. Your warning was timely, sir.'

The man tipped his hat to her. 'It was nothing really. So, do you stay long, Miss Fanshawe?'

'I am Lady Fanshawe and a widow,' Mariah replied. Something in his manner made her slightly uncomfortable, though she couldn't pinpoint exactly what it was about him that aroused her suspicions. 'We have not yet decided how long we shall stay.'

'Forgive me, I did not realise.' His eyes went over her, seeming to note that she was wearing a gown of white muslin trimmed with pink, her shoes white leather and her gloves white cotton, edged at the wrists with the same pink that trimmed her gown and was repeated in her stole. Regrettably she wore no hat, having ignored Sylvia's advice to put one on before she left. 'Perhaps we shall meet again, Lady Fanshawe.' He tipped his hat and turned away.

Mariah stared after him for a moment, biting her lip. She was so foolish. He had been perfectly respectable and she had offended him by her brusque tone. He could not have known she was entitled to the use of a title. Besides, she did not normally remind people of it. What was the matter with her? Did she think of herself as so worthless that every man must be a fortune hunter if they showed an interest?

Turning in the direction of the Huberts' villa, she walked quickly, blinking away the stupid tears. Was it too much to want to be loved for herself? What must a man do to convince her that he was uninterested in her late husband's fortune?

She had become suspicious of everyone and that was wrong. Wrong and foolish! Mariah must learn to trust again. If she wished to find happiness in marriage, she must give gentlemen the chance to win her trust rather than treating them all with the same level of suspicion.

If only Andrew Lanchester had shown some interest in her. Mariah was almost sure she was in love with him. He was the kind of strong, silent man that appealed to her nature—the kind of man who might succeed in keeping her interest above a few weeks. With a little encouragement she could have given him her heart, her person and her fortune—but after seeming to approve of her, he had withdrawn again and she did not know why. He was a friend, but it seemed he had no warmer feelings for her.

Shaking her head, she walked quickly towards the villa. There was no point on dwelling on the past. She had come to the conclusion that she needed a husband. If it was not to be Andrew Lanchester, then it must be someone else.

Next time she met an attractive man she would smile and keep an open mind. If she continued to refuse all offers, she would end a lonely old maid.

'Lanchester…' Andrew heard himself hailed as he left the inn at which he had chosen to stay for a few days while visiting the lakes. He stopped and frowned as he sought for recognition, then smiled at the younger man. 'What do you here, sir?'

'I am visiting a friend,' Andrew replied. 'I had some business in Naples, which came to naught, and took a detour to visit a place of outstanding beauty. Are you here alone?'

'No, with my aunt and uncle. I heard you had resigned your commission. I hope there is nothing amiss?'

'Why do you ask?' Andrew frowned, then recollected his manners. Lieutenant Grainger was not his enemy. They had been friends of a sort, though the younger man was his junior. 'Yes, I decided that the time had come to settle down and look after my estate. I heard you might be up for promotion?'

'It was on the cards, but I may also be leaving the service soon. My uncle suffered a severe illness some months ago and needs to spend more time in the sun. My aunt asked me to help them get settled out here—and, as they have no other heir, her husband wishes me to take up residence at their estate in England and assume the running of the place.'

'Shall you oblige them?'

'Yes, I think so. Where are you staying?'

'Here at the inn.'

'That won't do, Lanchester. We have plenty of room at the villa. I know I speak for my aunt when I say we should be happy for you to join us. Come and have dinner with us this evening. If you should care for it, you could stay with us for a few days. To be honest, I wouldn't mind your advice about a few things...'

'I am unable to dine this evening,' Andrew said. 'But if I can be of any help I shall be delighted to give whatever advice or practical assistance I may.'

'I am glad I ran into you, Lanchester. My aunt will be delighted to meet you. She is feeling a little lost, anxious about finding the right place. They have rented a villa, but may also need something in Milan. My understanding of the language is not as good as I would like.'

'Then I may be able to help,' Andrew said. 'I shall come back with you now and we may talk...'

Andrew was thoughtful as he matched his steps with the lieutenant's. His meeting with Mariah that morning had been less promising than he'd hoped. It had been in his mind to tell her about his problem, because he was aware that at one time she might have been justified in believing he was considering making her an offer. If he told her that he could not think of marriage until he had cleared his name of this shadow of doubt, she might understand why he had let her down.

Mariah was beautiful, intelligent and wealthy. How could he expect that a woman like that would be prepared to sit around twiddling her thumbs while he floundered about trying to discover an enemy—an enemy who might or might not be Lieutenant William Gordon? The answer was that of course he could not expect it. Mariah had made it clear that she wanted to marry soon.

Even if he were free of the stain on his character, was she the woman he wanted above all others? At times he was so certain that his inability to speak almost choked him with frustration, but at others...at others he was not quite as sure. Mariah needed a husband—but would any man do? She'd married once for money and her husband had spoiled her. Would she expect to be indulged and given her own way again? Was that quite what Andrew wanted from a wife?

Dismissing his confused thoughts, Andrew turned his attention to his companion. Peter Grainger was a fellow officer. It was just possible that he might know where William Gordon was to be found, though he must be careful how he put it. Until he was certain who was behind this business, he must make no accusations.

Chapter Two

'That rose silk becomes you so well, dearest,' Sylvia said as they prepared to go down and welcome their guests that evening. 'I am so glad that you have decided to wear colours again.'

'As you have told me many times, Winston would not wish me to mourn him for ever,' Mariah said and smiled at her. Sylvia was a pretty, diminutive lady with a charming smile and good manners, and sincere in her affections. 'I have decided to put the past behind me, Sylvia. I shall cease to look at every gentleman I meet with suspicion and enjoy being courted. I do not wish to live alone for the rest of my life and I cannot always be in the company of friends. It is my intention to marry soon.'

'As to that, you know you are welcome to live with us, Mariah.'

'You are so generous. Andrew told me that Lucinda has said much the same. She wants me to consider returning to Avonlea when I've had enough of Italy—though how anyone could ever be tired of such a glorious place I do not know.'

'I do so agree with you,' Sylvia said, looking fondly at her.

'If Hubert had no estates to worry him I should prevail on him to stay for another six months at the very least. However, two months more is as long as he can spare and so we shall have to leave in a few weeks so that the journey home is achieved in easy stages.'

'Yes, I know. Besides, there are pleasures to be had at home,' Mariah said. 'Winston has a beautiful country house. I have no desire to live there and shall probably let it to tenants, but they must of course be the right tenants. I think I would prefer to live in London with visits to Bath, Avonlea—and, of course, Italy, whenever I can prevail on someone to bear me company.'

'I would not turn down the chance another year. We could always travel with friends if Hubert could not find the time to accompany us,' Sylvia said. 'But you may be married by then, dearest. Your husband will wish to travel with you no doubt.'

'Perhaps…' Mariah looked wistful. 'Andrew kindly offered to vet my suitors for me. I think I shall accept his help. I have made up my mind that I would be more comfortable married to a decent man. I wanted to fall in love—but perhaps I should settle for a comfortable arrangement.'

'Would you not regret it?' Sylvia raised her brows. 'Surely you are young enough to hope for a little romance in your marriage this time?'

'I think Winston was the most romantic man I've ever met,' Mariah said and laughed as she saw her friend's surprise. 'No, truly he was. Everyone saw the age difference between us and believed the worst—but he was so gallant and so loving to me. He kissed my hand every morning. Every night I found either a rose or a flower of some kind on my pillow. Even when he was ill he had the gardener bring in a perfect bloom to place in my room for him.'

Sylvia blinked hard. 'You bring tears to my eyes, my love. Of course I knew that Winston adored you but I did not realise that he was such a sweet man. It is little wonder that you hesitate to marry for a second time. I do not think it will be easy to find a man like Winston again.'

'No, I think I shall not,' Mariah agreed. 'But perhaps I should seek someone rather different this time. I was utterly spoiled in my first marriage, but I am older and wiser now. It is time for me to grow up, to move on.'

'I do not think you could do better than Lord Lanchester himself,' Sylvia said. 'He is handsome, respected and has no need of your fortune—besides, I think he likes you, my love.'

'Yes, I think he likes me,' Mariah agreed and sighed. She might never find such devotion as she had from Winston again, but she was so tired of being a widow. 'However, Lord Lanchester shows no sign of making me an offer. I did think at one time—but he did not speak and I think I lost my chance. Something must have made him decide that I was not the wife he wanted, though he is still concerned for my safety and well-being.'

'Perhaps the right moment has not yet presented itself,' Sylvia suggested. 'Be patient, Mariah. He may speak when he is ready.'

'I fear patience is not my best virtue.' Mariah laughed at herself, for she knew her own faults. 'Once I make up my mind to something, I must act—and I have decided that I need a husband, or the promise of one, before we return to England.'

'Think carefully, my love,' her friend advised. 'If you marry in haste, you may regret it.'

'I have been a widow for nearly two years,' Mariah said. 'I have thought of contenting myself with affairs, but I think it would suit me better to be married.'

Seeing she had shocked her friend, Mariah laughed again and took her arm.

'No, really, dearest, it would not be so very terrible, would it?'

'Well…if one were discreet.' Sylvia shook her head. 'You have been married… I know you are teasing me—but Hubert would be most shocked if he heard you. You might lose all chance of a decent marriage, my dear.'

'Yes, I dare say,' Mariah said, slightly impatient, for she thought her friend's husband a little pompous at times. 'But I am so tired of sleeping alone.… I want to be courted for myself, loved.'

What would Sylvia think if she knew that her marriage had remained unconsummated? That she was, in fact, still a virgin? It was something she could never tell anyone, even her best friends.

A little later that evening Mariah stood by the open windows of the salon looking out at the night. The sky was velvet dark with only a faint light from the moon, which was half-hidden by clouds, but the air was much cooler after the heat of the day. She was tempted to walk in the gardens, but if she did, someone was sure to follow—and she could not be sure the right man would join her.

'Mariah, my dear, I want you to meet some friends of Hubert's,' Sylvia said, causing her to turn round and look at the newcomers. With a little shock she recognised the man who had saved her from a fall earlier that day. 'This is Sir Harold Jenkins, Lady Jenkins—and their nephew, Lieutenant Grainger.'

'What a surprise to see you again, Lieutenant,' Mariah said, extending her hand with a smile. 'Good evening, Sir Harold, Lady Jenkins, I am pleased to meet you.'

'Good evening, Lady Fanshawe,' Lieutenant Grainger replied and kissed her hand, looking into her eyes with such warmth a moment later that Mariah was surprised. 'I am so pleased to meet you again.'

'You met earlier? You did not tell us,' Lady Jenkins said archly, throwing her nephew a fond look.

'I met Lady Fanshawe walking towards the spot where a rock fall had taken place and was able to warn her that it was dangerous to go farther in that direction. I have since spoken to the authorities and they assured me a fence would be put in place immediately.'

'Ah, that is just like you, Peter,' Lady Jenkins said and looked directly at Mariah. 'My nephew is such a correct young man, Lady Fanshawe. Many would simply ignore something of that nature—but Peter always thinks of others.'

'You are too partial, Aunt.' Peter Grainger looked slightly embarrassed. 'You must forgive her, Lady Fanshawe. I assure you that I did only what anyone would have done in the circumstances.'

'I am sure that many would not,' Mariah said. 'Tell me, sir—how do you like Lake Como? Do you prefer it to Lake Garda?'

'I think all the lakes have their merits—but I believe the situation of Como makes it most agreeable to those who prefer a little more tranquillity. There are more visitors—or it seems there are more at Garda.'

'Yes, that was my feeling also,' Mariah said, warming to him. He seemed a sensible man. She had no doubt that his aunt was aware of her fortune, but Lieutenant Grainger did not seem overly anxious to impress her. Indeed, he had taken himself off at once after she'd revealed her status to him earlier that day and she was inclined to think he was in no particular need of her fortune. 'I think we have time for a turn in the garden before dinner, sir. Would you care to oblige me?'

He looked a little startled, as if her boldness had surprised him, but immediately offered his arm. 'A little air on the terrace would be perfect. I believe Count Paolo's gardens are reputed to be very fine?'

'Yes, indeed they are. We are fortunate that he allows us to stay here.'

Andrew watched with narrowed eyes as the pair disappeared out through the open doors onto the terrace. They stood talking in full view of the room so there was nothing particularly clandestine or intimate about their behaviour, but he found the sight oddly disturbing. Mariah had promised to take his advice in the matter of a husband; he did not think that Grainger was wholly suitable, but, as yet, he had not managed to think of anyone he could recommend to her wholeheartedly.

Watching her, he was aware of how lovely she was, the perfection of her figure and the enchanting way she held her head to one side when she teased or laughed at one. She was, he thought, a beautiful, sensual woman and his pulses quickened at the sight of her looking up at her companion. Something must be done. She was too vulnerable to unscrupulous rogues, though he had no real reason to think of Grainger as a rogue.

'Are you well acquainted with Lieutenant Grainger?' his host asked. 'Lady Fanshawe seems on good terms with him. She looks happier than she has for a while.'

'I was not aware that she knew him,' Andrew said. 'I had not seen him for years, though I remember that his regiment joined ours in Spain. He was a new recruit then…' He turned to look at Lord Hubert. 'Do you know him at all?'

'We have met once or twice. I am not well acquainted with him.'

'I am in similar case myself, though we had mutual friends in Spain.'

'I know his aunt and uncle,' Lord Hubert continued. 'Very good sort of people. Sylvia likes them—and I usually like my wife's friends. I dare say we shall see quite a bit of them while we are here. If Grainger and Mariah were to take to one another, it would be the very thing.'

Andrew scarcely heard him. He had found the younger man pleasant enough company earlier in the day, but now his hackles rose as he went out of the open doors and heard Mariah laugh. It seemed an age since he'd heard her laugh in just that way—and, looking at her standing there in the moonlight with the young lieutenant, he was struck once more by her beauty. She was a fine, spirited woman, perhaps a little reckless at times. Her restless nature would lead her astray without a strong hand to guide her.

Mariah became aware of Andrew as he reached them. She turned her head, a smile on her lips. 'Andrew, how are you? Lieutenant Grainger was telling me about a visit that the Regent paid to his regiment, when they were stationed in Brighton.'

'Indeed?' Andrew looked down his patrician nose. 'Prinny enjoys playing soldiers. I dare say you made him an honorary colonel or something of the kind, did you not?'

Lieutenant Grainger stared at him doubtfully. 'I believe he is our Colonel in Chief. He seems knowledgeable enough.'

'In his way, perhaps,' Andrew said. 'I have been meaning to ask you, Grainger. Would you happen to know the whereabouts of Lieutenant William Gordon?'

'Forgive me. I'm not perfectly certain whom you mean?' The younger man seemed hesitant, a little uneasy, then, 'There was a lieutenant of that name with us in Spain, I believe, but I thought he resigned his commission after being reprimanded a few times…but why you should think I might know him is beyond me. I was not acquainted with him.'

'Then you will have no idea where he is now? I was hoping to find him in Naples, but it came to nothing. For the time being, I must continue my search.' He glanced towards the room behind them, which was now brightly lit. 'I think Lady Hubert is looking for us, Mariah. I dare say dinner is ready— and she may wish to close these doors. The insects will invade the house now that the candles have been lit.'

'Yes, we must go in,' Mariah said and arched her right eyebrow at Andrew. 'I believe you are to sit on my right hand this evening, Lord Lanchester.'

Lieutenant Grainger had gone in just ahead of them. Mariah grabbed Andrew's arm, lowering her voice to a whisper.

'Why did Lieutenant Grainger look at you so oddly when you mentioned that officer—Lieutenant Gordon?'

'I have no idea,' Andrew replied. 'I should not have mentioned Gordon in his hearing had I known it would upset him.'

'There is a mystery. I know it.' Mariah's eyes mocked him. His secrecy had set her on her mettle for he knew that she liked a challenge. 'I shall get it out of you, Andrew—just see if I don't.'

He smiled and shook his head. She had seemed low in spirits that morning, but now she was the old Mariah. At times she aroused his protective instincts and he was inclined to throw caution to the winds and snap her up as his wife before someone else did, but then, when she was in a teasing mood, he wondered if they would not be at each other's throats in a fortnight. As a girl she had been very provoking, a nuisance, following a fellow about and wanting attention when he had better things to do. Mind you, when he thought of it, she had always been ready to go fishing or to play the fielder in ball games. A boisterous, bold girl whose reckless behaviour had landed them all in trouble more than once, for what was a chap to do but take the blame when Farmer Johnson's bull had got in amongst the young heifers when Mariah left the gate open.

He could not contemplate the idea of her married to a rascal, but marriage was a big commitment. Andrew knew that once he made it he would not stray; it would be a union for life and he must therefore be sure of his feelings before making an offer to any woman.

Besides, there was still the faint cloud of suspicion hanging over him. Unless he could prove his innocence to his commanding officer, he might be formally charged with the theft. Someone had taken the silver while he was the duty officer in charge of such things. He had not been expected to actually guard the valuable treasures, which lived in a locked cabinet in a locked room, but that it should happen on his watch was bad enough. The letter pointing the finger at him was an added complication and one that had given him many uneasy moments.

Major Henderson had suggested that his enemy might be Lieutenant Gordon, but there was no proof that he had even been in England at the time. Besides, why wait all this time to strike against Andrew? It did not make sense to his way of thinking.

'Something is worrying you,' Mariah said as they entered the dining room. 'Won't you tell me, Andrew? I promise not to plague you if it is important. I am not an unruly girl now. I can be sensible, you know.'

'Yes, of course you can,' he said, wrenching his thoughts away from his problem. He caught the smell of her soft perfume and felt desire stir in his loins. In that moment he wanted her badly. She was a beautiful woman and intriguing. If he could simply bed her and make her his mistress there would be no problem as far as she was concerned, but that was impossible. She was a lady and deserved his respect. 'I think you like Lieutenant Grainger. I have no reason to think him other than he seems—but be careful, Mariah. For your own sake, trust only those you truly know.'

'Very well.' Mariah looked into his eyes. 'I have reason to be grateful to him—he prevented me from coming upon a rock fall earlier today and warned me to change direction. However, I am sure that caution is best. You shall advise me.'

Alone in her room later that evening, Mariah let her various conversations with Andrew drift through her mind as she prepared for bed. He had talked animatedly of their friends at home and of the beautiful scenery. Of Lieutenant Grainger he had not spoken one word after his warning to her.

She puzzled over his reticence. Lieutenant Grainger had seemed embarrassed when a certain officer had been mentioned. Why had Andrew introduced the subject of the other officer and why should it make the younger man uncomfortable?

Andrew had followed them outside deliberately. Why had he done that? Was it to protect her from a man he was not certain of or...surely he could not be jealous because Mariah had been enjoying his company?

What had brought Andrew to Italy—and what was bothering him? She was certain that he was very worried about something, but did not know what it might be. Could he possibly have financial troubles? Was that why he had come—to ask her to marry him, because he needed money?

The thought made her blood run cold. No, she would not allow herself to think ill of him. He was her friend. He had promised to help her find a suitable husband. She had given him a list of her requirements in a husband and stressed that she did not wish to marry a fortune hunter.

If he wanted her for himself, he would surely give her a sign. Even if she acquitted him of wanting her fortune, which she had immediately, she had to admit that he showed no sign of being madly in love with her. A little voice in her head told her that Andrew might well make a convenient marriage with a suitable lady for the sake of an heir. Many gentlemen in his position did so. Would he consider her suitable—or would he think her too flighty, not serious enough?

Or was there another reason entirely for his reticence? Was Andrew hiding something he did not wish even his friends to know?

Mariah sighed as she slid between cool linen sheets and settled into a soft feather mattress. She loved uncovering secrets and a mystery to solve was a pleasant way to spend her days—and it would stop her wondering why Andrew had not come to the point. Sometimes he looked at her as if he might gobble her up, as if he wanted nothing more than to get her into his bed, but at others he was polite, cool and reserved.

Just what had she done that had made him hesitate? Perhaps it was because she'd shot the man who had been trying to kill Lucinda. Being a crack shot and keeping a cool head in a crisis were perhaps not the most feminine of traits. Men often wanted a sweet docile woman they could protect and dominate. Mariah was too spirited, too bold. Andrew had been attentive to her when she was recovering from her ordeal at the hands of kidnappers, but then, quite suddenly, he had drawn back. She must have done something to make him think her unsuitable—but what?

Thumping her pillow in sudden pique, Mariah felt both frustration and disappointment. She was almost certain that Andrew was the only man she could truly love and she longed to be taken in his arms and kissed until she melted for pleasure, but all he offered was friendship. She might have taken a dozen lovers had she wished or accepted as many offers of marriage. Why must she want the only man who seemed utterly indifferent to her charms?

'You provoking man,' Mariah muttered, blew out the candle and closed her eyes.

Mariah was not the only one to lie sleepless for some time after extinguishing the light. Andrew frowned as he lay on his back, staring up at the ceiling, his head filled with thoughts of Mariah. He knew that she was tired of being a widow. He had over the years seen her flirt many times. She was entitled to flirt with as many admirers as she pleased. Rich, unattached and as intelligent as she was beautiful, he imagined she was pursued wherever she went. The mystery was that she remained single. She must have had many offers of marriage and many others of a more dubious nature. As far as he knew she remained aloof—why? What kept her from indulging in love affairs? Was she still faithful to her husband's memory?

She was too young and lovely to remain a widow all her life and he knew it was not her intention. She had asked his advice because she wished for a husband who would treat her as she deserved. In his heart Andrew knew that if he did not speak soon he would lose her.

Yet how could he speak when he did not know who his enemy was? Thus far he had been accused of theft, but Harrison had done nothing. If someone felt bitter hatred for Andrew, they were hardly likely to stop there. His very life might be in danger. It would be wrong to involve a lovely young woman in his life at the moment—however much he wanted to kiss and touch her.

He had experienced jealousy on seeing her laughing with Grainger that evening. Was he a fool to hold his silence? She was beautiful, well connected and charming—what more could he want from a wife?

Remembering how soft and moist her lips had looked, he felt an urgent desire to feel them beneath his, to crush her soft body to his and… This was ridiculous!

Groaning at his frustrated thoughts, Andrew threw back the covers and got out of bed, going to the window to look out. He had accepted Lady Jenkins's invitation and removed his baggage here earlier in the day, though in view of his feelings that evening he was beginning to regret the decision. The inn might not be as comfortable as this room, but he had been well enough.

The moon was high overhead, shedding a bright silver light over the gardens. Something caught his eye in the shrubbery—a flash of white. A man's shirt, perhaps? Whoever it was seemed to be hiding…watching the house. Was there someone out there skulking in the bushes?

If some rogue was hoping to break in and steal valuables, he was going to be in for a shock. His instincts alerted to danger, Andrew dressed quickly. This needed investigation.

He left through a window at the back of the villa and made his way round to the front gardens, keeping close to the wall and in deep shadow. He was alert, his finger on the trigger of his concealed pistol, but even after his years of training in the army, he was not aware of the man behind him until the last moment. Someone lunged at him as he turned and grabbed for his arm. They struggled for a few moments and Andrew's pistol fired into the air. The next moment he heard a shout from the house and the door opened.

'Andrew—are you out there?'

Hearing Grainger's voice, the assailant suddenly shoved Andrew backwards, causing him to stumble and fall. Before he was on his feet again the shadow had run off, disappearing into the darkness. Andrew fired another shot in the direction he'd gone, hoping to scare him. He heard a faint curse and then nothing more.

'I'm over here, Grainger,' he called. 'There was someone lurking in the bushes. I came out to investigate and we fought. My pistol went off—unfortunately, it was pointing in the air and not at him. I may have winged him with the second shot, though.'

Grainger was dressed in breeches and shirt and had clearly not been to bed. He had a pistol in his hand as he came to join Andrew.

'It may be just as well,' he said. 'If you'd killed him, we should have had trouble with the authorities. Did you catch a sight of his face? Could you identify him?'

'No, I caught a glimpse of him, nothing more. He was acting in a furtive manner and I feared someone might be trying to break in and rob us while we slept.'

'You were not sleeping?'

'No. I had something on my mind.'

'Does it concern Lieutenant Gordon?'

'It might. Why do you ask?'

Grainger hesitated, then, 'I wasn't quite truthful earlier. At one time I was on terms with him, but then I realised that he was a rogue—and a thief. I caught him stealing from a fellow officer's kit.'

'You did not report him?'

'No...' Grainger looked uncomfortable. 'I ought to have done so—but he was supposed to be courting a young lady I know. She is my cousin on my father's side. Gordon had asked her to marry him and she had promised she would when she was eighteen. If I'd accused him of being a thief, it would have broken Thelma's heart.'

'She must have suffered when he left the army and disappeared?'

'Yes, she went into a decline. For a time we thought she might die, but thankfully, she is recovering at last. My aunt told me she is thinking of marriage to a decent man this time.'

'I am glad to hear it. So, you have no idea where Gordon is now then?'

'If I had, I should find him and thrash him.' Grainger frowned, but his eyes did not quite meet Andrew's. He had a feeling that he had not been told the whole story. 'Did you come out here to find him? Is that why you are here?'

'It was one of my reasons for coming out.'

'The other... Forgive me, was the other reason Lady Fanshawe?'

'Why do you ask?'

Grainger shook his head. 'She is beautiful, but I hardly know her. I dare say she would not look at me.'

Andrew would have answered him, but at that moment Lady Jenkins called to them from the house.

'The shots must have wakened your aunt. Go and reassure her, Grainger. I shall take another walk about the grounds, make certain there is no one lurking. We shall continue our conversation another time.'

Andrew frowned as Grainger went off to soothe his aunt's fears. It was clear to him that the young officer liked Mariah. As yet it was no more than that, but it might become more in time. As far as Andrew knew, Grainger would be a good match for her. His background was adequate and he had prospects. He did not have to marry money because his aunt and uncle were very wealthy and had already named him as their heir. Mariah could do worse than marry Grainger.

'A picnic,' Sylvia said the next morning when Mariah entered the salon. 'Lady Jenkins has invited us for tomorrow afternoon. She has arranged it on the lake shore and there will be boats to take us out on the lake should we wish it.'

'That sounds pleasant,' Mariah said. 'I believe I should like to go out on the lake. It is cooler and the weather has been very warm of late.'

'Yes, it has…' Sylvia looked at her, noticing faint shadows beneath her eyes. 'Has it been keeping you awake? If so, I can arrange for a net over your bed so that you may have the window open.'

'No, I do not think the heat kept me awake,' Mariah told her. 'I slept later, but I must admit I was restless for a time.'

'Were you thinking of Lord Lanchester?'

'Yes, for a while.' Mariah laughed. 'Is it not foolish of me? I do not think he has any intention of asking me to marry him, therefore I must look elsewhere if I am to find a husband before we leave Italy.'

'You are not serious in your intention?'

'Why not? I may have met a gentleman I rather like.'

Sylvia questioned her with her eyes. In her early thirties, she was a pretty woman, good-natured and much loved by her doting husband. The fact that she had not as yet given him an heir seemed not to bother him one bit, though Mariah suspected it was a source of some distress to her friend.

'I must suppose you to mean Lieutenant Grainger? He certainly has prospects, Mariah—if you care about such things.'

'Money is immaterial. I have far more than I need.'

'Can one ever have too much?' Sylvia asked and laughed.

'No, but I have enough. I want something more from my marriage—excitement, laughter, respect and children.'

Sylvia frowned. 'And love? You say nothing of it, but I suspect it means more to you than you will admit? Did the lieutenant give you reason to hope?'

'He was polite, friendly, but not overly attentive. I think his aunt would like him to make a push for my notice. She knows of my fortune and thinks me an excellent catch for her nephew, but he is more circumspect in his approach. He has given me no sign as yet. I do not think him a fortune hunter—which counts in his favour.'

Sylvia shook her head as she saw the speculative look in Mariah's eyes. 'I believe you are serious. You will really accept a proposal of marriage from him if he asks?'

'I might,' Mariah replied innocently, then gurgled with laughter. 'Or I might decide that an affair would suit me better. I am not sure whether he would suit me as a lover...' She tipped her head to one side, a sparkle in her eyes. 'It would be exciting to have an affair, do you not think so?'

'Now I know you are misbehaving,' her friend said with a shake of her head. 'You do so love to tease, dearest. I know you too well to believe you serious, but others might not. Be a little careful, Mariah. I should not like to see you hurt.'

'As yet I have met no one who is anxious to engage me in a clandestine affair,' Maria admitted ruefully. 'Most seem interested in getting a ring on my finger for the sake of controlling Winston's fortune.'

'Well, your unpleasant experience has given you a terrible shock,' Sylvia sympathised, 'but you must not think everyone the same. If you were to receive a proposal from someone you could like sufficiently, it might be the best thing for you. After all, business is a chore—why not leave it to a man you may trust? He would, of course, secure a generous settlement on you.'

'Yes, I believe marriage might suit me best,' Mariah conceded and turned away for fear her friend should see too much.

It was time she lost her virginity. Mariah had made up her mind that she would either marry or take a lover. Sylvia had been shocked, but many married ladies had clandestine affairs—why shouldn't she? At least she would not wake up one day to discover that her husband cared nothing for her and had run through her fortune at the card table.

That would be humiliating and something that she did not think she could accept. Rather an affair with a man who admired and excited her that she could end when she chose than marriage with a man who wanted only her money. Yet she was tired of living alone. She could not always be in the company of friends and there were many lonely hours, often in the dark reaches of the night when she could not sleep and longed for someone she could talk to as a friend.

Andrew Lanchester would never treat her so badly. Were he to offer for her she would marry him, even if he was not madly in love with her. He would be honest, generous and considerate. All the qualities she needed. The provoking man! Why could he not oblige her?

What she truly needed was for Andrew to care for her. She might think of marrying others in an idle moment, but in her heart there was only one she wanted.

Why would he not tell her he cared and ask her to marry him?

Chapter Three

It was yet another perfect day by the lake. In the warm sunshine the water looked impossibly blue and at times the sunbeams seemed to dance on the surface like a shower of diamonds. Mariah looked around her. Theirs was not the only party to take advantage of the coolness to be found by the lakeside and several ladies and gentlemen strolled arm in arm. Out on the lake itself there were various kinds of small boats: some being rowed by eager amateurs, as well as those plied by professionals eager for trade.

'My nephew was so distressed to miss the picnic,' Lady Jenkins said, taking a seat next to Mariah. 'He met with an accident while out walking this morning and was obliged to visit the doctor.'

'I am sorry to hear that.' Mariah looked at her in genuine concern. 'Did Lieutenant Grainger suffer a fall?'

'That is the most distressing thing about the whole affair,' Lady Jenkins said, lowering her voice. 'He begged me not to make a fuss. I was all for sending for the authorities, but he would not have it.'

'I fear I do not understand your meaning?' Mariah arched her fine brows.

'It is quite shocking. Peter was set upon by ruffians, my dear. He says there must have been two of them for they knocked him to the ground and kicked him. He fought back and they ran off, but he has suffered some injuries and was feeling unwell when we left him this morning.'

'Oh, what a shame,' Mariah said with ready sympathy. 'That is a great deal too bad. In the isolation of the hills one has to take care, for there may occasionally be bandits who will attack an unwary traveller, but here at the lakes—I have not heard of such a thing before.'

'It has made me uneasy,' Lady Jenkins agreed. 'I have almost decided to cut short our visit here and move on to Venice.'

'That would be a pity,' Mariah said. 'Though Venice is beautiful, of course, but…perhaps it might be best to speak to the authorities. If there are thieves in the area, they ought to be apprehended.'

'It is most odd. Peter says he was not robbed, simply knocked to the ground, beaten—and then abandoned.'

'How very strange.'

'Yes, I thought so. One would almost suppose him to have an enemy, but he will not hear of it—and he would not wish me to speak of the affair, but I wanted you to know why he had cried off. I know he was looking forward to seeing you again so very much.'

'It is a shame, of course. However, I am sure we shall meet again soon—unless you feel compelled to leave for Venice immediately?'

Smiling, Mariah rose from her seat, nodded to her hostess and walked slowly towards Andrew, who was standing with Sylvia at the edge of the lake, watching some children playing with a ball.

'It is a perfect day for being on the water, is it not?' she asked, then, frowning, 'Have you heard about the attack on Lieutenant Grainger? Lady Jenkins is quite distressed.'

'Yes, of course. Lady Jenkins was good enough to invite me to stay with them.'

'I had not realised that,' Mariah said. 'I might have invited you to stay with us.'

'Had I not already accepted Lady Jenkins's invitation I should have been happy to do so. I am pleased to tell you that Grainger's pride is more bruised than his arm, though he wears it in a sling for a slight sprain and was advised to rest.'

'What is that?' Sylvia asked. 'Lady Jenkins told me he sent his apologies, but nothing more.'

'I dare say he would rather not make a fuss—but apparently he was attacked while out walking early this morning. Some ruffians knocked him to the ground and beat him, then suddenly ran off.'

'Was he robbed?' Sylvia looked alarmed.

'I think not. It was a senseless attack for no reason—unless Lieutenant Grainger has an enemy, of course.'

'That is so shocking,' Sylvia said and looked at Andrew. 'I have not heard of such a thing happening here before—have you?'

'It is rare, I think,' Andrew replied. He hesitated, as if he would say more, then changed his mind. 'He was walking in an isolated area, I believe. You must be safe enough here amongst so many.'

'Yes, but still...' Sylvia shook her head in distress. 'It is disturbing none the less.'

'Yes, it is a little,' Mariah said. 'Lieutenant Grainger was obliged to seek the services of a doctor. Lady Jenkins is distressed and thinks of removing to Venice sooner than she had planned.'

'I do not blame her,' Sylvia said. 'Such things make one uncomfortable. I shall speak to Hubert later. We are engaged to Count Paolo later this week at his home in Milan. He is holding a masked ball in our honour, as you know, Mariah—but after that I, too, may think of repairing to Venice sooner than we had planned.'

'I should not let one incident overset you, ma'am,' Andrew said. 'I dare say it may have been some louts who'd overimbibed and thought to take their opportunity. Such things happen anywhere at any time, you know. Even in London there was a time when the Mohawks, marauding louts, some of them meant to be gentlemen, made the streets unsafe because of their drunken behaviour. I am certain both you and Mariah are safe enough, providing you do not walk alone at night—or in isolated places during the day.'

'Mariah walks alone sometimes during the day.' Sylvia looked at her anxiously. 'I think you should be more careful in future, dearest. If there are unscrupulous rogues about, you must wait until you have an escort.'

'I was thinking of walking to the far shore,' Mariah said and turned her bright gaze on Andrew. 'Would you oblige me, sir?'

'Yes, of course, if you wish it,' Andrew said and turned to

Sylvia. 'You will excuse us, ma'am—unless you wish to accompany us?'

'It would be too far for me,' Sylvia replied. 'Besides, Lady Jenkins spoke of taking a trip on the water and I think I should like to go, too. Enjoy yourselves, but please do not wear yourself out, Mariah. Remember that we leave for Milan in the morning.'

'I shall not be in the least tired. I have far too much energy. If I do not use some of it, I cannot rest at night.'

Mariah took Andrew's arm and they set out together, admiring various aspects of the scenery. She enjoyed the feeling of being close to him, her heart beating a little faster than normal. Not until some minutes had passed and they had seen no one else for a while did Mariah speak of what was on her mind.

'I have decided I must marry soon,' she announced and felt Andrew's little start of surprise. He glanced at her and she lifted her fine eyebrows, giving him a provocative look. 'I hope to announce my engagement on my return to England or perhaps before we reach Paris.'

He arched one eyebrow. 'Am I to wish you happy? May I know the name of the fortunate gentleman?'

'Oh, I have not yet decided who I shall marry,' Mariah said with an innocent air. 'I need a husband, Andrew. I am tired of being a widow and wish for the comforts of marriage. Tell me, what do you know of Lieutenant Grainger? I should like your opinion of his character and whether you think he would make me a suitable husband.'

'Has he spoken to you?' Andrew's gaze narrowed.

'Not in so many words,' Mariah said and dimpled naughtily.

'Lieutenant Grainger has been very complimentary and his aunt tells me he was devastated that he had to cry off today. I dare say a little encouragement from me might bring him to the point—but you shall guide me.'

'Does it have to be so immediate?' Andrew asked, a hint of impatience in his tone. 'Why the hurry, Mariah? Do you feel yourself in danger of being abducted again?'

'Oh, no,' she said airily. 'No, it is simply that I wish to be married again. I want someone I can rely on, a strong arm to support me—the kind of companionship that comes from living with a man.'

'Are you sure you are not reacting to that unfortunate business at home?'

'I do not think so,' Mariah said, considering. 'Yes, I was in some distress for a few days after the event. I was unfortunately unwell while I stayed with Jane and you, Andrew, and I did feel vulnerable for a time, but I have recovered from that now, I assure you.'

'When we met the other morning at your friend's villa, you seemed to be in some distress,' Andrew said thoughtfully.

'Was I? Yes, perhaps.' Mariah sighed. 'I still feel sad when I think of my late husband. Contrary to most people's belief, I loved Winston—perhaps not in the way I might love a younger man, but I was certainly very fond of him. I do miss him still.'

'Why did you marry him?'

'Partly because he asked when I was feeling piqued. You know Justin Avonlea asked me to marry him because his father had lost much of my fortune? I was annoyed because I knew he did not care for me—and there were other reasons.

However, I was happy in my short marriage and I have become bored with being a widow.'

'Might you not regret it if you married simply because you are bored with your present life?'

'Perhaps.' Her eyes sparkled with mischief. 'What else would you advise—should I take a lover, perhaps? Can you find me a suitable candidate who would oblige me without demanding too much?'

'I think you have a wicked tongue, Mariah.' Andrew gave a reluctant laugh. 'It is as well that I know you are jesting.'

'Am I? Are you perfectly sure? You do not know me that well, Andrew,' Mariah teased. 'I should like to know your true opinion of my character. Do tell, Andrew! Am I a wicked flirt? No better than I ought to be?' She tipped her head to one side, a challenge in her eyes and her lips slightly parted. 'Or am I a feather-brained goose?'

'You do not need me to answer that. If I were a vain man, I might think you were deliberately provoking me.'

'Perhaps I am.' Mariah tipped her head to one side. 'Yet I fear it is beyond me. You, my best of friends, are far too sensible to be turned from your purpose by such a flighty jade as I.'

'Had I not other things on my mind I might take you at your word, Mariah.'

'Indeed? I have sensed something, Andrew. Will you not tell me? If it is a matter of money, I might…' She faltered as he frowned. 'No? Yet I suspect something is bothering you— can you not unburden yourself to a friend?'

'My problem is mine to solve, Mariah. I fear if you look

for a proposal from me I cannot oblige, much as I might wish things otherwise.'

'That is plain speaking,' Mariah said, laughing to hide the sudden strike of pain. 'What a shocking disappointment! So, if you are not on the marriage market, for the moment that leaves Lieutenant Grainger... I ask you in all seriousness, what is your opinion of that gentleman? You did say you would help me to make a good selection when last we spoke of marriage.'

'I could not advise you on the merits or otherwise of that particular gentleman, Mariah. If you are serious, I will en-quire into his prospects and his background. Indeed, he seems respectable enough—but I am not certain he would suit you. You might find him a little worthy.'

'Damning indeed! Worthy? How dull, Andrew. While I would not wish for a black sheep, a slightly grey one might do well enough,' Mariah said, her fingers pressing lightly on his arm. Why could the foolish man not tell her what was troubling him? Any other man would seize the opportunity she'd given him to flirt and steal a kiss. 'Can you not think of someone you might recommend, Andrew? Will you not save me from taking the next fortune hunter that crosses my path?'

'Are you playing a game with me?' Andrew stopped walk-ing, turning to look into her eyes. 'If this is your idea of amusement, we may banter and then forget it—but if you are in earnest I shall give the matter some serious thought. How-ever, I think you must give yourself a little more time.'

Mariah pouted. 'Must I? Very well, I am prepared to wait a few months longer if I must, but please take me seriously. If you cannot help me, I may have to decide for myself—and then I might make a mistake. How would you feel with that on your conscience? I am a lonely widow at the mercy of un-scrupulous men—and I asked you for help. Ignore me at your peril.'

A gleam of amusement sprang up in his eyes and for a mo-ment she felt he was close to taking hold of her and giving her a good shake.

'You deserve a spanking, Mariah.'

'You wouldn't dare…'

'Do not be too certain.'

Mariah laughed. 'Very well, I shall not tease you, Andrew—but I am serious. I believe I shall not be happy until I find a husband I can admire and like.'

'You are serious now, I think.'

'Yes—and I need your help. Truly I do.'

'Very well. Give me two months after we all return to Eng-land, Mariah. If I cannot come up with a suggestion that suits you in that time…' He shook his head, a reluctant smile in his eyes. 'You are a minx, Lady Fanshawe. I wish I might speak freely…' He saw the question in her eyes. 'My hands are tied for the moment. Come, can you truly not wait a little longer to find a husband who will love and care for you?'

'If he was the right man, I would wait for ever,' Mariah said and for once she was not laughing. Her heart raced. Surely he must know what was in her mind? She could not be plainer. 'Do you think I might find love, Andrew? I have sometimes thought that I must be unlovable since no one seems to care for anything but my fortune.'

'Ridiculous,' he replied, a frown creasing his brow. 'You must know you are beautiful and charming. I dare say most men fall in love with you—but some are in desperate need of your fortune. Others are gamblers and you could not trust them even if they cared for you. However, I dare say there are at least twenty gentlemen I could bring to mind once we are in London.'

'Then you advise me to wait?' Mariah nodded. 'Well, I dare say I should need time to choose my bride clothes and have them made. Very well, I shall take your advice, my good friend.'

'Is there anything else your ladyship requires me to pack?'

'No, I do not think so…'

Mariah sighed as her gaze fell on the small trunk, which was to accompany them on their visit to Milan. They would stay at the count's large house in Milan for two nights before returning to his villa to complete their stay in Italy. In less than three weeks they would remove to Venice for a few days before leaving for France. Sylvia wished to spend a little time shopping in Paris and after that they would return home to England.

What was she supposed to do with her life then? Lucinda had said she would be welcome to make her home with her and Justin, but though Mariah would be happy to visit for a while, she needed her own home. She had paid brief visits to the country house Winston had left her, but it was too grand and impersonal. Of course she could fill it with friends, but she did not think it would suit her to live always in the country—at least, it might be bearable if she were married. As a widow she would do better in London or Bath. No! Bath was full of old tabbies who had nothing better to do than drink the foul waters and whisper behind their fans about the latest *on dit* in London.

Mariah thought she would rather be amongst the people making those scandals—or preferably making them herself. A mischievous smile touched her soft mouth. Andrew's manner was so frustrating to a woman who did everything impulsively. His eyes seemed to caress her, to dwell on her mouth, as if he found it attractive, yet she could not tease him into a kiss. She could have sworn he was on the verge of making her an offer as they walked by the lake the other day—or at least declaring himself—but he had drawn back once more. Her intuition told her that there was some mystery, perhaps some hint of scandal. Andrew was being so foolish. If he would only confide his problem to her, she might be able to help him. As if she would have cared for a little scandal!

'May I send for the porter, Lady Fanshawe?'

'Yes, please do, Lily,' Mariah said and smiled at her maid. 'Once the trunk has been taken you may go to bed. I am not ready to retire yet and can manage my gown myself when I wish to disrobe.'

'Very well, milady.'

Mariah left her maid to arrange for the luggage to be taken down to the porter's wagon. It would set off before them and her things would be unpacked and waiting for her when they arrived.

Mariah had not yet met Count Paolo, who was a personal friend of Lord Hubert and of his age group, she supposed. He had graciously loaned them his beautiful villa here at the lakes and must be a generous man. Mariah wondered if he were married. She had not heard Sylvia speak of his wife or family.

Shaking her head at the way her thoughts were taking her, Mariah went down to the spacious salon, which led onto a veranda. The windows were closed, but not locked, and she let herself out, deciding to take a turn about the lush gardens. The air was heavy with scent from a variety of flowers. Mariah thought she could smell jasmine, oleanders, roses and other more exotic perfumes that she could not name.

It was such a perfect setting. A night for romance and adventure, she thought, feeling wistful. How pleasant it would be to walk here with the man she loved, to feel his strong arms about her and his lips on hers. A surge of need and longing swept through her. She had so many friends and yet she was lonely.

She wanted someone special, a man she could lean on in times of trouble, a companion who would be with her throughout life, taking the good things with the bad.

Feeling the trickle of tears on her cheeks, Mariah swept them away impatiently. She would not give way to self-pity! Yet she wanted so much to be loved—passionately and without restraint. She was a fool to torture herself with thoughts of Andrew Lanchester. If he cared for her at all, he would surely speak!

Raising her head, Mariah felt angry. Why should she wait? If she were offered marriage by a man she believed more interested in her than her fortune, she would accept—and if a man she could like sufficiently offered an affair she might take a lover.

She was so tired of being a widow.

* * *

The journey to Milan was accomplished without incident and Mariah was delighted to discover that Count Paolo's home there was one of Milan's ancient palaces and had beautiful gardens and courtyards behind the rather faded facade. The entrance hall was large with high arched ceilings and marble floors, the sound of their footsteps echoing as the count's English butler greeted them and took them up to their apartments.

'Count Paolo will be with you in a short time,' the man said deferentially. 'He is with other visitors, but he will be with you very soon.'

'Yes, of course, Tomkins,' Lady Hubert said and smiled at him. 'And how have you been keeping since we last saw you?'

'Very well, milady. The climate suits me here and I have settled in nicely. I am grateful to you for recommending me to the count.'

'I was happy to do so. I knew you would get on famously.'

Sylvia beamed at him as he preceded them up the wide, rather worn stone stairs to the gallery above, then turned to Mariah.

'Tomkins worked for my father until he died, you know. He suffers with the rheumatics and decided he would like to live in a warmer climate than the east of England. Knowing that Count Paolo was looking for a major-domo for his house here, I suggested he might apply and gave him a reference.'

'That was kind of you.'

'Oh, no, Tomkins deserved it. He was very kind to Papa in his last days.'

They were led along the gallery to a suite of rooms that overlooked the courtyards to the rear of the house. Mariah went immediately to the window to glance out. The paved courtyard was very attractive with its slightly uneven and faded pink bricks that were interspersed with rose beds; there was a fountain with beautiful statuary and she could see a series of courtyards and gardens leading from the one below.

A man and a woman were walking at the far side of the courtyard. As she watched, the man kissed the woman's hand and she left him, going through an arched gateway to whatever lay beyond. A servant approached the man, who glanced up at the window where Mariah stood and nodded at something he had been told.

Was he the count? From this distance Mariah could see little except that he was dressed exquisitely in the French manner and his hair was a pale silver-blonde.

She drew away from the window as Sylvia called to her, 'This is your room, dearest. What do you think?'

Mariah went through the elegant sitting room to a bedroom. She gasped, for it was beyond anything that she had expected. Furnished in the French Empire style, which had become so fashionable during Napoleon's occupation, the furniture was imposing and grand rather than comfortable, made of light wood strung with ebony and gold leaf, the soft furnishings in purple and cream with touches of black. The mirrors were flamboyant with gilded rococo-style frames, as was a picture that looked as if it were an Old Master. Perhaps not da Vinci, but of the same period, and the ceiling was painted with ridiculously fat cherubs, ladies of ample proportions and a satyr.

'Good gracious,' she murmured, a naughty gleam in her

eye. 'I am overwhelmed. Do you suppose this chamber was meant for royalty?'

'I think Napoleon may have stayed here, though I am not certain he had this suite,' Sylvia replied and laughed. 'That was in Count Paolo's father's day, of course. He has only recently inherited the estate, you know. Hubert was the late count's friend, but we met Paolo at the funeral and he was gracious enough to offer us his villa whenever we wished to stay near the lakes.'

'He must be a very generous man.'

'Yes, I dare say,' Sylvia replied. 'He would accept no payment—but I believe Hubert and the count have some business together. The count also has vineyards and wishes to import his wines to England.'

'Ah, yes, a mutually beneficial arrangement. I wonder—'

Mariah broke off as she heard a knock at the door and then the sound of Lord Hubert's rather loud voice greeting their host. Drawn by curiosity as much as politeness, she walked back to the sitting room with Sylvia, glancing at the man standing with Lord Hubert. Her breath caught, for he was an extraordinarily handsome man, his eyes a greenish-blue and his hair a pale blonde, but not quite the silver it had looked in the sunlight. His nose was patrician, his forehead high, his chin not square but strong and his mouth soft and sensual. He was older than she had expected after hearing that he had only recently come into his title, being nearer thirty than twenty and of a slender build. His clothes were extravagant, very French, his cravat exquisitely tied, his coat a deep shade of violet and his breeches a paler shade of the same colour; his long fingers were crowded with expensive rings. From his accent as he spoke, she thought he must have spent much of his time in France prior to his inheriting the estate in Lombardy.

She became aware that he was staring at her in a way that made her body tingle from head to toe. This was one of the most sensual, aggressively masculine men she had ever met despite his foppery. His eyes were the eyes of a predator and she knew immediately that he found her physically attractive. The smile on his lips sent a little shiver down her spine—he was a hunter and she sensed that she had been added to the list of his prey, which she imagined to be substantial.

She must be on her guard with this man or he would gobble her up! How very exciting to be sure. Life would not be dull for a few days.

'Lady Hubert. *Madame*, I am delighted to welcome you to my humble home—and your friend, the so-delightful Lady Fanshawe.' He moved towards Mariah with the grace of a large cat on the prowl. Politeness made her offer her hand. The count took it between his own for a moment, then lifted it to his lips, depositing a kiss on the palm. It was such an intimate gesture that Mariah found herself suffused with warmth. She glanced up at him and saw the challenge in his eyes.

'Such beauty leaves me without words,' he declared. 'Had I known what to expect, but even your friend did not do you justice…*magnifique*…'

'You flatter me, sir,' Mariah said, but she smiled and did not withdraw her hand too quickly. His overt flirting made her want to laugh and she was intrigued. She could not imagine that Count Paolo was in need of a fortune. This house and its contents were worth a fortune alone, to say nothing of the beautiful villa at the lakes and his vineyards. No, he was not a fortune hunter, but perhaps something more dangerous. He hunted for a different kind of prey, but he oozed sensual charm. She was certain he would seduce her if she let down her guard.

'No, I never flatter,' the count denied. 'I say only what is in my mind—and you are one of the most beautiful women I have met. It is a great pleasure for me to have you at my home.'

'I am overwhelmed, sir,' Mariah replied. 'Your house is astonishing—such splendour and grandeur. I do not think I have seen anything like it in a private home before.'

'There are many such palaces in Lombardy and Rome. Venice is renowned for its beautiful palaces, of course—but for me there is nowhere quite like Paris. I lived there for many years. My father and I did not always agree and I had interests in Paris. My wife is French and I have a house there still.'

'Your wife? Do you have children, *signor?*' Maria was surprised. *So he was married. Not a possible candidate for her husband, then.*

She was not sure whether she was disappointed or relieved.

'A daughter only.' A look of disappointment or anger passed across his face. 'I should say that I had a wife. She died in an unfortunate accident some months ago. I am a widower...' He spread his hands. 'It was very sad, you understand. However, we were not—compatible is, I think, the word. It was a foolish marriage undertaken when we were both too young. Our daughter will remain with her mama's family—but I require a son, naturally. In time, when I find a lady I can both admire and love, I shall marry again.'

'I am sorry for your loss, sir. I hope you will find happiness one day.'

'Yes, it is very sad for the child, because she misses her mama. I have promised her that one day I shall find her a new mama and she will have brothers and sisters to play with.' He smiled. 'You may wonder why I chose to speak of such private matters? I feel empathy between us, *madame.* You have lost a doting husband, I have lost a wife. I hope we shall be good friends—perhaps more in time, who knows?'

Something in his tone made Mariah's spine tingle. She had never known a man to speak so directly at a first meeting, though many pursued her hotly.

'I hope we shall be friends, sir. I have heard much of you from Lady Sylvia. I shall enjoy making your acquaintance.'

The count smiled oddly. 'I have spoken too boldly, perhaps? It is my way, *madame.* Forgive me, your beauty swept away all caution and I feel as if I have known you all my life—have been waiting for this moment.'

He spoke of it as if it was his destiny—hers, too, perhaps. His smile was charming and all feeling of boredom had fled. Mariah had been longing for something to happen and now it had. If she wanted an adventure, the count would be more than willing to provide it.

Mariah was aware of a mutual attraction, for she had seen his interest immediately and felt something herself—but he went too fast. His eyes seemed to unclothe her and she read his thoughts so easily that she could not meet his gaze for more than a moment. This man was charming and exciting, but she felt slightly out of her depth, as if she did not take care she would be swept away out of her control.

'You flatter me, sir. I think you like to tease and provoke.'

'Do not be misled, *madame.* I am in earnest, I assure you—

but I am a terrible host,' he said, becoming aware that they had an interested audience and letting go of her hand. 'You must come down and meet my friends—unless you would prefer refreshments to be served here so that you may rest?'

'Oh, no, we need just a few moments to freshen ourselves,' Sylvia replied. 'I am looking forward to exploring your gardens, Count Paolo. I imagine they are different to those at the villa?'

'Yes, indeed, far more formal,' the count replied, turning his attention to her. 'It will be my pleasure to show both you and Lady Fanshawe after we have taken some refreshment. If you will excuse me, I must welcome other guests. Please come down and join us when you are ready.'

'Well,' Sylvia said as the door closed behind him, 'how very odd. For one moment I thought—he looked as if he could devour you, Mariah.'

'Nonsense,' her husband said. 'I have found the count both direct and honest in his dealings. He was making his situation clear. He is clearly looking for marriage and Mariah is beautiful enough to make most men lose their heads. The fellow was bowled over. You have made another conquest, m'dear. I almost pity the poor man.'

Sylvia arched her brows at Mariah, as if to say that a man would not understand. Such a direct approach was meant to have significance of some kind. Mariah was inclined to think the count bent on seduction. She was, after all, a widow and as such he probably thought her fair game. He couldn't have been hinting at marriage when they had only that moment met for the first time. She had read too much into the count's words. Lord Hubert was right. He had been struck and his tongue had run away with him; it was not the first time, though most young men became tongue-tied and foolish, staring at her with calf eyes. The count was very different.

Her pulses throbbed. He was certainly very attractive and she might not be averse to a brief flirtation, though she sensed that it might be dangerous to become more intimately involved with him.

Becoming aware that her friend was waiting for an answer, Mariah laughed softly. 'He is a surprising man,' she said. 'However, I must reserve judgement until I know him a little better.'

Chapter Four

Count Paolo certainly knew how to charm, both ladies and gentlemen. After a mere day spent in his company, Mariah had to admit that she liked him. She also found him physically attractive, though something warned her to be wary of showing it. He had given them a tour of his gardens in the cool of early evening, when the perfume of flowers wafted on a slight breeze filling the air with sweetness and the sun's fierce heat had abated.

'English ladies have such delicate complexions,' he said, offering his arm to Sylvia as Mariah followed with Lord Hubert. 'You must always be careful to stay out of the midday sun or you may spoil your beautiful skin, *madame.*'

'Oh, I never go out without a hat and my parasol during the day,' Sylvia told him. 'Mariah will do it, but she does not seem to burn as I do.'

'Lady Fanshawe has the kind of skin the sun loves,' Paolo said, directing a look at Mariah that she felt far hotter than any sunshine. 'I think perhaps she may have Latin blood in her somewhere.'

'Oh, no, I do not think it,' Mariah replied, a little smile on her mouth. 'My mother and father were both of English descent—unless one of my ancestors strayed...' There was a hint of mischief in her manner as she deliberately teased. 'I must admit that I do love to walk in the sun without my hat. Sylvia is forever scolding me.'

'I should not like you to be ill,' Sylvia said fondly. 'You are as a sister to me, dearest. I had brothers, but no sisters, something I regretted, and you have become more to me than most sisters could ever be.'

'I am very fond of you, too,' Mariah said. 'I do not know how I should have managed after Winston died if you had not come for me.'

'You speak of your husband?' Paolo's left eyebrow arched. 'He was, I believe, some years your senior?'

'Yes, but the kindest, sweetest man I have ever known.'

Paolo inclined his head. 'Of course you must miss him, but you are too young to grieve for ever, I think?'

'Winston would not expect it,' Sylvia said before Mariah could answer. 'We have been speaking of Mariah's marrying again. She will not wish to remain a widow for ever.'

'No, that would be a waste,' the count said, his gaze smouldering as he looked her way. 'Such beauty in a woman is meant for pleasure, to be enjoyed and savoured by the man who adores her.'

Mariah swallowed hard and then ran the tip of her tongue over her bottom lip. The expression in his eyes was setting little butterflies of apprehension fluttering low in her abdomen. Count Paolo was one of the most sensual men she'd ever met. If she wanted an affair, he would certainly oblige her.

For a moment her thoughts returned to those few precious moments by the lake when she'd thought that Andrew Lanchester cared—that he would ask her to marry him. He had not spoken, even though she'd tried to provoke him by suggesting that he help her to find a husband.

Andrew Lanchester was the man she wanted. Why could he not look at her like this?

'You have a beautiful home here, sir. I think if it were mine, I should not wish to leave it often.'

'I have always preferred my houses in France. I lived there for many years as a child and a young man. However, a house is but a house unless it contains a special person who makes it a home.'

'Yes, that is perfectly true.'

Mariah felt herself warming to him. He seemed to think as he ought and despite an instinctive feeling that she should be careful of him, she found him attractive. Marriage with such a man would certainly leave no time for moping or feeling lonely.

'I would be willing to live almost anywhere with the woman I loved. No sacrifice is too much when one loves, do you not agree, *madame?*'

Mariah nodded, making no answer. His eyes seemed to convey so much and her breath caught in her throat. She could not doubt that he was pursuing her in earnest. There was a small silence before Sylvia drew the count's attention to a particularly fine specimen of lily.

Mariah had seen the faint lift of the count's eyebrows. The signals were clear; he waited only for some sign of encouragement. She was afraid to give it, afraid of the intensity in his eyes.

'You have not yet told us if there are any other English guests attending your ball, Count,' Sylvia said. 'We must know who is coming or we shall not be able to speculate about their costumes. Part of the fun of a masked ball is guessing who has come as what—do you not agree, Mariah?'

'Oh, yes, certainly,' Mariah said. 'I always found that vastly amusing.'

'Well, I believe you may know Sir Harold and Lady Jenkins—and their nephew, Lieutenant Grainger. Also Lady Mary Soames, Mrs Sandford, Colonel Roberts—and a gentleman I have but recently met who is staying near you at the lakes. Lord Lanchester... I believe you may be acquainted with him, Lady Fanshawe?'

'Yes, I know Lord Lanchester quite well.'

'Oh, are they coming, too?' Sylvia looked surprised. 'Had we known, we might all have travelled together.'

'They are not due until tomorrow,' Count Paolo replied, an odd expression in his eyes. 'You have only recently met Lieutenant Grainger, I believe? What do you think of him?'

'As for myself, I cannot claim an intimate acquaintance,' Sylvia said. 'He seems a pleasant young man. Mariah said he had been of service to her, did you not, my love?'

'He kindly saved me from coming upon an unexpected rock fall, but I hardly know him.'

'You are a particular friend of Lord Lanchester, perhaps?'

'Yes. We were neighbours when I lived at Avonlea.' She wrinkled her brow, sensing something odd in him, an intensity as he waited for her answer. 'How did you come to meet Lord Lanchester?'

'Oh, he had some business in Milan,' the count replied

vaguely. 'He is looking to buy fine wines, amongst other things, to import into England for his own use, I understand. I invited him to the ball on impulse. He will be able to try our vintage and may wish to visit the vineyard to place an order before moving on.'

Mariah was intrigued. Was that the excuse Andrew had given the count for being in the Lombard region? It might be the truth, of course, but she suspected that the story was merely to cover his true purpose—whatever that might be.

'I have heard your wines are exceptional, Count.'

'You sampled one of our wines at luncheon. Tonight you will have the chance to sample more, but of course the best way is to visit the vineyards. I should be happy to escort you if you cared for the idea—perhaps tomorrow morning?'

'Oh, no,' Sylvia replied before Mariah could form an answer. 'It would be too strenuous on the morning of a ball, Count Paolo. However, we should be delighted to visit another day before we return to your beautiful villa.'

Mariah was certain that he had been inviting her alone, but if Sylvia's intervention had annoyed him he hid it behind a polite smile, asking her to forgive him for being foolish enough to suggest it.

She was intrigued and yet nervous. Sylvia had foiled one attempt by the count to get Mariah alone, but she did not imagine he would stop there.

Indeed, the count did not stop trying to get Mariah alone. After dinner, when the gentlemen had rejoined the ladies, having spent the shortest time over their port, Count Paolo found

Mariah standing by the long windows facing the garden, gazing out at the night sky.

'We have some stars tonight,' he said as he came up to her. 'I think there is nothing quite as romantic as the stars—do you not agree, Mariah?'

The way he spoke her name sent tingles down Mariah's spine. He was wearing a sharp fragrance that reminded her of citrus and something rather subtler that she could not name.

'Moonlight is also romantic,' she agreed. 'But we see the moon more often than the stars—at least that is so in England, I think.'

'You have too much cloud in England,' the count said. He reached out, tracing one finger down her bare arm. 'Surely you do not thrive in that grey country?'

'England is my home, sir. I do enjoy the sunshine of Italy—and, like you, I love Paris—but I was born in England.'

'Yet you could live happily in Italy. I have heard that you stayed on for a time after your late husband died?'

'People were so kind to me and I had no one particular at home.'

'Then why return there? I am sure you could find a new life here.'

Mariah replied honestly, 'Perhaps. Though I have many friends there and might find the life here a little lonely.'

'I am certain you would not be lonely. I have a wide circle of friends. If you made your life with me, you would not lack for company.'

'Forgive me? You cannot think that I…' Her cheeks felt hot because of the burning looks he was directing at her. 'I may be a widow, but I am not lost to propriety.'

Count Paolo laughed. 'You cannot have misunderstood me. I believe I have made myself clear from the beginning. I wanted you the first moment I saw you. You take my breath away, Mariah—I meant no disrespect. What is mine is mine. I never share. I would put my ring on your finger. We would be married, of course.'

'Married? We hardly know one another!' She was shocked, her spine tingling as she stared into his hot eyes. 'I would need time, sir. To give up my home and friends…to live here with you. I should need to care for you deeply.'

'You feel something. I sensed it at the start. Live a little dangerously, Mariah. I shall show you how to take the most from life. You have scarcely tasted its pleasures…'

The sensual purr in his voice made her heart race. He was persuasive, his eyes hypnotic, like a cat. She felt almost as if she were in the grip of a tidal wave that was lifting her, sweeping her away.

'I would need to think carefully…'

'You have told me yourself that you have no family.' He smiled at her. 'I have perhaps been in too much of a hurry— yes? I thought there was an attraction when we first met and I sensed something…a need for physical comfort. Perhaps I am wrong?'

Mariah caught her breath. How could he know so much about her? Had he seen the vulnerability she tried to hide? His voice was soft, caressing, and the look in his eyes was so very persuasive. It was hard to resist when she *was* so lonely.

There, she had admitted it to herself. The word was one she disliked. How could she be lonely when she had so many good friends? It was foolish to dwell on the thought and she would not give in to self-pity.

'I believe we might be good friends, sir.'

'Surely we could never be just friends? You feel it, but you fear it—admit the truth, Mariah.'

She glanced away from the count's eyes, because she was afraid that he would see how uncertain she was. How had he seen that she needed love? She prided herself on keeping a shield in place, but it seemed that he had instantly seen beneath it.

Mariah lifted her head proudly. 'It is much too soon to think of marriage, sir.'

'Yes, I am in too much hurry. Forgive me. I am impulsive—a man who feels deeply, passionately. As soon as I saw you I knew I wanted you—that you would be mine one day. In time you will accept it and realise that we were meant to love as only we can.'

'I suppose if one were in love it might be worth the loss of country and home,' Mariah replied, trying for cool indifference, though her pulses raced. Something in his manner dominated her. She was flattered, a little excited, but frightened, too. Instinct told her that this was the last man in the world she ought to trust, but she did not wish to offend him since she was his guest. 'I hardly know you, sir. Since we have only just met, you cannot know that we should suit—or that I would be the woman you require as a wife.'

'I knew of you long before we met today,' he replied. 'Besides, I had seen you before. You were with your husband in Paris, buying a necklace. I saw how he doted on you and the way you behaved to him, with love and kindness—even though he could not have given you the physical love you needed. The age gap was too wide. Had he not died, you would have wasted your youth as his nurse.'

Mariah went cold at this revelation. 'If you know so much about me, you must know that my husband left me a great deal of money. What can you offer me that I do not already have?'

'You do not need me to tell you that,' the count replied. 'When you lie in my arms you will no longer feel lonely. I can make you happy, Mariah—and you are not happy. Do you deny it?'

'No,' she said. 'I shall not deny what you have seen for yourself. I should like to be married to a man I cared for.'

'I shall make you love me, as I love you.' Count Paolo's eyes narrowed. 'You felt something when we met, as I did. Why deny your nature?'

His persistence was beginning to make her feel anxious. She said a little sharply, 'Allow me to know my own feelings best, if you please, sir.'

'But I do know you, Mariah. I know you much better than you could guess.'

'Then you have the advantage of me, Count. While you knew of me, I knew nothing of you. Before I could even consider such a marriage I would need to know you much better.'

Why had she not refused immediately? Mariah saw the pleased expression on the count's face and wished she had dismissed the suggestion out of hand. She had thought to avoid unpleasantness, but it was a mistake. He might have accepted her dismissal with good grace had she told him at once that her heart was engaged elsewhere, but if he discovered it now he would undoubtedly be angry.

'I simply wished you to know I was interested. I am an impatient man. I speak out once I know my own mind—and I have known what I wanted since I learned that you had become a widow.'

'How did you learn so much of me?'

'We have mutual friends,' he replied dismissively. 'I know that you suffered an abduction recently. The man is dead. He is fortunate that he died easily. Had it been I who dealt with the rogue, he would have wished he had never been born.' His eyes glittered with malice.

Mariah felt coldness at her nape. This was the man he kept hidden beneath the charming exterior. The count's proposal was outrageous, but, because she was lonely, she might perhaps have fallen into his clutches had she not given her foolish heart to another man.

No matter how much he charmed and flattered her, she loved Andrew. She must cling to the hope that he would speak and not let herself be swept away by the passion of a man she had only just met.

'If you know so much of me, you must know that I always insist on having my own way,' she said, a teasing smile on her lips. 'I fear it would be marriage on my terms, Count Paolo.'

Now he would see that her mind was set and draw back. If he did not the situation might become impossible, for she could hardly leave without upsetting her friends.

He inclined his head, his gaze intense. 'That might be arranged,' he said. 'If you gave me your promise, I would do my best to please your vanity.'

'My vanity?'

'Are not all women vain, wishing always to be pampered and adored?'

'You have an odd opinion of my kind, sir.'

'I speak the truth. Does it prick you, Mariah? I shall retract it if you are angry with me. Are you angry?'

'No, why should I be? I speak plainly. You must speak as you wish to me, sir.'

'Marry me. Give me time to show you how we live—how you might live here—and then make me the happiest man alive.'

'I must have time.'

'But you are not refusing me. I warn you, I do not like to lose.'

Mariah hesitated, then gave a little shrug. She had done all she could to convince him without making a scene and leaving his house.

A trickle of ice ran down her spine. She must find a way to answer without arousing his anger if she could.

'You may not like me when you know me better.'

'I always know what I want—and I always get it one way or another.'

Mariah began to be very uneasy. The look in his eyes was obsessive. It shocked her and she wished she had never let him believe for one moment that she would marry him in time.

'We speak of something that cannot be,' she replied and laughed softly. 'I find your proposition fascinating, Count— but I like my life too well and I should not like to lose my friends.' She reached out and touched his arm. 'You must look elsewhere for a mother for your sons, flattered as I am by—'

She gasped as he seized her wrist, holding it in an iron grip. 'Please, you are hurting me...'

'Do not play fast and loose with me, Mariah,' he said smoothly. 'You like your own way. I must tell you that is my nature also. When I want something I make certain it becomes mine in time. From the moment I saw you I have planned this meeting. You returned to England before I knew you were going, but I brought you back here to me. I shall make you fall in love with me and you will be all that I want you to be.'

Mariah pulled sharply away. She had tried politeness, but it had not worked. He seemed incapable of accepting her answer.

'I shall not listen to any more of this nonsense, sir. You forget yourself. I have friends who will protect me if you try to force your attentions on me.'

'If you mean Lord Lanchester, you should think again. He is a thief and more—and about to be exposed for his crimes.' The count smiled as she gasped. 'Yes, it is most scandalous, is it not? Your friend is on the path to ruin and disgrace. You should not expect him to help you. He cannot help himself.'

'You are lying,' she exclaimed. 'It cannot be true. Andrew would never steal. Why should he? He is a wealthy man.'

'I know a man who witnessed the theft,' the count replied. 'Would you accept his written testimony?'

Mariah shook her head. 'Letters can be falsified. I know Lord Lanchester to be an honourable man.'

'Then I shall bring the witness here to you.'

'Please excuse me,' she said and moved away from him. 'Sylvia is signalling to me. I think she is ready to retire.'

'Then I shall not keep you. You must be tired after your

journey here today.' He smiled at her. 'We shall not quarrel over this affair. The scandal will break soon and then you will know I was not lying.' His smile faded. 'I had not realised Lanchester meant so much to you. Had I known, I would have broken the news gently.'

'If it were true, there is no gentle way to tell me.'

'Believe me, Mariah, it is not a lie. I was as shocked as you are when I was told what happened.' His gaze narrowed. 'Ask Lanchester for the truth when he comes. He will not be able to lie to you—and if he does you will know.'

'Yes, I should,' she agreed. 'Very well, I shall ask him when he arrives.'

'Good. Forgive me if I have hurt you by this revelation— but it is best you know the truth. There is no one who truly cares for you, Mariah—no one you can rely on. Your former guardian is married and your friend will soon be disgraced.' His voice purred like a cat. 'You will be so much safer with me, Mariah. I shall protect and love you. You will have all you ever desired and more.'

Mariah was tingling all over. Her instincts were to run away from the count's house this very minute, but something told her that might be the worst thing she could do. If Count Paolo had done so much to find out about her and her family and friends, he would not be so easily denied. He might capture her and hold her prisoner until she did as he required. Her experience of such things was too vivid for her to risk it being repeated. She would be safer to stay close to her friends. She needed to talk to Andrew and ask his advice. Surely the count had lied. Andrew could not be a thief—but something was bothering him.

Walking to join Sylvia, Mariah knew that she must continue as if nothing untoward had happened. Could Sylvia and
her husband have any idea of the count's true nature? Mariah
was certain they knew nothing of his obsession for her, though
they must have unwittingly passed on information about her.

The count was indeed obsessed with her to an unnatural
degree. No sensible man would make such outrageous plans
for a woman he'd never truly met. As far as she knew, Mariah
had never spoken to him until they arrived at his house in
Milan. If she had passed the time of day at some time in the
past, it could have been no more than that or she would have
recalled his face.

It was two years since Winston died. Why had the count not
approached her before, courted her in the normal way? She
was not indifferent to him. Had he waited, courted her slowly,
sweeping her off her feet, she would no doubt have fallen for
him and married him. She might have regretted it soon after,
when she began to see the true man, but then it would have
been too late.

She had a feeling that the count liked to manipulate those
about him. It was as if he had spun a web around them, drawing in first Sylvia and her husband, because they could give
him so much information about Mariah. Then he must have
had her followed in England. He knew about Justin's marriage—and he had discovered a mystery concerning Andrew.

The tale was an invention of the count's to make her feel
isolated so that she would wed him. Andrew would tell her it
was a lie as soon as she asked. She could hardly wait to speak
to him.

* * *

Mariah heard the commotion downstairs as she was preparing to leave her room the next morning. Pausing at the top of the stairs, she realised that some guests had arrived. Almost at once she saw Andrew and her heart quickened, but then she realised that he was being supported by Lieutenant Grainger and bleeding over the marble floor.

The count's servants had arrived and two burly footmen helped support Andrew into the nearest salon, carefully placing him on one of the sofas.

'What happened?' Mariah asked as she followed them. 'Are you badly hurt, Andrew?'

'He sustained a wound to his head and another to his hand. It is his hand that is bleeding,' Lieutenant Grainger told her. 'He was driving his own curricle and someone fired on him. His groom did as much as he could to control the horses, but unfortunately there was an accident and the curricle overturned. We happened along shortly after and we took him into our carriage.'

Mariah looked at Andrew anxiously. 'How bad is it?'

'You may speak to me, Mariah.' Andrew's voice was faint but irritated. 'I am not dead yet. It is but a flesh wound.'

'You are still bleeding, therefore it is more than a slight wound,' Mariah replied and attempted to look at his head. Andrew motioned her away impatiently. 'It needs to be bound.'

'Then leave me to the physician. For God's sake, woman. It hurts enough without you fussing round. If I could lie down upstairs…'

'What is this?' Count Paolo entered the salon before Mariah could say more. 'Did I hear correctly—bandits attacked you on your journey here? Did you get a good look at the rogues? If you can furnish me with details, Lord Lanchester, I shall have the military make a sweep of the area. This kind of thing cannot be allowed to go unpunished. I shall not allow my guests to be treated with such disrespect.'

He sounded so indignant that Mariah might have laughed had the situation not been so serious. One of the count's servants had brought a bowl of water, another had bandages and various salves. She saw that Andrew was recovering a little as his head was bound and his hand examined. The wound looked red and there was a deep gash where the ball had ploughed across the skin; it was decided that a tight bandage should be applied while a physician was sent for.

'I imagine the culprits are long gone,' Andrew said in reply to the count's demand. 'But if you are sure they were bandits, it is probably your duty to report it for the sake of other travellers.'

Mariah's attention was caught. Something in Andrew's manner told her that he did not believe the attack on them was the work of bandits. Her gaze narrowed. Andrew was very worried about something. She had guessed there was some mystery, but Andrew had refused to tell her anything. Now she thought she understood why. He was involved in something dangerous and was trying to protect her.

She longed to tell him of the count's outrageous proposal the previous evening and of the allegations he had made against Andrew himself, but now was clearly not the time. He had survived a murderous attack by his own bravery in driving off the bandits and was hurt, though it seemed not as badly as she had first thought. He was sitting up now, apparently feeling better.

'Is there anything I can do for you?' she asked, but Andrew merely shook his head while the count smiled and assured her that everything was under control.

'My servants will care for our guests, Mariah,' he murmured and gave her a look that she could only call propriety. 'You must not bother your pretty head over this. Ladies must be upset by things of this nature and I would not have you distressed in my home.'

Andrew looked at her sharply for a moment, but his mind was clearly exercised by what had happened on the road and his injuries.

Leaving them to settle the unpleasant business between them, she went in search of Sylvia, whom she knew to be walking in the gardens. Men were incredibly stubborn about certain things. She was not likely to scream or faint at the sight of a little blood, and, had she been in her own home, would have tended Andrew. As for the bandits, it was not unknown for a coach to be held up by highwaymen at home and she knew that some of her friends had suffered similar experiences when travelling abroad. Why the count should imagine it might upset her she did not know.

Going in search of her friend, she found her in the rose garden, as she'd expected. Sylvia's passion for roses was well known and she had been given permission to cut some for the rooms of the female guests—a task she relished.

'Look at this beautiful damask rose,' she said as Mariah walked up to her. 'It has such a glorious scent, but there are only two bushes in flower so I must not cut too many blooms.

You shall have them for your room, dearest. Count Paolo insisted that I cut roses for you, Mariah.'

'He is very attentive,' Mariah said, wrinkling her brow as she sniffed the rose. 'Gorgeous. Tell me, what do you really know of him, Sylvia?'

'Apart from a brief meeting at his father's funeral I know very little about him, my dear. As I said, it was the count's father whom we considered a dear friend. He was such a lovely man, though I do believe there might have been a rift with his son. However, we found Count Paolo to be nothing but charming upon meeting him. He has certainly proved to be as generous as his late father and has shown himself to be as gracious a host.'

'Can you recall on your first meeting, did he ask about me?'

'I am not sure.' Sylvia frowned in thought. 'We may have spoken of you in passing, but not specially. No, I am certain he did not ask a direct question. I did not think you knew him.'

'I had never met him until we came here, to my knowledge, though he says he has seen me before with Winston in Paris.'

'He remembered you?' Sylvia was surprised. 'Well, you are beautiful, of course—but you must have impressed him.'

'Yes, it would seem so. He knows about the abduction and other things. He spoke of mutual friends, but if not you...' Mariah shook her head. 'It does not matter.'

Except that it did matter. If the count's information had come through an agent, it seemed more sinister. Why should he have gone to so much trouble to find out about her?

She felt uneasy about the whole business and wished that she might have confided her worries to someone. It would not do to worry Sylvia. Her husband was in business with the count and Mariah could not expect Lord Hubert to listen to her concerns. The only person she could talk to was Andrew, but for the moment he had too much on his mind. Sylvia's voice recalled her thoughts to the present.

'There, I believe I have enough roses for today. Shall we go and place them in vases? Tompkins will show us where to find what we need.'

Mariah agreed and, linking arms, they carried a basket each into the villa.

Chapter Five

Mariah spent the morning with friends and meeting more guests who had arrived for the masked ball. After luncheon she strolled in the gardens and courtyards until refreshments were served and then went upstairs to change. All the costumes for the ball were provided and each lady or gentleman found theirs waiting for them in their rooms.

Mariah discovered that her gown belonged to the sixteenth century and was in the extravagant French fashion of that day. The heavy silk skirts and panniers were wide and cumbersome after the simple but elegant gowns of the present time. Mariah thought the gauze band that framed her neck was rather delicate and pretty, but the costume was not particularly comfortable to wear. However, the cream-and-gold embroidery on a background of black was rather daring and, glancing at herself in a long cheval mirror, Mariah thought it gave her an oddly exotic look.

She might have been a queen of the French court—or perhaps a courtesan. She believed one of the king's mistresses had been famed for wearing black, though for the moment she couldn't quite recall which one.

Her mask was also fashioned of black, shaped like a pair of butterfly's wings and encrusted with gold and semi-precious stones. It added a touch of mystery to the evening and, seeing how different she looked herself, Mariah wondered whether she would be able to tell who was wearing what.

Sylvia knocked at her door and then entered. Her gown was simpler, more in the style of a medieval lady, and suited her very well. She gasped when she saw Mariah's costume and then clapped her hands.

'Oh, how clever of the count to see it,' she cried. 'You look wonderful, dearest. So beautiful and yet mysterious…perhaps even a little dangerous.'

'The black-widow spider?' Mariah frowned as she looked at herself in the mirror. She could not deny that her *toilette* was impressive, yet she wasn't sure it was the image she would wish to portray. Was that really her? She could quite easily have been Diane de Poitiers at the heart of court intrigues, wielding her power as the king's mistress.

It was no surprise to her, when they went down to the ballroom and found that the guests were gathering, to discover that the count was wearing a costume that matched and complemented hers. He was, of course, meant to be King Henri II and *she* his mistress. Clearly, the count was putting his mark on her, letting his friends know that she was his property. Had there been an alternative, Mariah would have changed immediately for she did not like the implication. He was laying claim to her, spinning his web a little tighter about her.

The bite of the black-widow spider was deadly to its mate. The thought brought a gurgle of laughter to her lips. If

Count Paolo imagined he could manoeuvre her into giving him his way, he was greatly mistaken. However, she did find the game amusing and the hint of danger involved was exciting.

'And who are you supposed to be—or can I guess?'

Andrew's voice made her spin round. She placed a hand to her mouth as the giggle almost escaped her.

'Well may you laugh, my lady,' Andrew said and the hard set of his mouth did not look amused. 'I have never felt so damned stupid in my life.'

'Forgive me. Are you feeling better?'

'Much, though I should do better to lie on my bed. I decided to make an appearance, though I shall not stay long.' He was frowning, obviously annoyed. Mariah's laughter was stilled.

'I did not mean to offend you—but that costume is not quite what I would choose for you, Andrew.'

He was dressed as a court jester in a parti-coloured costume of blue and silver, his long, strong legs encased in tight hose and the short jerkin barely covering his hips, revealing rather too much of his intimate proportions. On his head was a cap with a point that ended in a tassel and his mask reflected the colours of his costume.

'You have nothing to be ashamed of, Andrew,' Mariah assured him in a wickedly husky voice. 'Just be careful not to become too enamoured of any lady this evening.'

Andrew tugged unhappily at his jerkin, but it would not quite cover the source of his discomfort. She noticed he was wearing his riding boots, which did not seem a part of the costume, and enquired innocently whether no shoes had been provided.

'If you or Count Paolo imagines I am wearing those damned things, you can think again. The points were at least nine inches long.'

'Shame on you, my lord,' Mariah teased. 'I assure you I had no hand in planning the costumes.'

'No?' He sounded annoyed or disbelieving. 'You are so obviously matched with the count that I thought you must have known.'

'No, I had no idea what he planned,' she replied. 'I do not particularly care for the implication or the costume.' She hesitated, then, 'I should like to speak to you privately when you have a moment. I would have sought you out sooner, but I knew you must be feeling ill since you kept to your room all day.'

'My head ached for most of the day. It is better now, but I do not think I shall dance much this evening.'

'You suffered a bang to the head when your curricle overturned. It is a wonder that you were not killed. How is your hand now?'

'The surgeon stitched it for me. I have known worse injuries when I was with the army in Spain, but it would be awkward for dancing. If the wound should open, it might start to bleed again and ruin a lady's gown.'

Mariah nodded. 'Do you know why you were attacked?'

'For money, I imagine. Is that not why these bandits prey on unwary travellers?'

'Yes, I am sure that is so—if it was bandits.'

'Who else could it be? The count is looking our way, Mariah. He, of course, knows exactly what each guest is wearing. I think we should greet him, do you not agree?'

Count Paolo was the only person present not wearing a mask that evening. His costume was as splendid as Mariah's, exactly what a French king of the period might have worn at the balls and masquerades that were so popular at court. As host he had left off his mask so that his guests would know him and he could greet them all properly.

Everyone else had to play a guessing game. While it was easy enough to spot a familiar friend, it was more difficult to know who the other guests were.

'I see we are matched,' Mariah said as she greeted her host. 'I believe I am meant to be Diane de Poitiers and you are King Henri, I assume?'

'I thought it apt,' the count said, lowering his voice to a seductive purr. 'This is how it would be, Mariah. As my wife, you would stand with me to greet our guests and they would all pay homage to your beauty. The costume suits you very well.'

'It is a charming costume, if a little cumbersome,' Mariah replied. 'However, I think I might prefer to be Catherine di Medici if I were to choose that route.'

'Surely not? Diane was the love of Henri's life. He adored her.'

'But Catherine was his queen,' Mariah replied. 'I believe she was more dangerous than Henri ever understood—so perhaps you should beware, your Majesty.'

The count laughed, seeming amused by her banter. 'You will at least open the dancing with me this evening?'

'How could I refuse a royal command?'

Mariah passed on to mingle with the other guests. It was amusing to guess at other people's identity and she was successful in discovering Lady Jenkins and her nephew, Lieutenant Grainger.

'I have not thanked you for helping Lord Lanchester, sir,' she told him when he confessed that he had not been sure of her identity. 'I am sure he owes his life to your prompt arrival. Your aunt told me that ruffians had set upon you while out walking back at the lakes. It seems that travellers must learn to be more wary.'

'I can only agree,' Peter Grainger replied. 'I must speak with Lord Lanchester later. I have something to tell him that he may find of interest.'

'Something about the attacks?'

He hesitated, then inclined his head. 'Yes, I have thought of something that may have a bearing, but I should not worry you with these things, Lady Fanshawe.' He hesitated, then, 'Have you become…attached to the count?'

'Goodness, no,' Mariah denied instantly. 'The costumes are the count's idea, certainly not mine. I shall not deny there is some interest on his part, but nothing on mine. Indeed, I hardly know Count Paolo.'

'I am relieved to hear it. I should not have spoken if you had a partiality—but I would not advise… The count is not always what he seems. You would do well to be cautious in your dealings with him.'

'Do you know anything that I ought to know?'

'I have heard a rumour concerning his wife's accident… No, I should not. This is the wrong place to speak of such things. I am a guest here. Will you dance with me later, Lady Fanshawe?'

'I should be delighted. Count Paolo wishes me to open the ball with him, but I have an empty card otherwise.'

She offered him the card and he wrote his name in two spaces: the dance following the opening sequence and then another just before the supper interval.

Mariah thanked him and turned as Sylvia came up to her with another lady and gentleman and the conversation was changed. Lieutenant Grainger walked away, disappearing into the crowd. Mariah was suddenly surrounded by gentlemen asking for dances and her card soon became almost filled, though she saved one or two for Andrew if he should ask her. As yet he had not done so. Looking for him, she caught sight of him disappearing into the salon reserved for card play and smiled. No doubt he felt too uncomfortable in that ridiculous costume to dance—or perhaps his head had begun to ache again.

The opening series of dances were very stately and belonged to the time when ladies wore the kind of costume Mariah had been obliged to wear that evening. She opened the set with the count while everyone watched politely and clapped, gradually taking their places on the floor.

After the set of dances finished, the count bowed to her, wished her a pleasant evening and went off to attend to other guests. Mariah sighed with relief as Lieutenant Grainger claimed her. The dance was a waltz and she smiled up at him as he held her very correctly. His costume as a royal hussar was very apt for him and he looked perfectly at home as they circled through the room.

'You dance very well, sir,' she said. 'Is it your intention to seek a social life when you return to England—or will you remain in the army for a time?'

'I am thinking of resigning my commission. It was to be my chosen career, but my aunt has told me that my uncle would like help running his estate. Since I am his heir, I shall naturally oblige him.'

'Ah…' Mariah nodded. 'I believe you are a favourite with Lady Jenkins?'

'She has no heir and her younger sister died some months ago. Since then she has clung to me more than before. However, my position as estate manager would not preclude my marrying, for there is a fine house on the estate where I intend to live for the time being.'

'I am sorry to learn of Lady Jenkins's loss,' Mariah replied. 'I am sure you will find the life much to your taste.'

'Since the war with Bonaparte ended, life in the army becomes less interesting and is not particularly to my taste. Besides, there are other reasons why…' He shook his head. 'This is not the place, Lady Fanshawe, though I should like to speak to you privately another day. What I know has weighed on my mind and I must tell you—and Lord Lanchester.'

'You intrigue me, sir.' Mariah tipped her head to one side. 'Does this secret concern the count? Or perhaps Lord Lanchester himself?'

'It may concern both.' A startled expression came to his eyes. 'What do you know?'

'I do not know anything, but I know there is some mystery—and I wonder if it may be the reason why both you and Lord Lanchester were attacked.'

'Be careful, Lady Fanshawe.' He looked uneasy. 'Unguarded

speech here could be dangerous. Forgive me, I should not have spoken this evening. Perhaps we may meet privately tomorrow?'

Mariah would have pressed him further, but their dance was ending. As he led her from the floor, he whispered close to her ear. 'If you can, meet me outside the Duomo at noon.'

Mariah inclined her head. She was intrigued—she had known there was some mystery. Andrew was stubbornly refusing to tell her what was behind all this unpleasantness, but she believed Lieutenant Grainger was both prepared and eager to unburden himself of his secret.

She had no time to dwell on his mysterious hints, because she was claimed by one partner after another as the evening continued. Music and laughter was the order of the night and Mariah gave herself up to enjoyment of the evening. She looked for Lieutenant Grainger once or twice, but was unable to see him. Perhaps he had gravitated into the card room, as some of the other gentlemen were wont to do.

It was at supper that she had a chance to speak with Andrew again.

'Have you spoken to Lieutenant Grainger?'

He frowned as he met her enquiring gaze. 'No, did he have the intention of it? I saw him once when he danced with you earlier, but not since then.'

'It is a little strange. He asked me for the dance before supper, but did not come to claim me. I think he has something important he wishes to tell you, Andrew.'

Andrew muttered something under his breath, looking annoyed. 'If he has, he should come to me rather than hint something to you at such a time. Conversations may be overheard and misinterpreted at an occasion like this.'

'Oh, I assure you that he said nothing anyone could pick up or understand—he was quite mysterious, but I guessed more than he said.' She gave him a wicked look. 'Did I not tell you that I should get to the bottom of your mystery?'

'Please do not meddle in something you don't understand. It might be dangerous, Mariah.'

'Lieutenant Grainger said something of the sort.' Mariah frowned and looked about her. 'It is a little strange that he forgot our dance—you do not suppose that something has happened to him?'

'Good grief, no,' Andrew said. 'Why should anything happen here? I should have thought it was the last place...' He shook his head. 'I dare say he just became bored and decided to leave.'

'Without his aunt and uncle?'

Andrew frowned at her. 'He has probably gone out for some air. Excuse me, I must take something for my headache. I doubt I shall return. Do not concern yourself with my welfare. I have had enough of wearing this stupid costume.'

'You have not danced with me this evening.'

'Did you expect me to in this thing?' He scowled. 'You have partners enough. I dare say there will be other occasions. Unless you intend to make your home in Italy?'

'No, I do not think so,' Mariah said. 'Please go and rest. You should not have bothered to attend. Everyone would have understood—and Sylvia is looking for me, I think.'

Sylvia had found a table near the window and was signalling to Mariah. She inclined her head and began to walk towards her when she heard a slight commotion and saw that one of the servants was in apparently urgent conversation with the count. The man was gesticulating and speaking rapidly, the look on the count's face turning from astonishment to shock and then anger. Instinct told Mariah that something was wrong. She changed direction, going up to the count in time to hear him say, 'Do not tell anyone else, Carlo. I do not want my guests upset. Deal with it as I told you and I shall speak with you later.'

'Is something wrong, sir?' Mariah asked.

The count turned with an expression of annoyance, which changed to a false smile as he saw her. 'Just a small domestic matter that my servant felt I would wish to know. Nothing to worry about, Mariah.'

'You seemed distressed.'

'Annoyance merely,' he said. 'I trust you are enjoying the evening, Mariah?'

'Yes, very much. If there is nothing wrong, I shall join Lady Hubert for supper.'

Mariah walked away. He was lying, of course. It was quite obvious to her that something had happened, but of course she was to be excluded. Men were so very provoking. They imagined that ladies need to be protected when it was far more exciting to know what was going on. If Andrew would only tell her what he knew, she would find the whole thing less frustrating.

Bother! She would not let herself be provoked. Yet glancing round the supper room to discover that Lieutenant Grainger was nowhere to be seen was a little worrying.

* * *

'What is the matter?' Sylvia asked as she joined her at the supper table. 'The count looked a little disturbed.'

'A domestic matter he claims.'

'Ah…' Sylvia nodded. 'You haven't seen Lieutenant Grainger, I suppose? Lady Jenkins was looking for him a few minutes ago.'

'No. He was engaged to dance with me for the last dance but one before supper, but did not claim his dance. I have not seen him since early evening.'

'It is a little odd,' Sylvia said, 'but gentlemen often become absorbed in their card games, though not many would forget engaging you for a dance. I thought he rather liked you.'

'Perhaps…' Mariah frowned.

Would Lieutenant Grainger turn up if she kept their appointment the next morning?

'Mariah—where are you going?'

She paused in the magnificent hallway, glancing over her shoulder in surprise as she saw Andrew coming down the stairs towards her the following morning.

'I was going for a little walk,' she replied. 'How are you feeling today?'

'Much better, thank you. It was a slight wound, as I told you, and I had no fever.' He frowned. 'I do not think you should walk out alone, Mariah. Would you permit me to accompany you? Where did you wish to go?'

She hesitated, then, 'Did you happen to see Lieutenant Grainger last night after we spoke?'

'No. I think he must have returned to wherever he and his friends are staying.'

'He told me that he had something important to tell you and he wanted to tell me something, too—about the count, I believe, though I am not certain quite what he had in mind. He asked if I would meet him outside the Duomo at noon, which I was about to do—but I see no reason why you should not accompany me if you wish.'

'I should feel easier if you did not go alone,' Andrew admitted. He offered her his arm as they went out into the warm sunshine. 'I hope you will not be cross with me if I do not tell you what is going on, Mariah. It is not that I wish to exclude you, merely that I fear there might be some danger and I would not like you to be harmed. You suffered enough when you were abducted.'

Mariah shivered despite the warmth of the sun, her hand pressing on his arm for comfort. 'It was an experience I should not wish to repeat,' she agreed. 'However, I have recovered from it, Andrew. I might understand if you told me just a little. Lieutenant Grainger spoke of knowing something that might concern you—does that mean anything to you?'

'Perhaps. He may have information I need,' Andrew replied. 'I had an idea that Grainger might be involved in some business I am looking into. He pretended to know nothing of the affair, but may be involved in some way, which he feared to reveal.'

'He did tell me that Lady Jenkins's younger sister died a year or so ago and that she had clung to him more since. I do not know if that has any bearing on what he wished to say to you.'

'I cannot see how.' Andrew looked serious. 'It may or may not, but hopefully the mystery will be solved quite soon.'

'I hope it will, for you may then have less to worry you.' She looked at him, a wistful note in her voice. It was so pleasant when he really talked to her. He was a man she thought she would never grow tired of seeing each day. 'You asked me if I knew about the costumes last evening. Count Paolo planned them himself—it seems he makes many plans without consulting others.'

'What do you mean? Is something worrying you?'

'He has told me that he wishes me to be his wife—and refuses to take no for an answer. He seems to imagine that because he wishes it, it must happen.'

'Damn the impudence of the fellow!' Andrew gave her a shocked, incredulous look. 'Did he truly have the effrontery to say such things to you?'

'Perhaps not quite in those words, but he seemed to imagine I would welcome his advances since I have no family to protect me.'

'How dare he?' Andrew stopped walking and looked at her, a furious expression in his eyes. 'I shall call the rogue out!'

'No, no, my dear friend.' Mariah laughed, pleased with the reaction she had provoked. 'I believe he thought me lonely, a widow looking for excitement.'

'And are you?'

'Perhaps.' Mariah gurgled with laughter as she saw the disapproval in his eyes. 'No, no, Andrew. I assure you I have no intention of becoming the count's wife or his mistress. He is a very physical, attractive man and I might perhaps have been tempted had he courted me longer and not shown his impatience—but there is something about him that I think I should find distasteful. He is a man who expects to have his way in all things…perhaps a little dangerous?'

'Dangerous? Yes, I think he might be if he were crossed.' Andrew looked thoughtful. 'You must be careful not to walk out alone with him, Mariah. How soon were you planning to return to England?'

'We may leave as soon as next week,' Mariah told him. 'Sylvia was talking of a brief visit to Venice and from there we intend to travel to France. We shall visit Paris and then make our way home after buying some clothes.'

'I shall accompany you myself. I know you trust your friends—but they clearly believe the count a man to be trusted and might not be the best placed to protect you.'

'Thank you.' Mariah hugged his arm. 'I am glad the count was wrong—I do have some good friends, Andrew.'

'You should know that Avonlea and my sister and her husband are always concerned for your welfare.'

His eyes were warm as they rested on her, a little concerned—even protective, as if he might truly care for her.

'Yes, I suppose I do know, but I should not like to be a trouble to them, Andrew. Avonlea has Lucinda and his child to care for and Jane is recently married. I know that you have much on your mind…'

They had been walking for some time and were now close to the ancient palace. Mariah glanced at the little gold watch she had pinned to her pelisse and frowned.

'It is almost the appointed time,' she said. 'I can see no sign of Lieutenant Grainger.'

'It wants five minutes to the hour,' Andrew said. 'You are certain this is where he wished to meet?'

'He said that he wished not to be overheard.'

People were strolling in the sunshine, admiring the beauties of the ancient palace and other buildings of architectural interest. It was the ideal meeting spot, because no one particularly noticed anyone, everyone being more interested in taking in the sights.

They heard a church clock striking somewhere and then another, the bells ringing out, summoning the faithful to prayer. Andrew led Mariah to a little wooden bench beneath the shade of a tree and she sat down. He stood behind her, looking about him. There were several people passing but although they waited for some minutes Lieutenant Grainger was not one of them.

'It seems as though he has changed his mind,' Andrew said. 'You did agree to the meeting?'

'Yes. I thought it odd when he did not claim his second dance last evening,' Mariah said and looked anxious. 'Do you think something has happened to him? You said this affair might be dangerous...'

'I must be honest and say that I do not know,' Andrew told her, placing a hand on her shoulder. 'I know Grainger said he was attacked at the lakes, but I thought that might be a lie to cover something else...'

She turned her head to look up at him. 'To cover what— you are hiding something more from me, are you not?'

'Someone attacked me at the villa a couple of days before we had the picnic at the lake. I took a pot shot in the dark and I think I winged the rogue. I wondered if Grainger might have hired the rogue to frighten me off—and that his claim to have been attacked himself might be a ruse, but perhaps I misjudged him.'

'Why should he want you to be frightened off?'

'If I knew that, I should have the answer to my problem. I may be entirely wrong, of course. Indeed, his disappearance leads me to believe I was misjudging him. I thought he might be covering for a friend—now I think there is something far more sinister involved.'

'I suppose you will not tell me the whole.' Mariah stood up. 'I think I shall tell Sylvia that I would like to leave for Venice almost at once. Please, Andrew, tell me what is going on—as much as you can. I think I have the right to know.'

'Perhaps you do. There might be more to this business than I realised.' Andrew frowned. 'I have an enemy. He is set on ruining me and may not be satisfied unless he has my life.'

'Andrew!' Mariah was horrified. 'Do you know who your enemy is?'

'My commanding officer believes it may be a junior officer I was forced to reprimand some years ago.'

'Why did he do nothing then—why now?'

'I wish I knew,' Andrew replied. 'I heard he might be in Naples, but my search came to nothing. If I am unable to find him—or even the identity of my enemy—I may be in serious trouble.'

'You cannot tell me more?'

'For the moment I should prefer not to, Mariah. I will say that I am accused of something I did not do. I need to prove my innocence or I could face an official hearing.'

'Is this to do with an accusation of theft? Count Paolo hinted that you were about to be ruined, but I took his words for spite, believing he hoped to discredit you in my eyes and make me turn to him. But it's true, and now you face a court-martial?' She was shocked when he inclined his head in assent. 'That is ridiculous. I know you would not…do anything dishonourable.'

'Thank you for your faith in me, Mariah. I can assure you that I have never stolen anything in my life and it means a great deal that you believe in me. Major Harrison feels the same way, but without proof there will always be a doubt—a shadow hanging over me.'

'Yes, I see.'

She saw a great deal that had not been clear to her before.

Andrew was not telling her the whole truth, but Mariah knew that he was telling her far more than she could ever have expected—and that must mean he thought she needed to know.

'You are warning me, because you do not wish me to be affected by your shame—is that not so?'

'If I cannot clear my name, I could not offer marriage to any lady—especially one I cared for.'

'Ah, now I understand.' Mariah nodded. 'My very dear friend. I should not care for a little scandal. I would be prepared to live abroad if you found it intolerable to live at home.'

'I could never ask such a sacrifice of you.'

'It would not be a sacrifice,' she assured him. 'But where does Lieutenant Grainger come into this—unless he is your enemy?'

'I think not. I believe he knows something he thinks I ought to know and has concealed it until now. However, I cannot see how you come into this, Mariah. Why should he warn you of the count in the same breath as telling you he had something to tell me? It makes little sense.'

'He warned me the count was dangerous. I believe it may have had something to do with the countess's accident…but he was afraid to say last night lest he was overheard.'

'I believe Count Paolo may be a dangerous man, Mariah. You must be careful, because he will not like being refused— but there can surely be no connection to this other business. No, the two are quite separate.'

'Yet Lieutenant Grainger spoke to me last night of something important he wished to say to you, which I believe did concern Count Paolo. He thought I might be involved with him, because of the costumes. However, he had something more he wished to tell me. I believed it concerned the attacks on you both.'

Andrew glanced about the square. 'Well, whatever it might have been, it seems Grainger is not coming. Perhaps we should return to the count's home?'

'Yes, perhaps we should.' Maria took his arm. 'Is this mystery the reason why you asked me to wait until we were in England to make my decision, Andrew?'

He turned to her with a smile. 'I have been in some turmoil, Mariah. Yes, of course. I have had it in mind to ask you if you would do me the honour of becoming my wife, but I could not speak while this shadow hangs over me.'

'I assure you I do not regard a little scandal, Andrew.'

'It was not only that,' he replied. 'I am not yet certain who is behind this, Mariah. I would not like you to be caught in the crossfire if things become dangerous.'

'I did think once last summer that you might ask me to marry you, but then you withdrew and I wondered if I had displeased you—that business of the shooting...?'

'You were very brave and undoubtedly saved Lucinda's life,' he said. 'You have done nothing to displease me, Mariah. I am almost certain we should suit. I do not think either of us requires a love match particularly, but there would be no lack of respect or passion on my side. As yet I am not free to ask and may never be, but if I can clear this scandal that attaches to my name then I should like to discover how we feel about each other. We are friends, but do we wish to be more to each other and should we suit? I need a wife who is content to give me children, but should not wish her to remain always in the country if she wished to travel or even to live in London.'

Mariah kept her face turned away. So he thought her a suitable wife, but his implication was clear—he was not in love with her.

Well, she supposed she might live with that, though she had hoped for far more. Deep inside her there was a little hurt voice that demanded she weep, but she held it at bay and forced a careless laugh.

'Oh, I think I could manage that, Andrew. I might even live in the country for a few months each year, but I certainly wish for children.' She smiled up at him, a hint of challenge in her eyes. 'If we should discover that our feelings were involved, and you should ask me, I see no reason why the answer should not be yes.'

'Then we have an understanding,' he said and nodded.

Mariah turned to him with a smile. 'Yes, we have an understanding.'

They had an understanding of sorts.

It seemed her future might be in a way to be settled at last, because she knew that she cared deeply for Andrew, far more than she had expected to care for anyone. If he offered her passion, respect and children, it would be enough.

She turned to him, gazing up into his face. 'You may kiss me if you wish.'

'In public?'

'No one will notice.'

Andrew laughed, caught her about the waist and drew her to him. He lowered his head, taking her lips softly, but with a hint of passion.

'You are a temptress, Mariah. Do not imagine I have not been tempted. I am a man like any other and I have oft wanted to kiss you until the breath left your body and you surrendered to me.'

'Had you told me I should not have denied you.'

Her eyes sparkled with mischief. His kiss had aroused such dreams, such longing that had she not seen a couple looking at them in amusement she might have thrown her arms about him and declared her love.

'You are a minx, Mariah. I have told you before that you deserve to be spanked.'

Mariah pouted at him, taking his arm again. They walked on in silence. For a moment he had been provoked to passion, but now he was her sensible, dependable friend again. She was such a fool to want more, but she longed to lie in his arms and throw caution to the winds. Despite having shared a part of his secret with her, Andrew was still concerned about her reputation and behaving in an honourable manner. Why did he simply not make love to her and place his ring on her finger? If he loved her as she loved him, he would surely do so?

It was as they entered the count's house that Mariah sensed an atmosphere of alarm and upset. She was taking off her bonnet when Sylvia came down the stairs towards her.

'Oh, thank goodness you are back, my love,' she exclaimed. 'Lady Jenkins has been here, looking for you. She is in such distress. It seems that her nephew has disappeared. He accompanied her to the ball, but then went missing. She thought he might have returned to their hotel, but no such thing. He has not been seen all night. She thought you might know where he was.'

'No, indeed I do not,' Mariah said. 'He did ask me to meet him today, but he did not keep his appointment—or his engagement to dance last evening.'

'What could have happened, do you suppose?' Sylvia asked. 'Count Paolo was distressed that one of his guests should simply disappear that way. He has given orders that the house and grounds should be searched—and enquiries are to be made throughout the city.'

'Is Lady Jenkins still here?'

'She returned to the hotel in case he should go back there. After all, as the count suggested, he is a young man and men will sometimes go off on affairs of their own.'

'I doubt that Lieutenant Grainger is so ill mannered as to worry his aunt,' Andrew said. 'I dare say he may have met with an accident. I shall speak to the count and ask what is being done, and of course offer my assistance to Lady Jenkins.

In fact, I think I shall visit her hotel first to see if there is any sign of him.' Andrew glanced at Mariah, a warning look in his eyes. 'I shall do my best in this matter, but it is my intention to leave for Venice soon—and I would advise you to do the same.'

'Oh, could we travel with you?' Sylvia asked. 'After all that has happened I should feel safer if we could all go together. I think I shall send a servant to collect our things from the villa. I am sorry to curtail our trip, Mariah, for I know you were enjoying yourself—but I really do not think I wish to continue in such uneasy circumstances.'

'I am perfectly ready to leave when you are,' Mariah replied. 'I think we should all go tomorrow. A day or so in Venice will refresh us before we leave for France.'

'Yes, that is my feeling,' Sylvia said and took her hand as Mariah reached her. 'It is such a shame. I know Count Paolo feels it dreadfully—he feels responsible because his guests have been treated so ill. First that attack on Lord Lanchester and now Lieutenant Grainger has disappeared. I really do not know what is happening.'

'You must not distress yourself,' Mariah said and squeezed her arm. 'Whatever has happened is none of your making. We must not let it spoil what has been a delightful trip.'

'No, indeed. Count Paolo has been such a generous host. He was distressed when I told him I wished to go straight home. He told me that we should always be welcome to return, but I am not sure that I shall…' Sylvia blushed. 'I have not told Hubert yet, but I think… I really think that I may at last be in an interesting condition.'

'Sylvia, dearest.' Mariah kissed her cheek. 'I am delighted

for you—and you must not be anxious. This unpleasant business can have nothing to do with us.'

'No, I do not see how it can.' Sylvia looked relieved. 'The attack on Lord Lanchester was the work of bandits—and I do not know what can have happened to Lieutenant Grainger, I am sure.'

'He may just have gone off and had too much to drink,' Mariah said. 'He is a new friend and a pleasant gentleman, but you should not concern yourself too much, dearest. His aunt will no doubt engage an agent to search for him if he is not found immediately.'

'Will she know what to do?'

'I am sure Lord Lanchester will do whatever he can to help her. He is resourceful and has some knowledge of these things.'

'Ah, yes, your troubles…' Sylvia looked at her in concern. 'This must bring it all back to you?'

'No, it is not the same,' Mariah said. 'I do not believe I am in any danger. Let us take a little walk in the rose gardens, dearest—and then we shall instruct the maids to begin our packing.'

'Yes. How calm and sensible you are,' Sylvia said, some of the anxiety clearing from her eyes. 'I had hopes you might form an attachment while we were in Italy…'

Mariah considered telling her of her understanding with Andrew, but something warned her to keep the information to herself. It might be best to say nothing until they were safely on their way home to England. Andrew had not actually asked her and he might never do so if things went badly.

Chapter Six

'Grainger has not been seen at the inn and his things are just as he left them,' Andrew said when Mariah spoke with him later that afternoon while strolling in the courtyard garden.

Mariah's eyes widened. 'Do you think something unpleasant could have happened to him?'

'I told his aunt that he might have had an accident or perhaps become involved in a long card game—which is still possible, though why he should leave the ball without taking his leave of her I have no idea.'

'You do not believe it to be that simple, do you?'

'No. I think he may have been kidnapped or worse.'

Mariah caught her breath. 'I think I shall be glad to leave in the morning. I wish we might go sooner, but Sylvia is already distressed and I would not wish to alarm her further.'

'The morning will be suitable. I think we are all safe enough for the moment. If Lieutenant Grainger has been abducted or murdered, it is because he knew something I don't—to prevent him from telling me or you.'

Mariah shuddered. She would have pressed him for more, but saw the count striding through the courtyard garden towards them. He looked serious, a frown creasing his forehead as he came up to them.

'My servants have completed their search of the house and grounds. Grainger is, as I expected, nowhere to be found. However, one of my servants thinks he recalls a gentleman a little the worse for strong wine leaving halfway through the evening. His description matches the costume I know Lieutenant Grainger to have been wearing. Therefore we may assume that he grew bored with the company and went off to look for drinking companions. I dare say he may return when he has slept his excesses off.'

'Yes, I dare say he may. I shall hope for Lady Jenkins's sake that he has come to no harm by his foolishness,' Andrew replied smoothly. 'I must thank you for your hospitality, sir. As you know, we are leaving early in the morning. I shall not see you this evening, as I have promised myself to Lady Jenkins. I must do all I can for her before we leave.'

'I shall be sorry to see you go, Lord Lanchester.' Count Paolo inclined his head as Andrew turned to Mariah.

'We shall be ready to leave at seven in the morning. I trust that will not be too early, Lady Fanshawe?'

'Thank you, sir. I know Lady Hubert is anxious for an early start. We shall be ready.'

Mariah turned her gaze to the count as Andrew walked away. Her heart was beating a little faster than normal, but she managed to smile and look carefree as she said, 'I have to thank you so much for your hospitality, sir—both here and at the lakes. We enjoyed our stay there so much and the ball was delightful.'

'It distresses me that this unpleasant incident should have

given Lady Hubert a dislike of Milan. I shall be sorry to see you leave, Mariah—I cannot press you to stay on as my guest?'

'You know my answer, sir. I shall not deceive you. I fear I should not have settled here. I value your friendship, of course, but my life is elsewhere. I have good friends in England and I shall make my home there.'

He moved towards her and for a moment she thought he would take hold of her violently. She took a step backwards, not for the first time feeling fearful in his company. The intense look in his eyes told her that he had not given up hope of persuading her.

'I cannot force you to stay, but I think I know what I must do,' he said and his smile sent a shiver down her spine. 'I shall allow you to leave me for now, Mariah—but this does not end here. When I want something, I do not let go easily.'

Mariah shook her head, fighting to keep her smile in place. She wondered why she had ever thought he was a charming man—he was like a snake, potentially venomous and deadly.

'Forgive me, my mind is made up. Nothing can change it— no alteration in your circumstances. I know what I want from life and that does not include living here—as your mistress or as your wife.'

His eyes narrowed in anger and she drew a sharp breath, fearing that she had gone too far. Perhaps she had been rude, but she needed to make sure he understood there was no possibility of anything between them. However, he merely inclined his head and smiled coldly.

'A lady as beautiful as you is never easily won, Mariah,' he said and his voice was like the silken purr of a cat. It had fascinated her when they first met, making her pulses race, but now it left her cold. He was dangerous and she would be glad to see the last of him. 'I shall win you yet, my love.'

Feeling it would be unwise to say more, Mariah smiled and inclined her head. She walked towards the house, knowing that she must not look back lest he took it as an invitation, yet knowing also that his eyes were on her. Was he angry, plotting his revenge? She sensed that he might be violent if provoked and trembled inwardly, half wishing that Andrew had not promised to dine with Lady Jenkins that evening.

No, she was not a timid girl to be intimidated! Her abductor, Captain Blake, had thought to break her spirit and failed; the count would fare no better. She would stay close to Sylvia for the remainder of their stay—and she would lock her bedroom door!

The night passed without incident. Mariah dressed and went down with Sylvia and Lord Hubert. The count had come to bid them farewell; he was the perfect, handsome, smiling gentleman she had first met and she was not surprised that her friends believed that he was all that was generous and kind.

'I hope to see you in England very soon, Lady Fanshawe,' he said. 'I wish you a safe journey but I am sure you will meet with no more accidents on the way. I am sending two of my grooms to escort you to Venice. They will see you safely there.'

'Thank you, you are most kind,' Mariah said, for she could say nothing less.

The count said no more, turning instead to Lord Hubert on a matter of business. Andrew was waiting for them outside in the street with the carriage. Andrew had chosen to ride, but looked pale, though seemed in good spirits. He refused when she asked if he would not like to ride inside the coach.

'I am well enough to ride. My hand pains me a little, but I can manage.'

'If it hurts too much, you must stop the coach and ride with us.'

'I shall manage—' He broke off as Sylvia was helped into the carriage. 'Attend to your friend, Mariah. I do not need coddling.'

'Of course not,' Mariah said and pouted at him. 'Growling will get you nowhere, Andrew.'

'What was that all about?' Sylvia asked as she sat back against the squabs.

'Andrew is grumpy this morning. I think his hand pains him.'

'The foolish man should ride with us. I dare say it is his pride that prevents him.'

'I believe he wants to be outside, to help keep watch lest we should be attacked.'

Sylvia shivered. 'Please do not! Surely with the count's grooms to accompany us we shall be safe enough?'

'Yes, I am certain we shall.'

'I cannot wait to be out of Italy.' Sylvia shivered.

'I think we shall all be glad of a change of scenery,' Mariah said. 'Is Lord Hubert to ride, Sylvia?'

'Yes, he prefers it—though should it rain he would wish to ride with us.' Sylvia sighed and reached for her reticule. 'To be honest, I cannot wait to be home again.'

'In that case we might forgo our visit to Venice and make

straight for France and Paris instead. We need only stop in the city for a couple of days at the most before we head to the coast and the boat to take us back to England,' Mariah suggested. 'I should be quite content with that, dearest.'

'Yes, well, it is what Hubert decided when I told him my news,' Sylvia said, a faint blush in her cheeks. 'He is a little concerned for me and I thought it best to agree.'

'Yes, indeed.' Mariah smiled at her fondly. 'It will be good to be at Avonlea again.'

'Is that where you shall go?' Sylvia asked. 'I had thought… but, yes, perhaps it would be best. I dare say you have things to concern you.'

'I have some estate business that ought to be attended and I shall do that better with Avonlea's help. The duke is no longer my guardian, but in matters of this nature I value his advice. Besides, it is close to Lord Lanchester's estate.'

'Oh…' Sylvia must have seen the sparkle in her eye, for she nodded and smiled. 'I had not realised, Mariah. I am happy for you, dearest.'

'There was nothing to tell you. We have an understanding, but nothing is to be announced for the moment—it is merely a private arrangement for the future and may not come to anything.'

Sylvia reached for her hand. 'Well, I am glad of it—I have worried for you, my love.'

'You have been the best of friends and as soon as anything is settled I shall of course write and perhaps visit.'

'Yes, of course you must. I fear I shall do little visiting for the next several months. Once I am home I intend to stay there.'

'Yes, you must take great care of yourself.'

'As you must, dearest. I shall be happy to see you wed.'

Mariah agreed it would be the best thing that could happen to her.

Smiling to herself, she settled against the squabs and prepared for a long journey.

Mariah had wondered if the journey might prove too much for her friend, but Sylvia seemed very much better once they were clear of Milan. The weather was kind to them and they made excellent progress, quickly crossing the border into France.

'We shall certainly buy some new dresses in Paris,' Sylvia said. 'No one gives a *toilette* so much style as a French seamstress. I shall need gowns that will let out to allow for my condition and I may as well have them made rather than try to adjust my old ones. Besides, I am perfectly well. It was a mere irritation of the nerves.'

Mariah smiled, for she doubted her friend ever wore a gown that was older than a year. Her husband spoiled her and her wardrobes overflowed with beautiful clothes.

'I shall order a few gowns for the winter. They will send the order to Avonlea for me and Lucinda will have the gowns taken care of should I not be there.'

Sylvia looked at her coyly. 'Are you buying a trousseau, my love?'

Maria smiled and shook her head. 'Sylvia, dear, it is an understanding. I do not expect to announce our intentions for a while. Andrew has some affairs to set in order first and I have agreed that it shall remain private, known only to our close friends. We shall use this time to get to know each other better. I shall, of course, tell Avonlea and Lucinda and Andrew will tell Jane and George, but I think we do not need to announce it to the world.'

'You are very calm about things,' Sylvia remarked. 'Are you in love with him, dearest?'

'Love?' Mariah arched her right eyebrow, giving her friend a look of mischief. 'Andrew is very attractive and I am sure he will make me an excellent husband. I am attached to him and I like him—perhaps that is enough. Do you not think so?'

Sylvia murmured something about her knowing her own mind best. Mariah laughed. Her pride would not let her admit to anyone that it was a love match on her side when it was so obviously not on Andrew's. He treated her as a good friend, caring for her comfort and her safety, which she knew he would do for any lady of his acquaintance. However, he showed no sign of being a man driven by passion or love.

Mariah knew that he had been in love with Lucinda Avonlea the previous summer. Was he still coming to terms with his loss? Did he still carry a torch for the young woman he'd befriended when she was unhappy and uncertain of her husband's feelings?

She recalled a walk they had taken on their recent journey; it was one of the rare chances they'd had to be alone since they had come to their agreement.

'You have not told me what the count said to you that last morning before we left?' Andrew looked at her. 'Did he try to persuade you to stay on?'

'He knew that he could not. I tried to make it clear that there could never be anything between us, but he did not seem to accept it. He said he knew what he must do and would see me in England—he also said that a woman as beautiful as I was never won easily.'

'The man knows how to flatter.' Andrew scowled. 'You must tell me at once if he turns up and begins to pester you, Mariah.'

'It might be best if we did not delay our plans too long,' she said without looking at him. 'I know you fear the scandal over these unfounded accusations, but I should not regard it.'

'I should mind for your sake,' Andrew replied. His eyes narrowed. 'Did you encourage the count to think you might accept him?'

Mariah felt her cheeks heat. She raised her eyes to his and spoke bravely. 'I may have flirted with him a little at the start,' she admitted. 'I was feeling lonely, as I told you at the lakes. I considered marriage to be preferable to being pursued by fortune hunters. I was serious in that—and I suppose I also considered an affair. I am tired of being alone, Andrew. I know I was married for a short time only, but Winston was my friend as well as my husband and I still miss him.'

'Yes, I dare say you do,' he said and reached for her hand, pressing it to his lips. His action, though casual, sent a ribbon of fire through her, making her long for much more. He had large shapely hands and she imagined how good it might feel to lie close to him and feel his fingers stroking her flesh. 'I am certain we shall be good friends as well as husband and wife, Mariah. I have been aware of a lack in my life for a while. I think, if you are agreeable, we shall announce our happiness quite soon. Just give me a week or two once we are home so that I may settle my affairs.'

'Are you able to clear your name?'

'Nothing has changed since we last spoke. As yet I have no clues as to the identity of my enemy. However, I shall speak to my commanding officer, tell him that I believe the letter to be slander and little more. After all, there can be no proof for I know that I am innocent of any crime against my regiment. The regiment must decide whether to take my word or court-martial me. I have tried to find Lieutenant Gordon, but for the moment I have no idea of where else to look.'

'It is a matter of your word against an anonymous letter?'

'I fear it is all I can do at this moment. I have hopes that the matter will be dismissed.'

'Dismissed, but not completely resolved? Will you be happy with that outcome?'

'It is the best we can do in the circumstances. If I submit myself to my fellow officers' judgement, I shall stand or fall by their decision.'

'Supposing there is more behind this than an attempt to blacken your name? Your carriage was attacked on your way to the count's house in Milan—and you were attacked at the villa. Your enemy may want more than your disgrace.'

'You are suggesting that he hates me enough to kill me?'

'Has that not crossed your mind, Andrew?'

He stared at her for a moment, then laughed softly. 'How astute you are, Mariah. Yes, I have wondered if my life is in danger. That is why I have hesitated to speak of marriage. I should be distressed if harm were to come to you because of me.'

'I think that is hardly likely.'

'If I have a ruthless enemy, he might well feel the best way to strike at me is through you.' He reached out to touch her cheek. She sighed and moved closer. Andrew bent his head, his lips caressing hers softly, making her tremble with sudden need. 'If you were harmed, I should never forgive myself, Mariah. I just wish I knew who sent the letter...'

'You have no idea?'

'None at all, unfortunately.'

'You have not broken a lady's heart? That kind of trick is something a spiteful woman might do. Did you allow someone to think you meant marriage and then withdraw?'

'Apart from a few convenient arrangements, which were ended by mutual agreement, there have been no significant ladies in my life—until I met you. I do not suspect you of having sent it.'

'Are you sure of that, Andrew?' Mariah inclined her head teasingly. 'The letter is one thing, but the attack on your life is quite another—and why did Lieutenant Grainger wish to tell us both something?'

'I believe it concerned the count,' Andrew said. 'We have discussed this before. Yet I fail to see how the two are connected. If he knows something incriminating about Count Paolo, it may account for his disappearance—but can have no bearing on my problem.'

'There can be no possible reason for...' Mariah shook her head. 'This Lieutenant Gordon still seems the most likely culprit—does he have friends or family who might blame you for his disgrace?'

'I suppose that is a possibility. I believe he might have had a widowed mother and a younger sister.'

'Could one of them have been the writer of the letter?'

'Yes, that is possible,' Andrew admitted, looking thoughtful. 'You have given me some fresh ideas. As you say, that kind of letter might be a woman's weapon. I shall discover what happened to them after he left the service. If they are in trouble, I will offer to help them. Perhaps they may know where he has gone.'

'Yes, they may be able to help.' Mariah nodded. 'I do not know why—but I must tell you that I feel the mystery is more complicated than we yet realise.'

His eyes quizzed her. 'Because you wish it to be? You enjoy solving puzzles, Mariah. I recall that as a girl you loved to get lost in Avonlea's maze for hours. The old duke had it pulled down in the end because you spent too much time there and he was afraid you really would get lost one day.'

'I was a contrary girl and utterly spoiled,' she admitted with a laugh. 'Are you changing your mind, Andrew? I may not be the most convenient of wives.'

'I have no illusions concerning you, Mariah. You have been thoroughly spoiled for most of your life. I dare say you will expect to have your own way in most things.'

'Do not look so cross,' Mariah said and laughed even though she felt hurt inside. Did he really have such a poor opinion of her? 'They all enjoyed spoiling me. I assure you I can be perfectly sensible if I choose.'

'Yes, I am certain you can.' He smiled and her heart jumped because in that moment she felt that he truly cared for her. 'If I am honest, I dare say I like you as you are, dearest Mariah.' He reached out to caress her cheek with one finger, bringing her body leaping to life and pulsing with the need to be in his arms once more.

It was the closest he had come to showing affection for her in an age, but though his eyes seemed to convey a need of his own, he did not take advantage of the moment to kiss her. What a very annoying gentleman he was, to be sure! Mariah's throat closed with emotion, but she tossed her head and refused to let herself cry.

Since Sylvia had come up to them at that moment the mood had been broken and it had not been repeated, because for the rest of their journey to Paris they were never alone.

'So many pretty dresses,' Sylvia said as she stroked the material Mariah had chosen for a ball gown with the tips of her gloved fingers. 'You will hardly wear the half of them this Season. One never does in the winter at home.'

'Oh, I think I may find a use for them,' Mariah said. 'I have been clinging to the colours I wore after Winston died for too long. It is time I wore the rich colours that suit me—and, of course, white with spangles is always so good in the evening.'

'Well, I have decided to be sensible and buy not more than six new gowns,' Sylvia said. 'I shall not need to be bang up to the mark for my period of confinement, you know—and there are bound to be new ideas for when we go up to town next year.'

'Yes, I am certain there will be,' Mariah agreed.

She spoke to the seamstress once more about the delivery of her gowns, which were to be brought to Avonlea by the lady herself. For a customer of Mariah's importance such a journey was necessary—imperative—so that any last-minute alterations could be made. Lady Fanshawe's patronage would bring many new clients to her door, for she was much admired.

'It should be no longer than two weeks, milady. Of a surety all my girls will work on your order and I myself shall do the special embroidery on the ball gown.'

'Then I am certain it will be perfect. The last one you made me has been much admired, *madame.*'

'Ah, yes, when you came here with milord—a gentleman most fine and comfortable.'

'My husband was a good, kind and generous man,' Mariah agreed.

She took her farewell with Sylvia, who had chosen to have her gowns made elsewhere so that the orders should not bring a conflict of interest. They left the exclusive establishment, going out into a pleasantly warm afternoon despite the advanced time of year.

'We shall know the difference when we are home again,' Sylvia said. 'After so much sunshine the winter will seem long and dull.'

'Oh, I quite enjoy Christmas around a log fire,' Mariah said. 'I think it will be rather special this year and I am looking forward to seeing Lucinda and Justin's baby.'

'Yes, of course.' Sylvia brightened. 'I have my baby to look forward to and I must be at home for that, of course—' She broke off and clutched Mariah's arm, directing her to glance towards a certain café. 'Do you think that rather odd man is following us? I noticed him when we arrived. It is strange that he should still be here.'

Mariah glanced at the table outside one of the many cafés in the area. The man had long dark hair, a black patch over one eye and was wearing a large coat that looked too big for him. He was sipping a glass of wine, seemingly minding his own business, yet she felt that he was aware of them staring at him.

'He does look odd,' she agreed. 'However, I cannot imagine why he would wish to follow us, dearest. He is just enjoying a bottle of wine in the sunshine.'

'Yes, of course. How foolish of me! It was all that nonsense in Milan, of course.' Sylvia shivered. 'I cannot tell you how glad I shall be to be home again.'

'Well, we are leaving tomorrow,' Mariah comforted. However, she made up her mind to tell Andrew about the rather odd man, as soon as they returned to the hotel.

'I dare say it was just coincidence,' Andrew said when Mariah recounted the incident. 'I should not let it worry you.'

His innocent air made her suspicious and she caught his arm as he would have turned away. 'Are you having me watched? That ridiculous hair and the patch—really, Andrew! Surely your man can do better than that? Sylvia noticed him at once.'

His face reflected amusement. 'He does look a trifle obvious. I shall find someone less intrusive when we are home, but I did not want to forbid you to go shopping with your friend without an escort or to alarm you. However, I should have known you would find me out.'

'Do you think I am in danger of being abducted again?'

'It has crossed my mind.' He frowned. 'I am almost certain we were watched on our journey—and I think we were followed to Paris.'

'Count Paolo's men?'

'Yes, possibly. I cannot think of anyone else who might be following us, can you?'

'Was it one man all the time?'

'He changed his appearance, but, yes, I would say it was just one man.'

'Why would the count do such a thing?' Mariah shivered as the tiny fine hairs on the back of her neck stood up. 'I refused him and he said he would see me in England—but to have us watched...' She shuddered. 'It is unnatural.'

'It is certainly obsessive. The count is a man who likes his own way and there is nothing so very wrong in that—but perhaps he goes to extremes to get what he wants.'

'He did say something odd. I dismissed it as nonsense, but it made me feel uneasy. He spoke of seeing me with Winston when I was first married and never forgetting me. I think he may have been having me watched for a long time, even before our visit to the lakes.'

'Do you recall precisely what he said?'

Mariah shook her head. 'At first I thought he was flattering me, dallying with me, and I laughed. It wasn't until he made me that outrageous offer that I began to dislike certain things in his manner.'

Andrew looked thoughtful. 'I think I shall continue to have you watched for your own sake, Mariah—but I will ask my man to be more discreet. If, of course, it was my man...'

'It could have been the count's spy.' Mariah felt slightly sick. 'I shall be glad to be home again, Andrew.'

'Yes...' He hesitated, then came to a decision. 'If you think we shall suit, I believe we shall tell our friends at once, Mariah. Should there be a scandal, you could always withdraw...' She shook her head. 'Very well, I shall send a notice to the papers and I shall hold a ball, at which you will be my hostess.

It may be best to get the business of our marriage out of the way. Until we marry you will always be at the mercy of fortune hunters. Even Count Paolo must give up when we are married.'

'Yes, I believe you are right.' Mariah smiled and leaned forwards to kiss his cheek. 'Thank you, my best of friends. I shall not want a wedding trip that takes us abroad. Perhaps somewhere quiet where we can be alone for a while? I shall make no demands that take you from your affairs, for I know you have a great deal on your mind.'

'We could go up to my maternal grandfather's hunting lodge in the lowlands of Scotland. It belongs to my cousin, but he will loan it to us should we wish,' he said. 'By the time the banns are read I should have settled most of my affairs. I think I have dragged my feet too long. I should have asked you months ago, then much of this unpleasantness could have been avoided for you.'

Mariah said nothing because her friends had just entered the private parlour and it was time to order their supper. In the morning they would take a carriage ride to the coast, board the ship for England and there they would go their separate ways. Mariah thought that when she saw Sylvia again she would be married.

She was conscious of a tiny ache inside because her marriage was to be a matter of convenience. Andrew was being kind and she knew he felt something for her, but she wanted him to sweep her off her feet and carry her to his bed. She wanted him to declare that he was madly in love with her and could not live without her—but it seemed unlikely to happen. She knew him to be a passionate man and could only think that some part of him still remained devoted to Lucinda Avonlea.

She tossed the hurtful thought aside. Andrew would make her happy. She would have companionship and children—what more could she want?

It was very late when their travelling carriage drew up in the courtyard of Avonlea, but lights were blazing from all the windows in the house and all the candelabra had been lit. They were expected and both Justin and Lucinda had stayed up to welcome them home.

'Mariah, my dearest,' Lucinda cried and came running to embrace her as she stepped down from the carriage. 'We had begun to think you would not arrive before morning. Did you have an accident?'

'No, not at all,' Mariah assured her. 'The roads were not good, but we made reasonable time once we left Dover. There was some delay before our luggage was released and one of Sylvia's trunks was missing. We could not desert her until everything was sorted out, of course. She and her husband have been so good to me.'

'Yes, your letters were so informative,' Lucinda said. She glanced towards Andrew. 'Is it settled at last, Mariah? Justin wasn't sure from Lanchester's message, but it seemed to imply that we should expect to read the notice of your engagement in the papers.'

'Yes, we are to be married,' Mariah replied and was swept up into a warm embrace. 'Andrew thinks I need a husband to protect me.'

'Andrew adores you, of course, as we all do,' Lucinda said

and drew her past the gentlemen, who were greeting each other on the doorstep. 'Was it wonderful in Italy? I should like to travel so much more than I have. Justin says we may take Angela and little Harry and spend some time in Italy or Greece next spring, before it becomes too hot.'

'Yes, the spring or late autumn would be best—the summer is too hot for a baby.'

'Then I shall not go until the autumn,' Lucinda told her. 'Harry is such a darling and Angela adores him. She spends hours playing with him.'

'Justin does not resent her?'

'No, not at all. He wants to adopt her and says we must not think about the past or the brute that forced himself on me. Angela is my daughter and Justin treats her as affectionately as he would his own child.'

'I am so glad. It is time you had some happiness. You were treated badly by your parents and that awful man.' Mariah slid an arm about her waist. 'You do not let what happened bother you now?'

'Oh, no, I have put it from my mind.' Lucinda looked at her intently. 'And you, Mariah? Have you truly recovered from what that wicked man did to you? I was sorry not to be able to come with you when you went to Italy. I thought about you so much, even though I was confined and had my baby to consider.'

'You are a good friend.' Mariah smiled at her. 'I am glad we shall be neighbours when I am married. It means we shall see each other often.'

'Yes, it does. I think Jane will visit often, too. Lord George has just purchased a small house no more than twenty miles distant. He was left an unexpected bequest from an uncle he hardly knew and decided that Jane should have a house of her own close enough to her brother and us to visit when she chose, though I think she is too much in love to care where she lives at present.'

'Yes, she is and that surprises me. Jane was always so certain that she did not wish for marriage. She was always so independent and so very sensible, never in scrapes as I was when we were younger.'

'Love comes unexpectedly and cannot be denied,' Lucinda said. 'Justin swept me off my feet, for I did not think I ought to marry. But despite everything I have found such happiness—and I am glad that you will, too, dearest Mariah.'

'Yes. You are like a sister to me,' Mariah said and looked at her lovingly. 'Now tell me, when may I see Harry?'

'If we are very careful, we may tiptoe in and peep at him now,' Lucinda said. 'We must not wake him, for his nurse has only just settled him after his feed.'

'I shall be as quiet as a mouse,' Mariah said. She glanced back at Andrew. 'Goodnight, my dear friend. Thank you for bringing me home safely. I shall go to bed after I have seen Harry.'

'Yes, of course. Justin insists that I stay the night and so I shall see you in the morning.'

Mariah smiled and nodded, then went up the stairs with Lucinda. She felt content to be with her closest friends again. At Avonlea she must be safe from Count Paolo's spies, especially since Andrew would have warned the duke to alert his men to strangers. Within a few weeks she would be married and that rather awkward episode in Milan could be forgotten.

Chapter Seven

'Are you certain that you wish to do this?' Justin Avonlea raised his brows at Mariah. 'It is a generous thing to do, of course, but hardly necessary.'

'I have found too much money a burden,' Mariah replied. 'Winston had large estates as well as a great deal of money in blue-chip investments, which give me as much income as I need. I would like to make the gift now before my marriage, Justin. The capital will be kept in trust for the child until such time as she is five and twenty when she will be able to use it as she chooses. The income will be hers as soon as she is nineteen.'

'Ten thousand pounds is quite a large sum.' He frowned. 'It is generous, Mariah—and you do not wish me to tell either Lucinda or Angela of this until she is nineteen?'

'Lucinda might feel awkward. I would rather it came as a surprise to the girl when she is old enough to understand and enjoy the gift. It is enough to make sure that she could live well even if she did not marry, but not enough to have the fortune hunters annoying her.'

'She already has a house of her own and the income to run

it—and it was my intention to do something more for her when she was older.'

'You have been more than generous to her,' Mariah said. 'You will see to the provisions for the beneficiaries of my will should I die before I marry. I know that they will not apply if I marry and we shall talk again then, because Andrew has already told me that I am to settle what I will on my children and do as I wish with my own income. He will help me with my affairs, but he does not wish to benefit personally.'

'No, I dare say he finds your fortune a little overpowering. He is wealthy enough despite some setbacks in his investments, but he would not wish to take advantage for himself. Any suggestion that he was interested in your fortune would offend his pride.'

'Andrew has had some investment problems?'

'Yes. Did he not tell you? I think it was a year or so ago, when he mentioned he had a debt he must settle. I think he may have had the intention of selling land, but he put himself right without doing so as far as I know. He has already told me that he wishes the marriage contract to be settled in your favour with provisions for your children and the rest to be at your disposal.'

Mariah nodded. She was surprised to learn that Andrew had had some money difficulty. Jane had never spoken of it—perhaps did not even know of her brother's need. She wondered why he had kept it so quiet, because Jane had been his estate manager for a long time while he was serving in the army with Wellington. Andrew had given no hint of any difficulty and the reception he'd thrown for his sister's wedding had been lavish, as, Mariah believed, had his settlement on Jane.

She dismissed the faint doubts as Justin went into the process she would have to follow if she wished to give ten thousand pounds away. Her husband's trustees would need to be informed and she might have to sell an investment—unless she had a capital sum to hand?

'Yes, I do, as it happens. Winston placed a large sum at my disposal when we married. After he died, I had the income from his estate and so I never used the money he gave me. I think it amounts to about twenty thousand pounds. I have spent a few hundred guineas on clothes, which must be settled when the seamstress comes, but that is all. The interest together with my income from the estate has been sufficient for my needs.'

'Then all you will need to do is to sign the papers and I can arrange that for you.' Justin stood up and poured her a glass of wine. 'May I ask what makes you wish to do such a wonderful thing for the child?'

Mariah accepted the glass from his hand. 'I have been so fortunate in life, Justin. Lucinda told me how Angela was treated when that awful woman had her working, almost as a slave it would seem. I could of course have done something for her later in life, but one never knows what might happen—if I should die and no one knew of my wish she would be that much poorer.'

'Lucinda would thank you if she knew—but you are right, she might feel overwhelmed by your generosity. It is best if we keep this between us. My man of business is coming here next week and I shall arrange for the documents to be drawn up before that so that you may sign.'

Mariah thanked him and sipped her wine. A few minutes later, she left him at his desk in the library and went in search of Lucinda. Looking out of the window, she saw that the sun was shining, though it would no doubt be cold out for it was early December. Andrew had arranged the wedding for early in the New Year. Before that they were to hold a Christmas ball and Justin and Lucinda had planned a large affair here at Avonlea on Christmas Eve.

She smiled, ignoring the faint doubts that Justin's words had conjured up. Mariah had assumed that Andrew had asked her to be his wife on two counts: one was to make her safe from fortune hunters and the second was because he wanted to settle down and start his nursery.

He insisted that she must order her finances to suit herself, placing most of her fortune in trust for their children—but once they were married he would legally be in charge of her fortune and could, if he wished, use the money she had at her disposal. Even the news that he was marrying a woman of considerable fortune would impress any creditors he might have and give him a breathing space should he need it.

No! It was despicable even to suspect that her money might have swayed Andrew's thinking. Had he wanted her fortune he might have asked her months ago. If he'd had some financial difficulty in the past, it was resolved. He must have found some way of paying his debts, for she did not think he was in any difficulty now. The engagement ring he had bought her was a magnificent square emerald surrounded by fine diamonds—and the suite of emerald-and-diamond collar, eardrops and tiara that he'd given her as a gift were surely worth a king's ransom. She believed they were heirlooms, for he had told her she might have them reset if she chose. Surely if he had been in debt he could have sold the emeralds?

Justin had it wrong. Mariah would not think of it again.

'It is so good to have you here for Christmas,' Lucinda said as she hugged Mariah's arm. They were taking a turn in the conservatory, because the sun made it feel warm behind the narrow glass panes and they were able to stroll up and down the long room, which faced south and was at the back of the house. There were scented plants in large pots, which had somehow been forced to flower at an unseasonable time and gave an illusion of summer. 'I am looking forward to all the dinners and balls. I have not been out much since my confinement and shall enjoy them all the more for having you here.'

'It is wonderful to be with you again,' Mariah said. 'It was lovely at the villa until…' She decided that her friend did not need to know about the unpleasantness and gave a little toss of her head. 'One tires of travel eventually. Christmas at home will be much nicer.'

'Next year you will have a home with Andrew. It will be an exciting year for you, dearest.' Lucinda looked at her when she did not immediately answer. 'Is something concerning you? You have been a little quiet. Justin did not scold you too much this morning? Or are you missing Andrew?'

'I am missing him, of course, but I knew that he had business in London. There is something he must settle. I am certain that he will return as soon as he has the time.'

Mariah wrinkled her brow. Andrew had seemed to think

he could settle the business just by talking to a colleague—
but would it be so easy?

She felt a shiver of fear, which started at her nape and began
to trickle down her spine. If anything should happen to Andrew now, it would break her heart. She had begged him to
take care. He'd dismissed her fears with an arch of his eyebrows, laughing it off.

'In Italy we may have been in some danger, but I believe
we are safe enough here, my love. You must not worry. Think
about the arrangements for the wedding and before you know
it, I shall be home again.'

Was he telling her the truth? Or was he merely protecting
her so that she did not become anxious?

Lucinda glanced at her. 'You seem a little quiet, Mariah. Is
something the matter?'

'No, nothing at all. I am missing Andrew, of course, but I
dare say he will be back before we know it.'

'You were unable to find any trace of Lieutenant Gordon?'
Major Harrison looked grim. 'I am sorry to hear that, Lanchester. The matter is becoming urgent since I have been asked to
make extensive inquiries into the disappearance of the silver.
By withholding the letter I am becoming an accessory to the
crime. I ought to report it to a higher authority.'

'I perfectly understand that, sir. I am grateful that you have
held back this long. Should it come to a court-martial I shall,
of course, be judged by my peers. I swear to you that I know
nothing of the theft, but as yet I do not know why I have been
accused—or who the true culprit is.'

'I trust you implicitly, Andrew. I shall give you another month—after that...'

'Yes, I understand, sir. I have discovered the whereabouts of Gordon's mother and sister. I am thinking of approaching them to ask if they know anything of him or the letter.'

'You may receive a sharp answer, but if you could obtain a sample of their handwriting, perhaps a case might be made—should one or the other be a culprit.'

'There is another possibility, though I hesitate to suggest it. I must say at once that I do not think he stole the silver—but he may know who did...'

'Of whom do you speak?'

Andrew explained what had happened in Italy. Major Harrison looked disapproving. 'Grainger is an excellent officer. I do not think he would deliberately seek to discredit a fellow officer.'

'No, nor do I—but he might protecting someone out of loyalty. He disappeared in mysterious circumstances the day after an attempt was made to kill me...'

'You are not suggesting...' Major Harrison raised his heavy brows. 'Surely not? Why would Grainger wish to kill you?'

'I have no idea—unless...' Andrew shook his head. 'A thought has occurred to me, but I have no proof. If Lieutenant Gordon's mother or his sister was responsible for the letter accusing me of theft, he might be protecting her—but where the rest of it fits I have no certain knowledge.'

'It is merely a theory and I do not like the implication of another officer, whose behaviour has thus far been exemplary.'

'No, nor I, for I would not wish to cast aspersions on another man's character without proof.'

'That would indeed be a pity. If you come up with any proof, I should be glad to have this matter settled. If the silver could be recovered, I should be glad of it. Some of those pieces were irreplaceable and important to the regiment.'

'Yes, I am certain of it,' Andrew replied. 'It is hard to believe that any member of the regiment would steal something of that importance—where would he sell it? No reputable dealer would buy silver with the regiment's crest unless there was a certificate of permission for the sale—it must have been melted down for a fraction of its real worth.'

'That is my fear.' Major Harrison sighed. 'Sacrilege! It may, of course, have been an opportunist from outside the regiment.'

'I shall continue to make enquiries.' Andrew offered his hand, which was accepted. 'If I discover anything of worth, I shall come to you, Harrison.'

'Thank you. I have also to thank you for the loan you made to Mrs Ransome. I have not mentioned it before, because I did not wish to muddy the waters while this business was still unsettled.'

'Captain Ransome's widow was left without enough money to return to England and set up house,' Andrew replied. 'I think we all felt that Ransome's death was a shocking waste of life and regretted his loss. The money I advanced to her was meant to be a gift and to remain a secret.'

'And it will as far as others are concerned. The truth is that Julia has done me the honour to accept an offer of marriage. She thought it necessary to tell me of the gift—and that there was never an involvement between you?'

'None at all,' Andrew said. 'Teddy Ransome was a good

friend. I could not see his wife without a home or allow her to live in poverty.'

'I am more grateful than I can tell you—but the debt becomes mine now. I shall repay you very soon.'

'There is no hurry, but you must do as you wish. I perfectly understand your desire to pay what you consider a debt.'

'I shall send you a draft on my bank.' Major Harrison looked awkward. 'I did wonder at one time…ten thousand is a deal of money to find at short notice…'

'I borrowed from my bank, as it happens. They were happy to advance me until I could sell a small estate.'

'Yes, of course. Forgive me. It was just a little difficult in the circumstances. You will let me know how this business goes on?'

'As soon as I have any news.' Andrew smiled. 'I must congratulate you on your marriage and wish you both happy.'

The two men said their farewells. Andrew was thoughtful as he left the major's office. He could see why Harrison had found the business uncomfortable—and why some doubt had lingered at the back of his mind even though he professed to believe Andrew.

He wished that he had been able to settle the matter, because he might then have married Mariah with a clear conscience. He did not enjoy having this shadow having over him and he was anxious lest it should bring harm to the woman he admired and cared for.

Having discovered that Gordon's mother and sister were living in Hampstead, he determined to pay them a visit on his way home. He would ask them if either knew of Lieutenant Gordon's whereabouts and ask for an address, if they could supply it—but he could not ask outright if they had sent the letter.

However, before he left London he must pay a visit to the jeweller at which he had placed an order. His gift for Mariah must be ready by now and he was anxious to see if they had managed to find what he wanted for her wedding present.

Leaving the jeweller he had chosen to patronise an hour or so later, Andrew had much to occupy his thoughts as he returned to his hotel. The pearl-and-diamond collar he had purchased for Mariah was costly and beautiful enough to please any lady, even one as wealthy and discerning as his bride-to-be.

He frowned slightly as he thought about Mariah's circumstances. He had told her that she might do as she wished with her own fortune—he did not wish her to imagine that he was one of the fortune hunters who had plagued her since her first husband's death. Indeed, her wealth was one of the reasons he had hesitated to ask for her hand. Mariah was undoubtedly a spoiled beauty. She had been given everything she wanted for most of her life and at times she tended to be contrary and perhaps a little too confident of her right to do just as she pleased. Andrew admired her spirit, but could not help wondering if perhaps they would strike sparks off one another once they were wed.

He admired her in many ways and found her amusing company—but he could not convince himself that Mariah was in love with him. She liked him and respected him, but he doubted that her feelings ran deep. For himself, he held her in warm affection and thought it could be a good marriage.

He would be an unnatural man if he did not feel desire for a woman as lovely as she, but as yet he was not sure how deep his feelings ran. At times he felt that Mariah was indeed the only lady he could ever love, yet at others he felt the prick of doubt. Was he perverse in wishing that it had been otherwise? Only a handful of his friends had made love matches, and he knew that most would envy him his choice of a bride. Undoubtedly some would think he was marrying her for her fortune, but they would be wrong. His loan to Captain Ransome's widow had left him temporarily short of available funds, though his estate had never been in danger. He had sold some property left to him by an aunt—a house and land, which he had never cared for—and that sale had restored his income to its normal levels.

What was wrong with him? He might have married years ago had he not been so particular. Unprepared for a marriage that turned sour after a few months, as often happened, he wanted a lady he could admire and respect—and one that would return his affection. At times when he was near Mariah he felt near mad with wanting, but he could not forget her love of flirtation. Supposing after they were married she grew bored and amused herself with others? He had little experience of women outside his sister, except for lightskirts who were willing to lie with almost any man for money and gifts. No, he was a fool to think it, but could not help feeling slightly jealous of the men she had known. Just how many lovers had she taken since her husband died—and would he be enough to content her? Yet he could not bear the thought of giving her up now that they had agreed to marry.

He found that he was missing Mariah more than he would

have expected and would be glad when his business was finished and he could go home and claim his beautiful bride.

Mariah stood reluctantly for the fitting of her wedding gown. In its early stages, it still had pins everywhere and the drapes in the skirt did not look as she wished. She pouted at her reflection in the long mirror and pulled at the front of the dress.

'This is not quite right, *madame.* I would prefer that it fell in a straight drop. At the moment it makes me look fat.'

'You could never look anything but beautiful,' Lucinda told her with a laugh. 'However, the front is tucked up and needs a little adjustment. Do you not think so, Madame Bonnier?'

'Ah, yes, I see what you mean,' the harassed seamstress said and gave the front a little tweak, smoothing out the wrinkle that had spoiled the line. 'There, is that not perfect, milady?'

'Yes, it is.' A smile touched Mariah's mouth. 'I am difficult to please today, *madame.* I think it must be wedding nerves.'

'Oh, no, I have the clients much more *difficile,*' the seamstress said and laughed. 'Milady is the perfect client with her so-beautiful figure.'

'You need not be so polite,' Mariah told her. 'I know I am a spoiled brat. Justin told me so years ago and I fear he is right. I was always given my own way and perhaps I have become selfish without intending it.'

'Everyone likes to have their own way sometimes,' Lucinda said. 'I fear Justin was harsh to you, Mariah. He takes such a scolding tone at times that it leads others to think he is a cold man, but I assure you it is not so.'

'No, he is a loving husband to you, Lucinda. You suit him

so much better than I ever should. It was a good thing I turned him down—had we married, we should both have regretted it.'

'Is something the matter, dearest? You seem unsettled...a little unhappy. You are not sorry you accepted Andrew, are you?'

'Oh, no, not at all,' Mariah said as she slipped out of her half-finished gown behind the screen and handed it to the seamstress. 'I am quite certain I wish to marry him. If I am in a mood, it must be because he is not here.'

'Ah, yes, I understand. I always feel the same when Justin is away.'

Mariah dressed in a pretty yellow morning gown, smoothing down the simple lines of the slim-fitting skirt. How could Lucinda understand how she felt? She was secure in Justin's love, for he showed his adoration every time he looked at her. Mariah's problem was that she was uncertain of Andrew's feelings for her. He had not pretended to be wildly in love with her and that was honest of him. She had believed that she could accept the situation, as long as he felt warm affection and liking for her, but it hurt more than she'd expected. At one time she'd thought she might accept any man who was honourable, amusing and not interested solely in her fortune, but since then she'd come to a better understanding of her own feelings and knew that Andrew was the only man she wished to marry. She wasn't sure when the desire to tease him and make him admire her had become so much more.

Just when had she fallen in love with the provoking man? Was it last year in the spring, when she'd returned to Avonlea—or in Paris when he had disappointed her hopes, or at the lakes when he had failed to rise to her bait? Mariah wrinkled her smooth brow. Was it only because he did not cast himself at her feet, as other men had in the past, that she felt this way? Was it merely pique? She knew that she was changeable and wondered if she would have fallen quite so hard if Andrew had declared himself in love with her.

Deciding that it made no sense to torment herself, she took Lucinda's arm and, after bidding the seamstress goodbye, they went out into the conservatory for a walk through the scented blossoms. The gardener had coaxed some exotic flowers into flowering, though it was nearly Christmas, and it was a pleasure to smell and touch the blooms.

'I think I shall ask Andrew if he will allow me to build a large conservatory at his home,' Mariah said. 'In the winter it is somewhere warm to walk even if the sun only shines for a little time. I do not mind walking in the cold, but when it rains one is confined to the house.'

'I am certain he will say you may do just as you wish,' Lucinda told her. 'Justin recently told me I could refurbish Avonlea to my taste, but there is very little I wish to do. One or two of the guest rooms may need a new décor, but my own apartments are perfect, because he had them done for me.'

'Lanchester Park needs a little refurbishment, I think,' Mariah said. She stood at the window, looking south, and frowned. 'Is that one of the gardeners, Lucinda? He is staring at us...'

Lucinda came to stand with her, following her gaze. 'I'm not sure. I have not seen him before. Yes, he is staring and rudely...' She gasped and pushed Mariah to one side just as the man brought his arm up and fired towards the greenhouse, shattering a pane of glass. The ball passed its target and buried itself in a wooden tub of camellias as Lucinda screamed.

In seconds servants had rushed into the conservatory and the man outside had run away across the lawns. He was being pursued by two of the duke's servants as he headed towards a small wood.

'Are you hurt, my lady?' a footman asked of Lucinda.

'The shot was meant for Lady Fanshawe,' Lucinda said. 'I saw that he was about to fire and pushed her to one side or he might have hit her.' She looked anxiously at Mariah, who was standing by the pot of camellias looking at the splintered wood. 'Are you all right, Mariah dearest?'

'Thanks to your prompt action,' Mariah said. 'I feel shaken but his shot went wide. Perhaps it was not meant to hit me, but only to frighten us.'

'What happened here?' Justin came striding into the conservatory. He saw the shattered pane and the servants gathered around his wife. 'I thought I heard a shot. Is anyone harmed?'

'No, Justin,' Lucinda said. 'Mariah and I were just admiring the camellias and she saw someone staring at us rather too intently. I looked at him and noticed that he had a pistol in his hand seconds before he fired.'

'She may have saved my life,' Mariah said, 'though I think it might just have been meant as a warning—to frighten me.'

'Why would someone wish to frighten you?' Justin asked. 'I understand why men might wish to wed you, Mariah, for your fortune or yourself—but why on earth should anyone wish to shoot you?'

Hearing a commotion outside, they saw that the duke's servants were returning with their prisoner. Justin frowned, nodded his satisfaction, warned the ladies to go back into the house and stay away from windows and then went out through the French windows to speak with his servants.

'Come, let us do as he says,' Lucinda said, taking Mariah's arm. 'Justin will wish to get to the bottom of this before he allows us to walk here again.'

'I cannot believe someone would dare to come here and shoot at the windows of your house, Lucinda. In Italy there was some unpleasantness, but I thought that was all finished. If I've brought this on you...' She shook her head. 'No, it is too awful. Andrew was attacked outside Milan and thought someone wished to kill him but...why would anyone wish to murder me?'

'Come and sit down and tell me what is troubling you, dearest,' Lucinda said and squeezed her arm. 'I shall order some tea—or perhaps you would prefer something stronger?'

'No, tea will be perfect,' Mariah said. She lifted her head, forcing herself to smile. 'They have caught the rogue who fired at us. It may be just someone who has a grudge against Justin for being sacked or thrown off his land, do you not think so?'

'Well, perhaps. I really do not know,' Lucinda said. 'However, I am quite certain that Justin will discover the truth very shortly.'

Mariah made no reply. She was trying to tell herself that the shot had not been meant to kill her, but she could not help thinking that it must have something to do with what had happened in Milan. Yet how could an attempt on Andrew's life, the disappearance of a young lieutenant and that shot be connected?

She smiled and murmured something comforting to Lucinda, but her nerves were tingling and she was uneasy.

Where was Andrew? She wished he would come back. Somehow she would feel safer if he were here with her, though she knew that Justin must be furious. He would not tolerate such a thing happening on his estate.

Justin was indeed furious. It took all his strength of will to prevent himself giving way to an urge to have the man beaten to with an inch of his life. His keeper had caught the man and brought him to his knees with a flying tackle and he had already received more than one blow when he was dragged before Justin and thrust to his knees.

'Let him stand up,' Justin said, remembering that he was a gentleman. 'Now, sirrah, tell me why you have just tried to kill my wife and Lady Fanshawe?'

The man was visibly shaken, his face white, eyes wide with terror, having been threatened with hanging several times already in Justin's hearing.

'You had best tell me what you know,' Justin told him in a deceptively gentle voice. 'If you are helpful, I may save you from hanging—but if you remain silent I shall see that you receive the death penalty.'

'No, sir.' The man fell to his knees despite having been allowed to stand. 'I beg you to forgive me. I never meant to harm the ladies. I was told to come here and fire at the beautiful lady, not to hit her, like, but just to frighten her—but I didn't know which one and so I fired at the plant pot.'

'Who gave you such an order?' Justin's tone hardened. 'Why

did you accept an order that you must have known would land you in trouble?'

'He gave me twenty guineas and promised me another twenty if I did my work,' the man said in a trembling voice. 'I were starving, sir. Me and the missus and kids, we wus all starving 'cos the mill closed last winter and I couldn't find work.'

'You should have come to me with your story and I would have given you money,' Justin said. 'Tell me the name of the man who paid you and I will see that you receive a lighter sentence for your crime.'

'I don't know his name, sir. He were a gent like you, that's all I know—tall wiv dark hair and rich, I should think.'

'Was he English?' Justin frowned as the man shook his head. 'French, German or Italian perhaps?'

'He might 'ave bin French, sir. I ain't sure. I met him at night and he told me where to come and what to do. I was to meet him again ternight at an inn and he wus ter give me the rest of the money. I ain't sure his 'air was dark, 'cos he might 'ave bin wearing a wig, like. His 'air were a bit odd now as I think on it.'

'Then you shall meet him,' Justin said. 'I shall come with you—and if you point him out to me I shall give money to your wife and you will serve six weeks in prison instead of the ten years you undoubtedly deserve.'

The man stared at him for a moment, then started snivelling. 'Me missus will starve if I goes to jail fer ten years, fer I'll niver come out no more. If I take yer to 'im 'e'll kill me, so I'm done fer whatever I does.'

'Conduct yourself like a man,' Justin said sternly. 'You will be protected. Once I know who paid you to do this foul deed, he will not trouble you again.'

The man looked at him uncertainly, then nodded once. 'I ain't got much choice, 'ave I, sir?'

'You have no choice at all,' Justin said and smiled benevolently. 'My men will take you to the kitchens, where you will be fed. You will give my man your name and where he can find your wife so that food and money can be provided. You may think yourself lucky that your shot harmed no one but a rather beautiful camellia, otherwise you would never see your family again.'

'What did the rogue say to you?' Lucinda asked her husband when he joined them in the parlour a little later. 'Has he told you why he shot at us?'

'He was paid by someone to frighten the beautiful lady, but, uncertain of which beautiful lady, he fired at the plant pot,' Justin said grimly. 'He claims not to know the name of the man that paid him, but I have hopes that we may discover the rogue tonight. They were to have met again.'

'Justin!' Lucinda looked at him in fright. 'This man must be dangerous, whoever he is. You will take care?'

'Yes, of course, my love. I have far too much to lose,' Justin said and bent to kiss the top of her head. 'Apparently, the rogue may be French, though Jacobs, as he calls himself, really has no idea. I do not know why anyone should wish to frighten either of you—unless one of your rejected suitors has taken it badly, Mariah.'

'No, of course they would not...' Lucinda cried and then

frowned as she looked at Mariah's face. 'Would they? Do you think that you may have made someone angry, Mariah?'

'It is possible,' Mariah said, 'though I can hardly believe that anyone would wish to shoot me just because I would not marry him.' She looked uneasy. 'I am sorry to have brought this trouble on you, Justin. I cannot think of anyone—except perhaps Count Paolo...'

'Count Paolo? Was he not a friend of Lady Hubert and her husband? I thought it was his villa that you stayed at while you were out there?'

'Yes, at the lakes,' Mariah said. 'He wished to marry me and was angry when I refused.'

'Surely he would not have you murdered for such a reason?'

'It sounds ridiculous when you say it like that,' Mariah agreed. 'Yet the look in his eyes... He was like a large predatory cat, prowling his territory. I may have injured his pride. I sensed something dangerous in him and I fear that he is capable of doing anything.'

'He sounds a most unpleasant gentleman,' Justin said. 'Naturally you turned him down instantly.'

'Well...I did think it might be amusing to have a mild affair, but only for a short time. Yes, I did turn him down almost at once, though vaguely so as not to offend, as we were his guests. I told him I would not consider marriage, but, before I left Milan, he made it clear that he had not given up the hunt. I think my refusal made him more determined to have me in the end.'

'He does sound dangerous.'

'He seemed to think he could persuade me to do what he wanted in time. He had costumes made to match for the ball and told me his friends would honour me when I became his wife. In the end I found him a little menacing and could not wait to leave, especially after Lieutenant Grainger went missing.'

'Yes, I see. Andrew did mention something. He wondered if Grainger's disappearance might have some bearing on the regiment's missing silver, but I cannot see how any of this should affect you, Mariah. If that shot was aimed at you, it must be a disgruntled suitor. Unless...' He shook his head. 'You do not think your late husband's trustees... Would his sister inherit if anything happened to you?'

'No, I do not think so. Winston left everything to me. His sister has a house in Bath, which he gave her when she married, but neither she nor her husband can hope to inherit for they are not named in my will.'

'Then it seems we may rule them out.'

'I know she was a little annoyed that everything came to me under the terms of his will, but I am certain she would not do anything as sordid as to have someone shoot at me.'

'No, I thought not—then I think it must be one of your suitors, Mariah.'

'Unless he was shooting at me,' Lucinda said. 'Perhaps we have an enemy, Justin. You cannot be certain he meant to frighten Mariah.'

'No, I cannot be certain, and that is why I have arranged for more armed men to patrol the grounds. I am furious that anyone dared to come right to the house and take a shot at you while you were in the conservatory. I shall not rest until this thing is settled.'

'I wish—' Mariah broke off as she heard something and

then the door opened and Andrew's tall figure walked in. 'Oh, thank goodness you are back,' she cried. 'Perhaps you will know what is going on, for I am sure I do not.'

Her voice was emotional, causing Andrew to frown and demand to know what had been happening in his absence. Justin told him and he swore loudly, then apologised.

'Forgive me, ladies. I should not forget myself, even though I am shocked beyond belief that such a thing could occur. Lucinda, I am so sorry that you should have such a fright in your own house. You are not harmed—or you, Mariah?'

'No, I am not harmed,' Mariah said, feeling a little put out that his concern seemed more for Lucinda than herself. 'It was shocking, of course, and I feel terrible, because Justin thinks it must be one of my disgruntled suitors. I can think only of Count Paolo. He was determined that I should be his wife and I suspected that he was angry when I refused.'

'Yes, that is possible, of course. He is not a man I would trust,' Andrew said, his eyes narrowed in thought. 'You should never have encouraged him for a moment, Mariah.'

'I merely flirted a little,' she replied, stung by his criticism. How could she have known instantly that the man was obsessed with her—surely he must be if he had done this thing? 'I had no idea that he was mad... Well, he would have to be if he came all this way to pay someone to shoot at me in Justin's orangery.'

'Mad or obsessed,' Andrew agreed. 'From what you told me, his interest in you was far from natural, Mariah—but it does seem excessive to come all this way to take a pot shot at you. If he had attempted to ravish you at his house, I might have thought him madly in love with you—but this is ridiculous.'

'Completely,' she agreed. 'We shall dismiss it as a foolish idea. So what is the answer? Why would anyone wish to frighten me—or Lucinda?'

'It might be that either I have an enemy—or perhaps Justin has upset one of his neighbours,' Andrew said. 'If a man wanted to strike at you, Justin, what do you suppose he might do?'

Justin looked thoughtful, then his mouth drew into a hard line. 'If he could not get to me, he might seek to harm my wife or child.'

'Exactly.' Andrew nodded. 'However, I do not think you need concern yourself, Justin. If my judgement is correct, it is I who has an enemy and not you.'

'Do you have any idea who has a grudge against you?'

'If I did, I should have settled the business before this,' Andrew replied tersely. 'I had hoped to have got to the bottom of things by now, but although I believe I may know a little more I can be certain of nothing. Besides, I do not see why my affairs should cause anyone to shoot at Mariah.'

'Perhaps we should discuss this in private,' Justin said. 'There are certain arrangements we need to make that the ladies need not be bothered with.'

'Oh, fudge,' Mariah said, eyes sparkling with a decided militancy. 'Why do gentlemen always imagine we worry less if we do not know what is going on?'

'I agree with Mariah,' Lucinda said. 'We are not babies to be coddled. I would prefer to be told what is happening, rather than kept in the dark, Justin.'

'Indeed, madam?' Her husband glanced at Andrew and then laughed. 'We may as well discuss this openly since I, for one, shall get no peace unless we do. I was going to suggest that we send Jacobs in alone to meet the rogue who employed him this evening while we watch, and then catch him on his way out later.'

'Can you trust the rogue? Might he not betray us to his employer?'

'I think he has been suitably frightened,' Justin said with a grim look. 'Given the opportunity he might cut and run, but if the man who sent him is at the arranged meeting place, we shall have all the entrances covered. Neither of them will escape us.'

'I have a couple of ex-soldiers working for me at the estate. They know how to handle themselves and will prove handy in a fight. We must nip this in the bud tonight, Justin, or none of us will sleep soundly in our beds until it is done.'

'I am sorry that you had such a fright,' Andrew said to Mariah later. They were walking alone in the gallery on the upper floor of the east wing since he had judged it best to stay inside the house for the moment. 'I doubt there are more rogues waiting to attack you, but it is best to be safe until we have settled this thing.'

'It is such a nuisance and I do not intend to be intimidated, Andrew. I was startled at the time,' Mariah admitted, 'but truly it was all over so swiftly that I hardly knew what was happening.' She looked at him, her eyes dark with anxiety. 'Do you truly think it was your enemy, Andrew?'

'I fear it must be so,' he said and looked grave. 'Had I been certain of it, I should not have spoken, Mariah. I would rather you had not been involved in this sordid business. Indeed, I spoke only because I meant to protect you.'

What did that mean? Was he regretting his haste? Mariah felt a stab of hurt in the vicinity of her heart. It was not easy to love someone who felt only mild affection in return. However, it would avail her nothing to let her hurt feelings show. She turned away as she asked, 'Have they discovered what happened to the missing silver?'

Andrew frowned. 'I fear it is far from solved—though I may know who sent the letter accusing me. I called on Lieutenant Gordon's mother and sister. I was unable to see them both, but his mother received me. She was hostile at first and swore that she did not know where her son was. However, when I asked if she needed help, she thawed a little. She told me that she had not heard from her son for months, though she believed him to be in England. She clearly blamed me for his disgrace and hasty departure from the army. However, I do not think she wrote the letter. Something she said makes me suspect it may have been his sister.'

'She wrote to discredit you in the hope of bringing you to ruin?'

'Or perhaps because she wished to deflect blame from her brother.'

'You think he may have taken it?'

'It is possible that he did so and his sister knew. What she hoped to gain by pushing the blame on to me I do not know, but I think she may be responsible.'

'Surely she is not behind the attempts on your life—or the shot at me?'

'Perhaps that was Gordon himself.'

'Oh, Andrew...' Mariah shuddered. 'He must truly hate you to do something like that.'

'Yes—or he fears that I know he took the silver and will expose him.'

'He is already disgraced...' Mariah shook her head. 'Something does not quite add up. He may be your thief and his sister may have sent the letter—but would he follow you to Italy to murder you? Why not kill you here before you left? Why try to shoot or frighten me?'

'What are you suggesting?' Andrew's gaze narrowed. 'Why else would this person attack you other than to strike at me? I have not yet been disgraced—they or he may have been driven to desperate action in search of revenge.'

'If they are one and the same person,' Mariah mused. 'Might there not be some other reason for that shot, Andrew? I do truly think Count Paolo capable of something of the sort.'

'Well, we must hope that the perpetrator is caught tonight,' Andrew said and turned to her with a smile. 'This is distressing for both you and Lucinda, my dearest. You should be enjoying yourselves, looking forward to the wedding and having fittings for new clothes, not worrying your pretty heads about who is trying to shoot you.'

'Fudge,' Mariah said and pouted at him. 'New clothes become boring if one has too many fittings. It is exciting to be shot at—providing one is not harmed, of course. Life can be too dull at times, especially if one is a woman.'

'I do not think Lucinda felt the same way.' Andrew gave her a severe look. 'Neither of you is to follow us this evening.

I will not have you risk yourself out of a desire for some adventure, Mariah. Do you hear me? I mean what I say.'

'Are you scolding me?' Mariah's eyes sparkled, because she enjoyed seeing him aroused this way. It pleased her that he was concerned for her welfare, yet she could not resist the urge to provoke him a little. 'It would be vastly amusing. Could I not dress in a man's clothing and come with you to watch the fun?'

'Fun? Good grief, girl! Do you not know how dangerous it might be for all concerned? If this rogue is fighting for his life, he may shoot to kill. If I am worried for your sake I may become careless and give him the opportunity he needs.'

'Please do not, Andrew,' Mariah said, the smile leaving her eyes. 'I was merely teasing you. I want you to promise me that you will not take unnecessary risks.'

'I shall do nothing to endanger myself foolishly,' he said. 'Please give me your word not to sneak out and follow us. If I have to worry about you, my mind will not be on the business in hand.'

'I promise. I was merely teasing,' she said, chastened. 'Surely you know me by now, Andrew? I may say very foolish things, but I am sensible most of the time. I should do nothing that might place you or the others in an awkward situation, believe me. All I want is for us to be married and comfortable together. I looked for adventure once, but now I wish for children and marriage.'

'Do you, my dear?' Andrew gazed down into her face. 'Sometimes I fear that you may grow bored with marriage and wish for your freedom again. I want you to know that I should not hold you against your will, Mariah. If you ever decide that you wish to resume your old life, please tell me and we will come to an amicable arrangement. All I shall require is discretion.'

'Truly? You will make a very comfortable husband, Andrew.' Mariah laughed, though her heart was close to breaking. He seemed to imagine her a heartless flirt who could not be constant for more than a few days. 'You will not mind if I flirt a little?'

'Shall I not?' He frowned and for a moment she thought he would say something meaningful. Would he drag her into his arms and show her who was the master in no uncertain way? Excitement filled her at the thought of being dominated by him. Her heart raced, but he smiled suddenly and reached out to flick her cheek lightly with his fingertips. 'You do like to tease, Mariah. I must accustom myself to it, for it means nothing, I dare say. I meant what I said, however. If you wish to be free, you have only to say, but if you choose to remain my wife I shall expect you to be faithful to me.'

So he cared enough to dislike the idea of her taking a lover! It was some consolation for a sore heart. Earlier, when he'd learned of the shooting, his concern had been first for Lucinda. Was he still in love with her? Was he marrying Mariah to keep her safe from fortune hunters or in the hope of having an heir? She could not quite decide. At times he seemed to care for her and at others he almost seemed to raise a barrier between them.

'I do not think you need worry that I shall take a lover,' she told him. 'My constancy is in your hands, Andrew. If you give me no cause to wish for another's kisses...'

'Minx! I see you will push me to the limit.' Andrew caught

her about the waist, pulling her in close. Her heart jerked and raced madly as he lowered his head, his mouth taking hungry possession of hers. His tongue probed as she opened her lips, his tongue touching hers delicately, exploring and tantalising as she was pressed into his body. For a long moment his sensual exploration of her mouth seemed to draw her into him so that they seemed melded together, a part of one another— melting in a mutual fire.

Mariah had thought Count Paolo an attractive man, feeling the pull of his physical appeal, but she had not dreamed that she could feel such desire. Her body was heating, her pulses pounding as Andrew continued to kiss her. He slid his right hand into her hair at the nape of her neck, his fingers caressing the delicate skin, sending a shower of tingling sensation through her entire body. For a long time she had wanted to know what it felt like to be loved, truly loved, by a man who wanted and needed her. As Andrew held her clasped against his body she could feel the hardness of his masculinity and the urgent need in him. Her whole being burned with need and longing, a feeling so sweet and enthralling that she had never imagined it could be half as good.

She gurgled with laughter, looking at him with delight. Some of the shadow of hurt that his careless attitude had inflicted melted away as she saw the heat in his eyes. At least he wanted her in a physical way. She might be a virgin, but she was worldly wise in other ways and she recognised need when she saw it.

'Love me, Andrew,' she suggested on a sudden impulse. 'Take me to bed now and make love to me.'

'Temptress,' he murmured huskily. 'How much I should

like to oblige you, my lady, but I fear now is not the time. If I took you at your word, I should not wish to leave your bed this night.'

'Why should you? Justin and his men could manage alone. Why should you risk your life when others can take care of this stupid business?'

Andrew released her, an expression of disapproval in his eyes. 'I know you do not mean that, Mariah. You spoke without thinking. You would not expect me to leave Justin to deal with a man who wishes to kill me?'

Mariah sighed and moved away from him. 'Men and their stupid sense of honour. I cannot bear it if you are killed, Andrew. What shall I do if your enemy shoots you dead? You might have some consideration for my feelings.'

He looked at her severely. 'You will conduct yourself with dignity and in time you will marry someone else. You must excuse me now. I have arrangements to make for this evening.'

'Don't be cross with me,' Mariah cried as he turned and walked away, leaving her staring after him. 'You don't understand. I didn't mean it that way…'

She felt the sting of tears. Bother! He had made her feel guilty, as if she were being selfish—but it would hurt her so much if he died. Why couldn't the foolish man understand that she loved him?

Mariah dashed the tears from her eyes with the back of her hand. She wouldn't cry for him. He said he cared and his kisses told of a need for physical passion. She suspected that he might even be lonely—perhaps because he was still in love with a woman he could never have. A part of her wanted to take him in her arms and kiss away his sadness, but a part of her protested that he must love her as she loved him.

Mariah raised her head. Everyone said she was spoiled. They envied her, envied her life and her wealth, but all she truly wanted was to be loved—loved in a way she had never known. Winston had treated her like a little girl, spoiling her and indulging her every whim, but Mariah was no longer a girl. She was a woman, a passionate, healthy woman who needed the love of a man in every way. Andrew was the man who could give her all she needed. In his arms she had wanted to surrender her body, her very being, but he still saw her as a spoiled child.

How could she make him see her for what she truly was?

Dressing in the plain dark clothes he intended to wear that night, Andrew frowned at his reflection in the dressing mirror. He knew he should concentrate his mind on what was about to happen, because a lot might depend on his being alert. Justin seemed to imagine it would all be easy and straightforward, but Andrew was not certain. As yet he could not be certain who was behind all the unpleasant happenings of the past few months. The most obvious seemed Lieutenant Gordon and his sister, but somehow he could not think they were behind the attempts on his life—or that outrageous attempt to either harm or frighten Mariah.

She had suggested that he might have not one, but two enemies—but who else might wish him harm?

He had won a large sum from one or two gentlemen over the past couple of years, but on other occasions he had lost to the same men. Gambling usually evened itself out when it was fair and no one cheated, unless one was desperately unlucky. He had known men to have a losing streak that drove them to the verge of suicide, but to his knowledge he had not contributed to anyone's death—except the man who had abducted Lucinda, of course. He had certainly played his part in bringing Royston down, and so had Mariah, of course, though it was doubtful if anyone knew of her part since they had agreed amongst themselves to keep it private.

Could Royston have a friend or relative who wanted revenge? It was another possibility. Andrew cursed. He wanted the business over and done so he could attend to something far more important—his courtship of Mariah. That kiss had lit a conflagration that had almost raged out of control. He must not think of the reactions she had roused in him, for he had dangerous work that night.

A thoughtful smile entered his eyes as he glanced at his reflection once more and nodded, satisfied that he looked suitably nondescript and could blend into the background of the inn at which he hoped to discover the perpetrator of this foul attempt to frighten Mariah and Lucinda.

Lucinda had looked pale and shaken when Justin told him what had happened in the conservatory, but Mariah had shown no sign of nerves. He suspected that she was quite an actress, for he was beginning to realise that she often disguised her feelings. For a while he had mistakenly imagined her to be shallow, a woman who cared only for her own pleasures but recently he had come to realise that Mariah was adept at hiding her true emotions. However, she had held nothing back when he kissed her. There was fire in her, something that pleased Andrew, because he was a very physical man himself, but he would expect her to be faithful to him in marriage, even though he had hinted otherwise to test her.

How many lovers had she taken since her marriage ended? The knowledge that a woman of her temperament must have had lovers made him grit his teeth. He wanted her to be untouched, to have known only him, to be an innocent in love, but of course that was ridiculous. Andrew dismissed the stupid jealousy that seared through him when he thought of Count Paolo. Had she flirted with the man to such an extent that he thought he had rights over her? Had she allowed him to kiss her, touch her intimately?

Andrew felt a sudden spurt of rage. In that moment he would willingly have taken the count's neck in his bare hands and choked the life out of him. Mariah was his. He would allow no other man to touch her. She belonged to him.

He glanced at his reflection once more before picking up his pistols and leaving the room. The fury in his eyes shocked him. Where had that violence of feeling come from? He had thought himself in complete control of his emotions. Mariah was beautiful and a charming companion. She would be an excellent wife for a man in his situation and a good mother for his children—but he had never expected to feel such turbulence at the thought of her in another man's arms. Andrew had never considered himself a jealous man.

Walking down the stairs, Andrew realised that he had never truly had a serious love affair with any woman. He had been touched by Lucinda's plight when she and Justin had suffered a series of misunderstandings that made her terribly unhappy. Yes, he had loved her truly, but in a gentle protective way that made him want to knock her husband down for hurting her—

but had he ever felt such violent rage when he saw her smile and kiss Justin?

The answer was no: hurt, a little envious and wistful—but not this searing rage that made him want to tear Count Paolo limb from limb. Andrew was puzzled, because he had believed he was in love with his friend's wife. She was a lovely, generous and sweet girl, whereas Mariah was beautiful, capricious and...he would be damned if he would let the count near her again. If the man came sniffing round after they were married, he would send him packing in good order.

A smile on his lips at the thought, Andrew went outside to where Justin was gathering the men they were to take with them that night. Andrew's own men were already in place in the inn, where they could watch what was going on and take note of anyone who seemed to be hanging around waiting for someone to arrive.

Andrew would need to remain in the shadows and wait, because if his enemy saw him the game would be up and he would make a quick exit.

'Are you ready?' Justin asked as he reached him. 'Jacobs knows that if he plays his part well I shall do my best to keep him out of prison.'

'The damned rogue needs to be taught a lesson, Justin. He might have killed your wife or Mariah.'

'I think he has learned his lesson and his story has been checked. He did lose his job and he's had a hard time of it.'

'Doesn't excuse what he did,' Andrew ground out. 'If he'd harmed Mariah, I should have killed him.'

'I know how you feel.' Justin smiled oddly. 'I was so angry

that I could have broken his neck, but I've calmed down now. The man we need is the man who planned this and paid him.'

'Yes.' Andrew nodded grimly. 'I pray to God that we get him tonight, because only then can I be sure that she is safe.'

In that moment he knew that the woman he was speaking of was Mariah—the woman he wanted as his wife.

Chapter Eight

Mariah stood at the landing window and watched the men gathering in the courtyard below. She felt a clutching sensation in her stomach and knew that it was fear. It took all her will power not to run down to Andrew and beg him not to go, but she knew that such an action would make him angry. She had given her word that she would do nothing foolish, but she longed to mount her own horse and follow them. Andrew need not have been anxious for her, because she believed she was more than capable of defending herself should the need arise.

It was so much harder to be left behind than to be there and watch! Yet she had given her word and must keep it.

'Could you not rest, either?'

Mariah turned as Lucinda came towards her. They had parted earlier on the pretext of wanting an early night with a book, but neither of them was interested in reading.

'I wish they had sent someone else in their place,' Mariah said. 'Why must they do everything themselves? Surely what was done here warrants an arrest being made by the local militia? Justin need only have sent for them and they would have been glad to oblige.'

'Do you really think that either he or Andrew would do that when we are threatened? Neither of them would be satisfied to leave it to others.' Lucinda took her arm. 'Come, dearest, we shall wait downstairs in the parlour for their return. I am certain that they will manage the thing very well. Shall we play cards or would you rather play the pianoforte? You play so well, dearest.'

'I should strike all the wrong notes,' Mariah said and laughed. 'I am such a fool, but I keep thinking that...' She shook her head. It was impossible to explain her feelings even to Lucinda. How could she tell her that she had never confessed her love to Andrew? Impossible to say that she was not certain he loved her, because he might still be in love with Lucinda herself. 'No, I must be positive. Neither of them will be harmed. They will catch the rogue and all this horrid business will be over.'

'Yes, I am sure they will,' Lucinda said. 'They have planned it so meticulously that I am certain nothing can go wrong.'

The inn was a seedy affair, the kind of place that thieves and rogues might habitually patronise, but no honest traveller would ever set foot in. Its appearance was rundown, the windows grimy and steamy inside, and though a welcoming light spilled from a lantern outside, the surrounding area was dark with plenty of places that a man might hide.

'We must hope he is already inside and waiting,' Andrew said as they dismounted and left their horses out of sight of the inn windows. 'I shall leave you here, Justin, and make my way to the rear of the place. If he is my enemy, one sight of me and he will be away.'

'Yes, we'll split up and surround the place. Once Jacobs goes in to ask for his money, your men will identify the rogue he meets—and let us know when he leaves. We shall have him, whichever way he chooses to leave, be it a window at the side or the back door.'

Andrew nodded and left him to order his men as he would. His own plan was to keep moving, scout round the outbuildings and stables, where a man might be waiting and watching for Jacobs to arrive. The plan was to let Jacobs go in and then move quickly to surround the place, so that if his employer scented a rat they could grab him before he made a run for it. However, the man might be crafty enough to wait in the shadows and could perhaps escape before they could discover his identity or whereabouts. Andrew hoped that by using the experience he had gained in the army, where he several times went alone on reconnaissance trips to gather information concerning the enemy, he might be able to catch this rogue off guard.

His apparel was dark and the kind any man might wear for travelling. By keeping to the shadows and moving from place to place he might have the advantage. He saw Jacobs enter the inn. Justin's men waited for perhaps ten seconds before deploying about the inn. Andrew saw them moving silently, following their employer's orders to the letter, keeping to the shadows as much as possible and communicating by signs. He was moving towards the stables when he saw the man lead his horse out and mount it; then he was suddenly riding towards him, clearly in a hurry and in haste to escape. Andrew knew instinctively that their man had been too wary, perhaps suspecting something might have happened to Jacobs. Justin had moved his men too soon. He made a desperate lunge at the horse and grabbed the reins, trying to halt it. The rider brought his whip down hard on the horse's rump and it reared up, kicking at Andrew with its forelegs and knocking him sideways as it rushed by—but for one split second he looked up and saw the man's face and knew him.

'Grainger,' he grunted and cursed. 'Damn the rogue!'

He climbed to his feet as someone fired after the fleeing horseman and then Justin was there beside him.

'He was too crafty for us,' Justin said. 'I did not want to lose him, but I should have waited out of sight a little longer. Did you catch a glimpse of the rogue?'

'I saw his face just for an instant. He must have seen your men, Justin, but he didn't notice me until it was too late. It was Lieutenant Grainger. I told you he went missing in Milan during a masked ball at Count Paolo's house. His aunt was anxious about him and Mariah wondered if he might have been murdered, but I thought he had taken himself off because he was being threatened.' Andrew looked grim. 'It seems as if I may have been mistaken. If Grainger arranged that shooting at your home, he must be the one behind all that stuff out there—the prowler at the villa and the attack on my carriage. I was his guest at the villa and he may have invited me simply so that he would be aware of my movements...'

'Didn't you say he was with the regiment out in Spain? Did you do something that might have aroused his enmity?'

'Nothing that I know of,' Andrew said. 'I would have said we were friends. Unless he was a particular friend of Lieutenant Gordon. He denied it, said they were mere acquaintances—but he may have lied.'

'Yes, I see that,' Justin said. 'But why should he want to kill you? That part of it makes no sense to me, Andrew. He might have a grudge against you if he holds you responsible for a friend's ruin—but murder? It sounds too far fetched to me.'

'He may think I know something. Could he have been responsible for taking that damned silver? It sounds ridiculous, I know. I cannot imagine why anyone would have been foolish enough to think it was possible to sell it for more than a fraction of its worth.'

'I think we are missing something, Andrew. What could he hope to gain by killing you?'

'Perhaps he imagines I was in Italy to spy on him. There are gaps in the theory, but Grainger was here tonight, waiting in the shadows—and he was in a hurry to get away. He must be involved in that shady business somewhere, but I can't be sure how or why.'

'Damn! The mystery remains.' Justin looked frustrated. He turned as one of his men approached, bringing Jacobs with him. 'You saw nothing of your employer, of course.'

'He weren't there, sir,' Jacobs replied. 'He never meant to pay me the rest. He cheated me like everyone else.'

'Well, I shan't cheat you,' Justin told him with a tight smile. 'You are free to go home with money in your pocket and the promise of a job on my estate—with one provision. If you ever see this man again, you come to me at once and tell me.'

'I'll do that, yer 'onour. He deserves to 'ang, so he does, fer tryin' ter upset them fine ladies and you, sir.'

'It is my intention that he shall when we catch him,' Justin said. 'Whoever he may be, he will pay the price for what he has done. As for you, sirrah, you may go home. Report to my bailiff in the morning and he will find you work.'

'God bless yer, sir. May I drop down dead if I ever lift a finger against yer again, milord.'

'Believe me, you will,' Justin said and smiled as the man went off with some of the others from his estate.

'You repay evil with good,' Andrew said. 'I am not sure I should have had your forbearance, Justin.'

'We need the rogue on our side. You saw Grainger ride off and you have reason to suspect him of some involvement in your affairs—but that does not make him the man who paid Jacobs to fire at Lucinda and Mariah. I am for keeping an open mind on this until we know more.'

'Well, I dare say you are right,' Andrew replied. 'It never hurts to keep your enemy close where you can watch him.'

'That was my feeling. We may as well go home. I am quite certain that neither Lucinda nor Mariah have retired to their beds. They will be waiting anxiously for our return and we must put their fears at rest.'

'Unfortunately, we cannot tell them that this wretched business is at an end.' Andrew frowned. 'I have wondered if we should postpone the wedding for a while. I would not have Mariah widowed for a second time.'

'Well, that is your affair, but she will not like it—and I cannot see that it will help. Your only hope of ending this business is to draw your enemy out, Andrew. And the best way of doing that is to face him down, let him believe that you think he cannot touch you. If he loses his temper, he may make a mistake and then you may have him.'

'Well, I have drafted in more men to patrol my grounds and I know you have done the same. All we can do now is to wait and see what happens.'

'Thank God you are both home safe,' Lucinda said and ran to Justin as he entered the salon where they sat, toying with cards that neither of them was the least interested in playing. 'We have been on edge all night.'

'My foolish little love,' Justin said and kissed her. 'Go up now and I shall follow you very soon.'

Mariah watched their affectionate greeting and felt a pang of envy. She wished that she might run to Andrew's arms with the same ease and confidence. She lingered after her friend went out, looking at her fiancé.

'I am glad to see you unharmed,' she said. 'Did everything go as you hoped?'

'No, not at all,' Andrew told her bluntly and explained what had happened when Grainger's horse had knocked him down in the rush to escape.

'So he went missing of his own accord,' Mariah said with a little frown. 'What part do you imagine he played in this affair? I believe he is nervous of something or someone—but somehow I do not see him as a murderer, Andrew.'

'Well, he was certainly there this evening and in a rush to get away, but as yet I do not know where he fits into this business, Mariah. He was at the Lakes and in Milan at the time the incidents took place and I must therefore hold him suspect—but I shall keep an open mind. In the meantime we shall carry on with our lives as if nothing were wrong. I shall stay here this evening, but in the morning I shall go home and set the wheels in motion for our wedding.'

'We are to go on as before?' Mariah nodded. 'Yes, I see. We must hope that draws him out, Andrew. I need not ask, for I know that Justin has made certain arrangements that will ensure no one can reach us in the house again. Well, I am happy to ignore this rogue, whoever he may be—and since I do not believe Lucinda is at risk there is no need to feel anxious. I do not think she needs to know the whole affair.'

Andrew raised his right eyebrow quizzically. 'You are concerned for her, but not yourself?'

'Of course I am concerned for Lucinda. She is as a sister to me.' Mariah laughed huskily. 'I shall carry the pistol my father taught me to use when I was fourteen. If anyone attacks me, I shall not hesitate to use it. Had I had it to hand the day I was kidnapped, they would not have taken me so easily.'

'I believe you,' Andrew said and smiled. 'Go up now and sleep soundly, Mariah. No one will harm you in this house.'

'I am sure of it,' Mariah said. She went to him and kissed his cheek. Had Justin not still been in the room she might have thrown her arms about him and begged him to accompany her. 'Thank you for not postponing the wedding, Andrew. I am certain it must have crossed your mind.'

'We must not give in to this rogue. I am not certain who is behind this, Mariah—but if his intention was to force us apart we shall show him that his plan has not worked.'

'Yes, we shall,' she said and smiled at him. 'I shall write to Sylvia and invite her to stay for the Christmas dance. Lucinda has told me that I may invite as many friends as I wish to stay during this time, but the only friends I truly wish to have about me are Jane, Lucinda and Sylvia. I shall invite others, of course—Winston's sister and aunt must be invited to the dance and the wedding, but they are not my particular friends.'

'I see you have taken me at my word,' Andrew said. 'I am glad that this has not overset you. It worried me that you might fear another attempt at abduction.'

'If it happens, I shall be ready,' Mariah said. 'However, you are probably correct in thinking that Lieutenant Grainger was behind the various attacks.' She wrinkled her smooth brow. 'Do you suppose he might have had something to do with the missing silver?'

'What makes you think that?' Justin turned from his contemplation of his brandy glass to look at her.

'It was just a thought. If he held a grudge against you, might he not take it in the hope of having you blamed?'

'I suppose it could be that,' Andrew said. 'Yes, the thought did cross my mind. I dismissed it as unlikely, because each item of silver bears the regiment's crest and would be hard to sell. A man would need to be desperate to steal it. So it might have been taken for another reason entirely.'

'That is indeed a possibility,' Justin said. 'It makes a great deal of sense. You thought the letter came from Martin's wife or daughter, but it could well have been Grainger's work. Perhaps he thought someone suspected him and tried to shift the blame?'

'Yes, that could well be the truth,' Andrew said. 'He is certainly involved somehow.'

'We shall not solve the mystery tonight,' Mariah said. 'Excuse me, gentlemen, I shall seek my bed.'

She left them to drink a last glass of brandy together and went up to her room, feeling thoughtful. Andrew was right in believing that Lieutenant Grainger was involved in this murky business, but she had an uncomfortable feeling that there was more to it than any of them could yet see. Mariah suspected that she herself was involved here but she did not know how. Unless…

Could Count Paolo be involved in this somehow? She did not see how or why, but her spine tingled and the idea grew in her mind as she began to undress. If the count thought Andrew was his rival, he might do anything to be rid of him.

Mariah felt a tingling sensation all over her body. In that instant she was sure that she had hit upon the solution. No, she was letting her imagination fly. Surely she was being foolish, inventing a story to fit the parts. Andrew would laugh if she suggested such a thing to him—but somehow it made sense.

Mariah shuddered, because somehow she could believe that Count Paolo would be ruthless if he believed that another man stood in his way. Yes, he was the kind of man who would stop at nothing to intimidate or threaten another man.

Where did Grainger come into it? There were so many possibilities that Mariah's head began to spin. She laughed at herself. It was all nonsense, of course; she was inventing complications where there need be none. Yet even though she dismissed her ideas as nonsense, she sensed that she was close to the truth.

He had been going to tell her in Milan, but then something had frightened him off and he'd disappeared. The fact that he'd been waiting in hiding at the inn that night showed that he was still involved somehow—perhaps trying to find some way of communicating with her or Andrew.

Yet why had he tried to run Andrew down?

Mariah finished brushing her long, heavy hair and decided that she must put all the unpleasantness from her mind or she would never sleep. Instead, she would think of the coming dinners and dances leading up to her wedding. Her heart quickened as she remembered the look in Andrew's eyes earlier. Had she imagined it—or had there been something new in the way he'd looked at her?

She smiled as she slipped in between fresh sheets that smelled of lemon and flowers. She must ask Lucinda what her servants used for washing the sheets, because it was pleasant. Soon she would have her own home to run; although it was not a new thing for her, it would be very different. In the past she had had only herself to please, but in future she would have a husband—a very powerful, physical man who had decided opinions of his own. It was likely that they would argue, for their characters were strong, but Mariah smiled as she contemplated such a future. Being petted and given one's own way all the time was pleasant, but she rather thought she would enjoy a tussle of wills sometimes, especially if there were certain compensations when it came to making up a quarrel.

Settling down into the softness of her feather mattress, she sighed and closed her eyes, smiling as she thought of how pleasant it could be to make up a quarrel with Andrew by going to bed with him. Her body remembered the way it had tingled when he kissed her and she drifted into sleep, thinking of pleasures to come.

'Would you care to ride over to the house with me?' Andrew asked when they met the next morning in the breakfast parlour. Mariah had risen to take breakfast with him, because she knew that once he was at home she would not see him quite as often as when he'd stayed at Avonlea, though it was, of course, merely a short ride away. 'I thought you might like to look at the main apartments and discuss what repairs you would have me commission to be done while we are on honeymoon.'

'What a wonderful idea,' Mariah said and glanced towards the window. 'The sun is shining. A perfect day for a ride— and I should love to see your apartments, Andrew, though of course I would not dream of changing them, for I dare say you have had them refurbished to your own taste.'

'As it happens I have not touched them since my father died.' Andrew looked thoughtful. 'I was in the army for a long time and did not bother to take over the master suite until I resigned my commission. Jane had her own apartments done and when I came home I saw to some of the guest rooms. I did not bother with what was my father's room or my mother's. I fear that has not been touched since she died. My father would not allow anyone near it for years. Jane had it cleaned after he died and kept it fresh, but she did not change the décor. That will be for you to do, Mariah—unless you prefer that we use the best guest suite?'

'I shall tell you when I have seen them,' she said and arched her brow at him. 'Wait while I change my gown—fifteen minutes, no more.'

'I shall tell the grooms to bring the horses in thirty minutes.'

'Then we shall waste time. I shall be no more than a quarter of an hour.'

* * *

He had looked at her in disbelief, but Mariah was as good as her word and walked down the stairs in her riding habit no more than sixteen minutes later. The gown was fashioned of dark blue velvet and the slender bodice and skirt set off her figure to perfection, a jabot of creamy lace at her throat. A jaunty hat with curling black feathers sat to one side on her luxuriant hair, which was swept up into a net, and her immaculate York tan gloves finished the elegant ensemble. She looked every inch the wealthy fashionable lady she was and the look of admiration in Andrew's eyes caused her heart to beat faster.

'You look beautiful,' Andrew said. 'I took you at your word and the horses are waiting, my love.'

'Thank you.' Mariah bestowed a smile on him. It was an age since they had ridden together and it brought back memories of a time when they were young and she'd given her untried heart to a dashing young officer who had gone off to fight for his country without a backward glance. 'You are an attractive man, Andrew—even more than when you first joined the army. People will say we make a handsome couple.'

'Will they?' He gave her an odd look. 'You know that many will think me a crafty devil—that I covet your fortune like so many others?'

'I shall pay them no heed,' she replied and threw him a look filled with mischief. 'I have not yet discovered just why you wish to marry me, Andrew, but I acquit you of being mercenary.'

'Thank you,' he said and made a wry face. 'It was one of the reasons I held back, you know. There was a time when for various reasons I was a little short of the readies. It was not something that affected my estate; merely a temporary over-draft on my bank, which I was able to settle by selling some land I did not need.'

'I am glad to hear it. Should you be in any difficulty, I dare say I could advance you something, Andrew.'

'There is not the least need, I assure you. I have already told Justin that I shall be settling a sum of money on you as well as making a generous endowment should you be left a widow before we have children.'

'Please do not speak of it,' she said and shivered. 'I am wealthy enough, Justin. I do not need money. I need a hus-band who will give me children and a family life.'

The grooms had their horses waiting as they went into the courtyard. They stood waiting respectfully. Andrew put Mariah up and then mounted himself without assistance. They moved off, their horses' hooves clattering on the cobbles, the grooms following at a discreet distance.

Mariah realised that the grooms would not be the only ones watching over their lord and his fiancée, because An-drew would take no chances. He might speak of his intentions should the worst happen, but he would do all he could to pre-vent it.

'I am glad to hear it,' Andrew said in reply to her earlier comment. 'Though you will forgive me if I say that I hope we shall have some time to enjoy each other's company before the first child arrives. We shall go to Scotland for a few days after the wedding, as we discussed, but I want to take you to Spain, Mariah. I know you have travelled, but I think it was mostly Italy and France, am I not right?'

'Oh, yes,' she said and looked at him with interest. 'Winston spoke of Spain and Greece. His health would not allow it, as you know—but I think I should enjoy an extensive honeymoon before we return to your home.'

'I believe you will enjoy Spain. It may appeal to the adventurous side in you, Mariah, for there are many parts that have not yet been discovered by those of our acquaintance who enjoy Rome, Venice and Paris. Of course you must buy some clothes in Paris, should you wish it.'

'I have more clothes than any woman could possibly wear,' she said. 'The difficulty will be in deciding which I should take with us and which should be sent to Lanchester Park for our homecoming.'

Andrew laughed. 'You have been thoroughly indulged, have you not? I shall have hard work of it to impress you, Mariah. What may I give you as a present that you would truly like?'

'There are other ways to impress me,' she said, giving him a naughty smile that any red-blooded man could not fail to interpret. 'I loved the ring and collar of emeralds you gave me, Andrew—but all I truly need is to be your wife and to be appreciated for what I am.'

'And what is that, Mariah?' he quizzed with an arch look. 'I must confess that I have puzzled over you for many a day. I believe I am coming to know you a little better. You like to tease and flirt, I know that—but I believe you show only a little of yourself to the public gaze. As your husband I should wish to know more of the real you.'

'We shall learn to know each other,' she said, glancing away from his searching gaze, which made her heart behave so oddly. 'It is a perfect day for a gallop, Andrew. Shall we race for a time?'

'Yes, if you wish it,' he said. 'I shall give you a start, for your horse will not keep pace with mine, I think.'

'Will she not?' Mariah laughed and tossed her head. 'If that is true, you have found your wedding gift, Andrew—a horse that will match yours.'

'But could you ride it?'

'You must try me and see,' she replied and gave her horse a little flick with her heels. Her mare responded and she raced away, bending forwards over its neck in an effort to outpace him.

For a time she managed it, but gradually he caught and matched her, but did not seek to pass. Instead, they rode side by side, the wind in their hair, riding swiftly but well within the capability of both, until at last they stopped in consideration of the horses and the grooms who could not hope to keep up with their pace.

'Well?' Mariah looked at him, a challenge in her eyes. 'Should I match you if I had a horse of your quality?'

'I dare say you would outpace me,' he said, and his face was alight with laughter and something more, which she thought was desire. 'You have your wedding gift, Mariah. You shall have a horse the equal or superior to mine.'

'Now that is something I shall anticipate with pleasure,' she said. 'I believe there may be much to look forward to in our marriage, Andrew.'

'I shall try not to disappoint you, my love.'

She laughed and shook her head at him, but would not be drawn, merely giving him a look that might mean anything.

Now that they were on easier terms she delighted in their banter; knowing that she could bring that fierce, hot look to his eyes was truly pleasing.

Within a very short time, they had arrived at Andrew's estate. Once they reached the front of the beautiful house, with its graceful portico and Ionic columns of gleaming white, he dismounted, coming round to assist her so that she slid down into his arms. He held her for a moment and her breathing quickened, her mouth opening slightly as if to invite his kiss. However, grooms had come running to take their horses and the housekeeper was hastily assembling servants to greet them at the door. Mariah knew them all by name, because she had visited so often in the past and there were seldom changes amongst the staff, except for the occasional new maid. However, there was a new respect in their faces as she was welcomed to what would be her home in future.

'We were all so happy to hear the news, milady,' Crawford, Andrew's butler, told her. 'Everyone will welcome you as the new mistress at Lanchester Park.'

'Thank you. I shall be very happy to be the mistress here, and you may tell Mrs Crawford that I shall not interfere with her arrangements. Any adjustments may be made gradually after some consultation between us.'

'I have no doubt that she will be pleased to make any changes you require, my lady. She has gone out this morning or she would have been here to greet you. One of the maids is ill and she went to visit her at her family home, my lord.'

'Quite right, too,' Andrew said. 'This is just an informal visit, Crawford. You may dismiss the staff. We shall wander around the house ourselves—and you may serve a light nuncheon at half past twelve, if you will.'

'Certainly, my lord.' Crawford nodded and ushered the servants back into the house, where they soon dispersed.

'Well, where shall we start?' Andrew asked as they stood in the hall and looked at the imposing staircase leading to the landing above. 'You are familiar with the public rooms, of course.'

'Show me the best guest suite first and then your apartments,' Mariah said. 'I believe we can discuss the other apartments at leisure, but we should settle where we are to be private, Andrew.'

'It is the most important,' he agreed. 'The best guest suite is in the west wing. Shall we?' He offered her his arm and they walked up the wide staircase together, turning to the right at the top.

'Do you have a valet?' Mariah asked. 'I do not believe I have ever seen him.'

'I have not bothered to employ one,' Andrew said. 'In the army I had a batman, of course, but unfortunately he was killed in an accident just before I resigned my commission. I should have offered Parker the position, but in the circumstances I decided to manage without a valet. Crawford has made it a part of his duties to care for my clothes and assist me when I need it.'

'You should employ a man before we marry,' Mariah said. 'You cannot take Crawford away from his duties here and you will need someone when we are travelling.'

'It has been in my mind. I shall send for a man who once served with me under Wellington. I believe Manson might enjoy the position. He was my sergeant for a while, but we lost contact. I heard recently that he had suffered the loss of an eye, which may make it difficult for him to find work elsewhere.'

Mariah glanced at him, then nodded, a smile on her lips. 'I approve of that notion, Andrew. One should always do what one can for others less fortunate and, if he was an army man, you will find him useful in a crisis.'

'Yes, I imagine so,' he said, looking at her oddly. 'I thought you might think me foolishly romantic to think of offering the post to a man with only one eye.' He quirked an eyebrow at her.

'It should not affect his work. Besides, you have servants enough to assist him in his duties should he need it.'

'I doubt Manson would need help because he happened to lack the use of one eye.' His expression made Mariah raise her brows at him. 'I had not thought you would take an interest in the welfare of those less fortunate, Mariah.'

'Had you not?' Mariah refused to let his remark hurt her. It seemed to show once more that he thought her either selfish or heedless of others. 'Then you do not know me, Andrew. In the past I have consulted Justin about my charitable trusts, but when we are married you may like to help me. I am on the board of two trusts, one for the alleviation of poor women and their children, and another that works to find men, who have become disabled through accident or warfare, some kind of work they can reasonably do. We give them money to help them learn a trade or to buy tools so that they can set up a small business.'

Andrew's gaze narrowed. 'Why have you never told me any of this before?'

Mariah shrugged carelessly. 'Do you not think it boring to be forever prating of one's good deeds? I find that those who do so are usually less charitable than those who keep their own counsel.'

'In that I must agree with you,' he said and looked thoughtful. 'How many more secrets have you kept from me, Mariah?'

'Oh, hundreds.' She laughed and pouted at him. 'You should not ask, Andrew. Do you not find a certain mystery tantalising?'

'You are a wicked tease, Mariah.' He stopped outside a pair of double doors and then moved forwards to throw them open. 'This is the suite we offer to our most prestigious guests—but perhaps you would prefer that we should use it?'

Mariah moved into the first room, which was a rather lovely sitting room, adorned with furniture in the latest style; of satinwood, inlaid with fruitwoods and strung with ebony, the elegant chairs, desks and cabinets gave the apartment a light and airy feel, especially with the deep colours of crimson, gold and grey in the decor. She looked approvingly at the fittings and then moved into the first bedroom, glancing out at a view of the formal gardens, then went through the dressing room into an even larger room, which had similar furnishings, but a decor of cream, gold and rich blue.

'I can see that these rooms have been done recently and the decor is excellent. However, I should like to see your apartments before making a decision.'

'Yes, of course. You must do just as you wish. It will be my pleasure to please you.'

Mariah turned and saw his eyes intent on her. He was clearly interested in seeing her reaction to his home.

'Did you consult Mr Adam when refurbishing these rooms?' she asked as they left the west wing after peeping into various guest rooms, none of which quite matched the luxury of the apartments Andrew had had refurbished. 'I think the furniture is in his style.'

'No, I merely instructed a London company to come here and refurbish the suite in the style of Mr Adam. I think they did well enough, though I have wondered if perhaps the rooms are a touch impersonal?'

'Yes, but that can easily be changed with a few small changes. When one has one's own things about one, everything is more comfortable, do you not think so?'

'In the army we became used to having few personal possessions. You may think the way I live spartan, Mariah.'

'Well, we shall see.' Mariah laughed. They had progressed through the house and were now standing outside a pair of imposing mahogany doors. The wood gleamed with polish and the door handles were gleaming brass, but there was a different feeling as Andrew pushed opened the doors and invited her to enter.

The sitting room was furnished with a solid mahogany bookcase, also a pretty French cabinet made of fruitwood inlaid with patterns of flowers and ribbon stringing. Inside its glass panels a collection of Chinese porcelain was shown to advantage. There was a selection of comfortable but rather worn-looking chairs, a desk set with oddments of writing paraphernalia, an elegant elbow chair and a couple of wine tables with fluted edges. The colours in the curtains seemed to be dark but indistinguishable, as if they had faded into a muddy shade with age.

Choosing the door to the far left of the facing wall, Mariah found herself in a very pretty room, which had obviously belonged to Andrew's mother. It had been cleaned recently and smelled of lavender and beeswax. Here the decor was of various shades of lilac and blue, which were charming, but not the colours Mariah preferred. She discovered that the view looked out towards a wide stretch of lawn with graceful old trees and in the distance she could see what could only be the lake.

The furniture was good, but belonged to an earlier age and would need to be changed. However, the room was of good proportions and with the right decor and some of her own furniture, which she would have brought here, it would be comfortable. She walked through into what was clearly a lady's boudoir; it smelled faintly of perfume and was furnished in the French style in shades of cream and rose. From there she progressed into a gentleman's dressing room, which was exceedingly neat, everything tucked away into various chests of drawers and a heavy-looking tallboy.

She hesitated at the next door, for it could lead nowhere but Andrew's bedroom. Her stomach clenched and she glanced back at him. He nodded and she opened the door and went through. Immediately, she smelled the familiar scent of cedar with an underlying tone of leather that reminded her instantly of his scent. Her eyes went to the bed, which was huge, the imposing headboard in the style of Mr Chippendale. All the furniture was dark mahogany, but beautifully made with such style and charm that Mariah knew instinctively why Andrew had not bothered to change anything here. It was just right for a man of his character, solid and useful without being intrusive.

She turned to look at him, a smile on her lips. 'Yes, I think these rooms will do well, Andrew. I should wish to refurbish my room and change the soft furnishings in the sitting room—but very little needs to change here, I think.'

'I found it comfortable, though perhaps the curtains and soft furnishings could be replaced—would that be enough for you?'

'Yes, of course, but you must have it as you wish, Andrew. It is your room.'

'I was hoping you might be a regular visitor here?'

Something in his tone made her heart race. She raised her eyes to his as he moved closer, her lips parting in anticipation as he encircled her waist with one arm, bringing her body close to his. Smiling, she waited for his kiss, her mouth soft and responsive as his lips touched hers. A little shudder ran through him and he deepened his kiss, his tongue probing and exploring, touching hers as she responded, her body melting into him. Her hands moved at his nape, her fingers reaching into his hair, making little circling movements as she indulged her senses.

'Mariah,' he said huskily against her hair, 'seeing you here—it is what I have thought of so often. I have dreamed of you here in my bed. I want you so much, my dearest.'

'Andrew,' she whispered, gazing up at him, an unconscious invitation in her eyes. 'I long to be yours in all the ways a woman belongs to a man. Do we need to wait until the wedding?' A little gurgle of laughter left her as she saw the hot need in him and felt the response of his manhood as he held her pressed close to his body. 'I am very ready to be yours—now, if you wish it?'

'Temptress,' he muttered, his mouth against her white throat. His teeth nibbled at her skin and his hands slid down to cup her buttocks, pressing her closer so that she could feel his hardness and sense his urgent need. 'I am almost minded to take you at your word.'

'Why not?' she asked. 'We shall soon be wed, Andrew.'

'Yes, thank God. I'm not sure how much longer I can wait to have you.' His hands moved; his right hand caressed her breast through the silk of her gown, the other moving up the arch of her back to stroke the skin at her nape. He pressed his lips to the soft skin of her throat, licking at her delicately. 'You are so beautiful, Mariah. So many men have wanted you. I do not need to know how many lovers you have had since Winston died, but you must give me your word there will be no more, for I could not bear it if you were unfaithful to me. I shall not hold you here if you wish to travel later, when our children are born, but you must promise that you will not take lovers.'

'Would it truly matter to you?' she asked, giving him a teasing smile that hid her desperate need to know his true feelings for her. 'Surely you are not jealous, Andrew?'

Her teasing struck the wrong note. He released her and moved away, turning his back to toy with a trinket on the dressing chest. 'I know you were married to an old man who was too ill to satisfy you, and you may have thought it permissible to take lovers to supply the lack—but you will not find me so easy to deceive, Mariah.'

Mariah was stung. How dared he presume that she had betrayed Winston? For an instant she was tempted to punish him, but she bit back the foolish, careless words that must provoke a quarrel.

'I refuse to quarrel with you, Andrew. You may have no opinion of my character, but I assure you I do not give myself lightly. I may have flirted a few times, but I took no lovers while Winston lived—and I should not dream of betraying you.'

Andrew swung round to face her, his eyes burning with a deep fire that shocked her. 'I think I might kill you if you did,' he said, his voice shaken by passion. 'We should go down to the parlour, Mariah. Our luncheon will be served shortly— and I cannot vouch for my actions if we stay here a moment longer.'

Mariah was tempted to tell him that she hungered for his touch, not food, but his assumption that she was a wanton had made her cross with him. He would no doubt discover his mistake if she took him to bed, but he had hurt her feelings and she needed time to recover her composure.

'Pray go down and I shall follow in shortly. I should like to tidy myself a little before we eat.'

He hesitated, seeming unsure for a moment, then inclined his head. 'As you wish, Mariah. You will find anything you need in my dressing room.'

'Thank you.' She smiled at him. 'I can manage, Andrew. I shall not get lost, I assure you.'

'No, of course not. I need a word with Crawford. Take your time. I shall hold luncheon until you are ready.'

'I shall not keep you waiting long.'

After he had gone, Mariah went back to the dressing room. There she found water, a mirror, combs and other things necessary for her comfort. She smoothed her hair and her gown, satisfied that she looked as she ought, then glanced round her once more. Already, she felt at home in this room; she liked the aroma of masculinity and the feeling of permanence that had been lacking in her life. Tempted by a need to know a little more of the man she was to marry, she opened the first of the large drawers in the tallboy and discovered the shirts and a variety of stocks folded neatly inside. Knowing that she was prying, yet driven by a need to discover more, she opened the second drawer, which contained more shirts and inexpressibles, then passed on to the largest drawer at the bottom of the chest. As she saw the various items of clothing carefully laid between layers of tissue and scented shavings of some woody herb, she caught the gleam of silver. Turning back the layer that covered it, she saw a small shield, which, when she took it out, revealed a regimental crest, but no dedication.

A chill trickled down Mariah's spine as she held it before swiftly tucking it back into the drawer. Why had it been hidden away like that? Was it a part of the missing silver, which had been stolen from the regiment?

No, that was a wicked thought! She would not allow it to poison her mind. Andrew would never steal from his own regiment. Of course he would not. She could not imagine why he would hide something of the sort, for if it had been presented to him for bravery or some such thing it ought to have been out on display.

Going back into the sitting room and then out onto the landing, Mariah forced herself to think calmly. If she loved

Andrew, she must believe that he would never do anything underhanded. She did love him and therefore would not allow herself to doubt him or to imagine that the silver shield was part of a larger hoard of stolen silver.

She retraced the way they had come earlier and went down a small flight of stairs to the main landing, which she followed until she came to what she knew to be the family dining parlour. There was a grand one on the ground floor used for large parties; it opened out into a salon and together, when cleared of furniture, the two became the ballroom they would use for their dance. However, the small parlour on the second floor was used for intimate dining.

Andrew was standing with his butler as she entered. He looked at her, lifting his brows as if to ask if all was well.

'Tell Mrs Crawford we are ready to eat now,' he said. 'I think that is all for the moment, Crawford.' His gaze narrowed intently as the butler left. 'Is anything wrong, Mariah?'

'What could possibly be wrong?' she asked and laughed. 'I have been getting to know my home, Andrew—and I must confess that I could not resist opening a few drawers to see what was inside. Do you mind?'

'Not in the least. I have no secrets to hide,' he said. 'Were you looking for incriminating love letters, Mariah?'

'Do you have a mistress?' she asked. 'Should I be aware that I must share you with her?'

'I have no mistress at the moment and no intention of taking one,' he told her, a hint of laughter in his eyes. 'Is this retaliation, my love? I must beg your pardon for what I said to you earlier. I had no right to say such a thing to you.'

'No, you did not,' she agreed and her heart lifted. 'However,

I shall forgive you. It is as well to get these things out of the way now rather than brood over them, do you not agree?'

'Yes, I do as it happens,' he said. 'Will you have some wine, Mariah? I have some rather fine French wine—unless you prefer Italian?'

'Oh, no, I prefer French,' she said. 'Champagne is my favourite, but I shall be interested to try whatever you have to offer.'

'I believe you will enjoy this,' he said. 'One thing you have not yet seen is my cellar, Mariah. I have imported wines from Spain, Portugal, France and Italy, all of which have some merit. I shall teach you to appreciate the finer vintages. It is an interest we may share.'

'If you will share my love of poetry I shall share your interests,' she assured him.

As Andrew began to question her about the poets she liked and her tastes in general, her spirits lifted. She could see herself sitting here with him often when they were married, talking over the events of their day or news from friends, and she enjoyed the picture it created in her mind.

The doubts and anxieties had lifted and Mariah was conscious of feeling happy. The sooner her wedding day dawned, the better.

A little smile touched her mouth as she imagined Andrew's surprise when he first took her—would it please him to know that she was still virgin?

'Why are you smiling?' he asked, handing her a glass of wine.

'Perhaps I shall tell you soon,' she teased. 'Or perhaps you will discover for yourself....'

Chapter Nine

For Mariah the next week passed in a blur of pleasure. She went walking or riding with Andrew most mornings, and he normally stayed to nuncheon at Avonlea, or accompanied Lucinda and Mariah when they visited friends. Once he took her back to Lanchester Park to meet with the man who was to undertake the covering of chairs and sofas in their apartments and to choose silks for new curtains in several rooms. She passed a very happy hour or so mulling over rich fabrics and was well pleased with her choice. On another day her personal things arrived and were taken up to her rooms, which had been cleared of the old furniture. The change was remarkable and Mariah enjoyed being reunited with favourite pieces she'd had under covers for months, especially a very beautiful desk that she had once had made for her by Mr Robert Adam.

'I can hardly wait to move in,' she told Andrew with a smile. 'I have written all the invitations for the wedding. You must check my list and make certain I have not missed any of your friends.'

'I have sent out the invitations for our dance,' Andrew told her. 'I think you and Lucinda should come early on the day and you may all stay overnight rather than driving home afterwards.'

'Yes, that sounds an excellent idea,' Mariah said. 'Will Jane and George be here for the dance?'

'Yes, certainly. Jane wrote by return and said she would stay until the wedding. It will be pleasant to have the family together again.'

'Yes, it will.'

Mariah's eyes were intent on his face. She had a feeling that he was keeping something from her, but did not enquire too deeply. Andrew had presented her with several pretty trifles in the way of gifts: flowers, a leather-bound copy of one of Lord Byron's poems and a pretty Bristol-blue scent flask filled with the perfume she liked most.

'How did you know what I use?' she asked and was surprised at the colour that rose in his cheeks.

'I fear I am a thief. I took one of your kerchiefs that you left lying somewhere and sent it to my man in London. He took it to a top perfumery and they were able to trace it quite easily.'

'Andrew!' She laughed and pouted at him. 'You are a devious man and I shall have to watch you closely.'

The idea that he had taken one of her kerchiefs pleased her and she pictured him holding it to his nose before sending it off to discover the name of her favourite perfume.

'It was a charming thought, thank you.'

Sometimes in the afternoons, they entertained friends to tea. A constant stream of acquaintances had been visiting at Avonlea, bringing tributes of flowers, bonbons and other small presents for Mariah and wishing her happy in her coming marriage. At other times they took turns in reading to each other or walked in the orangery, which had been repaired the morning after that infamous shot was fired.

Nothing untoward had happened, either on their walks in the gardens or on their rides to Lanchester Park. Mariah was vaguely aware that they were protected. She had once or twice caught a glimpse of a burly man with a shotgun over his shoulder, and she rather thought there were more footmen on duty at Avonlea than had been the case in the past. However, nothing was allowed to intrude and she found life pleasant and peaceful.

'I do not think I have ever seen you look so happy, dearest,' Lucinda said when they were sitting together in the little parlour they favoured in the mornings. Andrew had sent word that he had some business that needed his attention and would arrive at about three that afternoon. 'There is a glow about you these days that was not there before, Mariah.'

Mariah laughed, her eyes dancing with amusement. 'I am happy, dearest Lucinda. I owe some of that to you, you know. Had you not welcomed me when I came to stay without asking I should have gone away again and perhaps this would never have happened. Andrew took a deal of time to make up his mind.'

'This was and is your home—or one of them,' Lucinda said and looked up as a footman entered bearing a silver salver. 'Yes, Jason, is it a letter for me?'

'No, my lady. It is for Lady Fanshawe.'

He offered the small tray to Mariah and she took her letter. 'I dare say it is an acceptance for the wedding. I believe this is Sylvia's writing.' She broke open the seal and read the first lines. 'She says she is well and will arrive three days before Christmas. So she will be here for the Christmas dinner, our dance and the wedding.' Mariah looked at her friend. 'I fear your house will be invaded by my friends, Lucinda.'

'I am happy to have them,' Lucinda assured her. 'I have only one aunt, though of course Justin has a large family, but we have plenty of rooms, dearest.'

Mariah had turned the page and gave a start of alarm. 'No! Oh, dear, I wish he had not…'

'Is something wrong?'

'Sylvia says that Count Paolo is staying with her and has invited himself as her escort for the journey. Lord Hubert will not arrive until Christmas Eve. She says that she is sure I shall not mind seeing the count again and… No, he would not!'

'Something is wrong. Pray tell me, my love.'

'Sylvia says that Andrew wrote to her asking her to the dance and told her that she might bring the count if he happened to be staying with her. Why would he do such a thing?'

'It would seem only polite to ask Count Paolo since he offered you such lavish hospitality at his villa and his home, Mariah. You cannot truly believe he was behind any of that unpleasantness? He is, after all, a gentleman. Andrew does not think it or he would not offer the invitation. Justin told me they believe they know the culprit—a lieutenant in the same regiment.'

'Yes.' Mariah bit her lip, hesitating. 'I suppose we ought to invite Count Paolo if he is Sylvia's guest—but I cannot help wishing that Andrew had not done so.'

Mariah got up and walked to glance out of the window. She

knew that everyone was convinced Lieutenant Grainger was behind the trouble in Italy and what had happened here. Nothing more had happened and perhaps that was because Grainger knew he'd been seen. He must know he was a marked man and would not dare to come near the house himself. It all fitted very neatly—but she could not rid herself of the idea that the count was involved in the murky business somehow.

Andrew must have acquitted him or he would not have invited Sylvia to bring the count with her. Mariah wished she'd spoken to Andrew of her doubts, but she had avoided the subject, knowing that it might provoke her fiancé's censure. She had only flirted a very little with the count, but Andrew had suspected more and so she had pushed the thought from her mind, but now it rose to haunt her.

'You should speak to Andrew if you are concerned,' Lucinda said. 'However, I do not think we can refuse to receive the count if he escorts Lady Hubert. It would cause offence to both her and her husband, for the count is a great friend of Lord Hubert's, I believe?'

'Yes, they have business together. I suppose that is why the count has come to England to stay with them.'

He had told her he would see her very soon. He had asked her to wait for him, told her that he always got what he wanted in the end. Despite her refusals, he seemed to think that she would give in and marry him. What kind of a man persisted when a lady had made her feelings known?

Mariah felt a cold prickling sensation at the nape of her neck. An icy droplet trickled down her spine, making her shiver. She had been enjoying herself so much, looking forward to all the excitement of the parties, dances and the wedding itself, and suddenly it was as if a shadow had been cast over her.

Mariah went back to her seat. There was no point in brooding over things. The count might give her reproachful looks, but there was little he could do. The date of her wedding had been announced and the invitations had gone out. He must know that there was no chance of her agreeing either to a proposal of marriage or anything else he might offer.

It was a little awkward, to be sure, and she might experience some uncomfortable moments, but she was safe enough here. Andrew and Justin were protecting her. Providing that she took care never to be alone with him, the count could not harm her or prevent her marriage.

'Why did you tell Sylvia that she might invite that man?' Mariah asked when she was alone in the conservatory with Andrew later that afternoon. 'You know I do not like him.'

'There will be quite a few people at our wedding whom I dislike,' Andrew said and made a wry face. 'In society one has to show a polite face even to one's enemies, my love. Count Paolo cannot harm you here. I shall take him off to stay with me once he arrives. After all, he is my guest, not yours. I owe him hospitality for that he showed me in Milan.'

Mariah frowned at him. 'You still will not take me seriously when I say he was involved in Lieutenant Grainger's disappearance. I know he is alive and you saw him that night at the inn—but I think there is more to this than you know. And I believe Count Paolo is involved. I do not trust him and…' She shook her head as she saw the amused light in his eyes. 'Are you laughing at me, Andrew?'

'No, my love, why should I?'

'You think my vanity has led me to believe he would murder for me, do unspeakable things to make me his wife.' She tossed her head. 'I am not imagining things, Andrew. That man is dangerous. I think he is mad.'

'Mad to risk all for your sake—to own you?' Andrew's mouth hardened. 'It is not unknown for a man's desire to drive him mad—but I dare say there is more to all this than we know.'

There the subject was dropped. Andrew wanted to talk to her of carpenters and stone masons, and repairs he was having done to the east wing. From there they went on to discuss the many gifts that had begun to pour in from their mutual friends, the thank-you letters that must be written, and where they would travel on their wedding trip.

Gradually, Mariah's mind was eased. Andrew was clearly not troubled by the knowledge that Count Paolo would be staying with them for several days. He seemed to have dismissed even Lieutenant Grainger as being unimportant in the scheme of things, therefore she was being foolish to let her doubts play on her mind. This was meant to be a happy time, a time of getting to know her future husband.

Mariah was learning so much about Andrew, things she had never guessed. They spoke of having dogs and Mariah confessed that she had always wanted one of those huge shaggy Irish wolfhounds.

'Papa had one when I was small. It followed me everywhere and once, when I had been away for some days, it was so overjoyed to see me that it ran at me so hard Papa thought it would knock me down, but it did not. They can be fierce with strangers, but are so gentle and loyal when they love, Andrew.'

'Yes, I believe I recall you telling me of your love of wolf-hounds some years ago,' Andrew said and smiled. 'Tell me, why have you not purchased one for yourself?'

'Had we returned to England to live I should have done, but since I married I have lived in Italy, France or other people's homes. I visited the house we were to have made our home once, but could never settle there.'

'Is that where the elegant cream-and-gold furniture for your bedroom came from?'

'Yes. I purchased it in France on my honeymoon and had it sent to England to be stored for me. It goes well at Lanchester, do you not think so?'

'It is perfect for you.' Andrew looked thoughtful. 'You have elegance and style, Mariah, but I am discovering that much lies hidden beneath the surface. Is there anything more you would wish to bring from Lord Fanshawe's house?'

'No, I think not.' She wrinkled her smooth brow. 'What do you think I should do with the house and the land, Andrew? I doubt that we shall ever wish to use it since you have your own houses, here and in London—also a hunting box in Devon, I think you said?'

'Yes, I have houses enough, but nothing in Bath. Do you like Bath, Mariah?'

'It is well enough for a short stay, but there are too many gossiping busybodies for my taste. I prefer London society,' she said and laughed as his eyebrows rose. 'Well, you asked. You would not wish me to lie over a thing like that?'

'Heaven forbid,' he said, amused by her straight speaking. He took her hand, playing with the fingers, his casual caress sending shivers up and down her spine. She felt a tingle of desire and wished that he would kiss her. However, he seemed content to touch her hand, his mind on practical things. 'So we shall not bother to buy a house there. What would you wish to do with Lord Fanshawe's house?'

'I think we should sell it. Perhaps we should offer it to Winston's sister and her husband. If they have no use for it, we can dispose of it as we choose—unless you think it should be kept for our children?'

Would he think her wanton if she wound herself about his body and demanded he make love to her? Mariah felt a hot flush spread through her body. If she was finding it difficult to control her need now, what would she do when they were married? Andrew might discover his wife demanded more than he had ever thought to give. For a moment she felt a prick of fear, as she wondered if she were doing the right thing. Andrew could be passionate—but did he want her with the same intensity as she wanted him? It was with difficulty that she brought her thoughts back to the task in hand.

'Shall we postpone the decision until we return from our travels? I can instruct my agent to overlook it for you, make sure all is well there from time to time. I shall inspect it myself once we are home again and see what I think you might do with it, Mariah. If you wish to be rid of it, of course, we could sell it immediately—but you might let it to tenants, perhaps.'

'I really do not know what to do,' she admitted. 'Most of the fortune I was left is in trusts or investments, but there are other properties, I believe. I think my agents let them, but I have not gone into things in detail for the income is sufficient for my needs without raising capital. Ledgers were never my favourite reading matter.'

Andrew looked at her thoughtfully. 'Has Winston's wealth been a burden to you, Mariah?'

'Yes, to some extent,' she agreed. 'I am glad to have it, of course, and I try to use some of the income to help others, but I do not know if my agents are as efficient as they might be—and I do not wish to be bothered with enquiring into things too deeply. If I discovered they had been cheating me, I should no doubt lose my temper and sack them all.'

'Then would you like me to talk to them for you? It is too close to Christmas to visit London now, but I could go early in the New Year, before our wedding—if you wished?'

'I shall admit that it would be a relief to me,' she said and smiled at him. 'Being able to buy whatever one wishes is a pleasure, Andrew—but the possession of great wealth is a responsibility. I know that once we have children we may put much of the money into trusts for them—and since I hope to have several it will be put to good use, for the girls should have an equal share with the boys.'

'You wish for several children?' Andrew's eyes sparkled with humour. 'I had no idea that you were such a domestic creature, Mariah. How many babies would suit you, five or six?'

'Oh, you,' she said. 'I do not mean all at once—but perhaps four—two boys and two girls.'

Laughter released her tension. How foolish she was to doubt.

Her life would be so much happier as his wife than it had been for many a year.

'I shall have to see what I can do to oblige you, my love. In what order would you prefer them?'

Mariah laughed and slapped him lightly on the shoulder, at which he reached out for her, drawing her close to him, his eyes hot with desire as he gazed down at her. Her heart raced with excitement. She lifted her face to receive his kiss, which was hungry and demanding, lasting so long that she was breathless when he let her go. Oh, how good it felt in his arms! Her body tingled with desire, the need in her so great that she thought he must see it. At times like this their wedding seemed too far away.

'You accuse me of teasing, but you do it, too,' she said. 'I was an only child, though I know I had a brother once. He died when I was still a baby and I cannot remember him. My father spoiled me, Andrew. He was lonely after Mama died and he treated me as the son he had lost. I have been lonely too often. I do not want that for a child of ours.'

Andrew's arms tightened about her. 'You shall not be lonely while I live, Mariah. I have a sister and I am fond of Jane—but I think that I, too, was lonely until you came into my life.'

He drew her closer, kissing her again, but this time with such tenderness that she felt tears sting her eyes. When he spoke to her this way and kissed her like this she almost believed herself loved—not as a spoiled darling, but as a woman, a partner who would share everything with the man she loved. If that were the case she would be so fortunate.

'Andrew…' Mariah's lips opened on a sigh. What she might have said then was lost as Lucinda's voice came to them.

'We have visitors,' Lucinda called. 'Lady Hubert and Count Paolo have arrived. I have had them taken to their rooms, but I know you would not wish to neglect your friend, Mariah. She has the green room, which is three doors from yours, if you wish to go up and greet her.'

'Here already?' Mariah said, startled. 'I thought they were not due for another two days?'

'I think she said something about intending to call on another friend on her way here. Unfortunately, the lady was taken ill suddenly and could not receive visitors so they decided to come straight here. Lady Hubert apologised and said she hoped her early arrival would not put me out. Of course I told her it was perfectly agreeable and we should be glad to have her company.'

'That is true if it were only Sylvia,' Mariah said and glanced at Andrew in a slightly accusing way. 'I rely on you to take the count home with you, Andrew.'

'Oh, was he to stay with you?' Lucinda looked surprised. 'Forgive me, I have given him a room in the east wing. I can hardly send him away now. His trunks will have been unpacked.'

'No, you cannot send him packing,' Mariah said and shrugged, ignoring the chill at her nape. 'Do not worry, Lucinda. I was being foolish earlier. The count is a guest here and a gentleman. I am sure I am perfectly safe in his company.'

Her words were meant to reassure her friend, but as she spoke them Mariah was mentally resolving never to give the count a chance to find her alone.

* * *

Mariah left Andrew to make his own way to the parlour. Tea would be served shortly but she must first go up and greet her friend.

Knocking at Sylvia's door, she was invited to enter and found her friend putting the finishing touches to her hair. She had clearly changed from her carriage gown, which lay discarded on the bed, and was wearing a yellow-silk tea gown, which Mariah recalled they had ordered in Paris.

'Your gown becomes you, dearest,' she said and kissed Sylvia's cheek. 'Are you well?'

'Yes, exceedingly so. Had I not been Hubert would not have allowed me to make the journey here, I dare say, but I told him that I could not miss your wedding, but would rest once I got home. It will be my last large social engagement before my confinement.'

'You are certainly blooming. I imagine Hubert is delighted with your condition?'

'Over the moon. We have been married some years, as you know, and we both feared it would never happen. The dear man cannot do enough for me.'

'I am sorry he could not come with you. I trust there is nothing wrong?'

Sylvia's brow wrinkled. 'I think he may have a little trouble over some matter of business, but he rarely discusses anything of that nature with me. It was just a chance remark that led me to think he might have a difficulty—something about perhaps selling his hunting box, which in truth he hardly ever uses these days.'

Mariah hesitated, then, 'Forgive me if I offend—but should Lord Hubert be in any difficulty I might be able to help...'

'Oh, no, my love, he would not dream of it, though it is just like you to ask,' Sylvia said. 'I am sure it is nothing—just a temporary lack of funds. I think Count Paolo asked for a larger investment in the business, but I cannot be sure. I have no head for these things.'

'Business is boring when there is so much more to enjoy,' Mariah agreed and smiled at her, but underneath her calm manner, an alarm bell was ringing. Was her friend's husband being cheated by the count?

Mariah bit back the words of warning. To speak of something she did not know for sure would be foolish and might be described as slander. She must keep her opinions to herself, but she would listen and observe, and if she suspected the count of being less than honest with Lord Hubert she would tell him in private of her suspicions.

'Come,' she said, holding out a hand to Sylvia. 'They will be gathering for tea in the parlour. You and the count are our first visitors, but there will be many more over the next few days. The duke has a large family and they descend in hordes over the Christmas period, because he holds such wonderful parties.'

Sylvia took her arm as they went out together. 'I am looking forward to your dance and the wedding. Have you had many presents yet? I wasn't sure what to bring you, but decided on some beautiful old lace that has been in my family for years. I had it laundered and I think you will love it, Mariah. You may use it to trim undergarments or perhaps the christening gown for your first child.'

'What a lovely idea,' Mariah said. 'I've often admired your lace, Sylvia. It is difficult to find such intricate work these days.'

Talking happily together of clothes and fripperies, the two friends went down the landing and the main staircase. In the hall below they discovered two gentlemen talking together. Mariah's hand unconsciously tightened on her friend's arm as she saw Andrew standing with the count.

Her heart raced as she walked towards them. Andrew smiled at her, but she sensed something in his manner as he greeted her—an air of...what? She might almost say ownership, as if he were determined to show the count that she belonged to him.

'Mariah, my love,' he said. 'I was just telling Count Paolo how pleased *we* are that he could come to *our* dance. I asked if he would stay for the wedding, but he says he must leave after the dance on account of business pressures at home.'

Mariah felt relief, but controlled her facial expressions. 'Nothing too serious, I hope, Count? We are, of course, happy you could come to the dance. You gave such a lavish entertainment for us in Milan.'

The count moved forwards. She was obliged to offer her hand. He took it and bowed over it, but did not kiss it as he had when they first met. Lifting her gaze, she caught the gleam of anger in his eyes and knew that beneath his charming manners he was seething with fury.

'It was my pleasure, Mariah,' he murmured in a low voice. 'I am glad you remember, for I forget nothing. Your beauty graced my home and you will be long remembered, I assure you. My house is empty without its treasure.' The last words were spoken so softly that she was certain no one else could hear them. 'It waits for the return of that which was stolen from me.'

Mariah shivered as she removed her hand from his. She had no doubt that his soft words were a warning, but delivered in such a way that no one else would suspect him of being anything other than polite.

'You are too gracious, Count.'

He murmured something indistinguishable and stood back. Mariah walked to Andrew and took his arm. Her hand trembled slightly. He raised his brows, but she gave a slight shake of the head. Impossible to say that she felt threatened even here with her friends about her. She was being foolish. Perhaps the menace was merely in her mind.

Sylvia had taken the count's arm and was following as Mariah and Andrew led the way to the large parlour where tea was to be served. She could hear her friend laughing at something the count was saying and wondered if she had made too much of a look and a few words that might mean anything.

Lucinda and Justin were already in the parlour, and a surprise awaited the newcomers. Jane and Lord George had arrived to stay at Andrew's home and driven over to take tea with their friends. There was a flurry of excited greetings, during which Jane was hugged and kissed by the ladies and the gentlemen shook hands and talked of various sporting matters and the favourite subject of wine.

When Mariah looked, she discovered that Count Paolo was the centre of attention and seemed to be extolling the virtues of wine from his own vineyards.

'I have formed a partnership with some of my neighbours

so that we can export in greater quantity to England,' he was saying to Lord George. 'It is an investment opportunity for discerning businessmen, though I know English gentlemen do not like to discuss trade.'

'Oh, we discuss it at the right time,' Justin told him, 'but not around the tea table, Count. Later, perhaps? We shall all sample some of the fine wines from my cellars and then we may talk business if you choose.'

Mariah saw the little nerve at the count's temple. He was annoyed that he had been put in his place by a man who out-ranked him and was of far more importance socially than he. Once again she wondered if he had cheated Lord Hubert in some way, and once again she put it from her mind, as the conversation became general, centring on the festivities and the forthcoming wedding.

Mariah studiously avoided catching the count's eye, though she was uncomfortably aware that he watched her through-out tea. However, with her friends about her, she was able to laugh and talk, enjoying the gossip Jane and Lord George had brought from town.

'Jane wanted to do her shopping in London,' Lord George said with an indulgent look at his wife. 'I dare say she has ruined me, but I like a little bit of shopping for Christmas myself.'

Jane's spirited denial and counter-accusations set the com-pany laughing and by the time she and Lord George took their leave, Mariah had managed to quell her nerves.

Andrew was right. The count was forced to be on his best behaviour in company of this quality and she was quite safe, providing that she did not allow him to catch her alone. However, since Andrew had decided to accompany his sister and her husband to his home, she felt a little less safe when she went up to change for dinner.

The gentlemen lingered over their port for half an hour or so and Mariah was at the pianoforte when they finally came through to the drawing room. Mariah wished that Andrew had stayed to dine, as he had most evenings since he returned home, but she understood that he had felt obliged to welcome his sister and her husband to his home and make sure they were comfortable. He could hardly dine here if they were not to join the company.

She was very much aware that the count's eyes were on her as she finished her piece and left the instrument to take a seat next to Lucinda. Sylvia had taken her place at the pianoforte and invited Count Paolo to sing with her. He had a pleasant, deep voice, and since the piece they chose was both witty and popular it was not hard to listen, even though Mariah felt as if an oppressive shadow hung over her.

After Sylvia had finished the piece and left the pianoforte the last drinks were served. Lucinda announced that she was tired and the ladies went up together, saying goodnight at the top of the stairs. Once in her room, Mariah locked her door, standing with her back against it for a moment. Then she shook her head and went through into her bedroom, ringing for her maid, who entered through the dressing room.

She was being foolish. The count would not dare to attempt anything while he was a guest in the Duke of Avonlea's house.

Mariah had decided that she would take breakfast in her own room the next morning. It was her usual habit to rise and breakfast downstairs after either a walk in the gardens or a brisk ride out, with or without her groom. However, since the weather had turned frosty, she had decided to forgo the pleasure. Her maid was a little surprised by the request, but Mariah was being sensible.

Only when Sylvia came to her room an hour or so later did she declare that she was ready to go down.

'Are you feeling unwell, dearest?' Sylvia asked. 'I thought it was your habit to ride or walk early in the morning.'

'Yes, it is,' Mariah agreed. 'However, I thought I would have a lie in this morning. It is only another three days until our dance and I wanted to be full of energy so that I can dance the night away.'

'You must be so excited,' Sylvia said as they went down the wide staircase together. 'I am surprised you have not felt the need to come up to town to buy things for your home. Perhaps you intend to do so once Christmas is over?'

'Oh, no, I think I shall remain here until the wedding,' Mariah told her. 'I shall have plenty of time to buy things on my honeymoon. Besides, I still have not unpacked everything I bought in Italy and Paris. Andrew told me yesterday that another crate had arrived at Lanchester—and I had my own furniture sent there.'

'Well, I suppose you have most of what you need. Winston did leave you such a lot of money.'

'Most of the capital is tied up in various trusts or property,' Mariah said. 'I have lived within my means—but he was very generous to me. I still have some of the capital he settled on me when we married, though I have given some to a friend.'

Mariah looked at her, because there was something a little odd in her manner. 'Is anything troubling you, Sylvia?'

'No, of course not, dearest,' Sylvia replied awkwardly. 'I would not dream of… No, nothing is wrong.'

Mariah took her by the arm, leading her into a small parlour where they could speak privately. 'I know you are hiding something. Are you in money trouble, Sylvia—is Hubert?'

'I do not wish to bother you…' Sylvia looked uncomfortable. 'Hubert has always been so generous to me and if I overspent my allowance he would settle my bills, but…he told me last week that I must keep strictly within my allowance for he could not advance me if I fell into debt.' She bit her lower lip. 'I did spend lavishly in Paris and now the merchant is dunning me and I cannot pay. His last letter was really quite abusive and I dare not tell Hubert.'

'How much do you owe?'

'No, Mariah, you can't,' Sylvia protested. 'I wouldn't dream of asking it. I did not mean you to know, but it slipped out, because I have been so anxious. Hubert has never refused me before.'

'Perhaps he has some trouble himself,' Mariah suggested. 'Please allow me to help you, my dear friend. If you wish, we shall call it a loan without interest and you may repay one day in the future when you are able. Tell me what you need.'

'I fear it is more than one thousand guineas.' Sylvia sighed. 'I know it is an exorbitant sum to spend on clothes, but I wanted pretty things for my confinement and I bought lace, silks and linen for the baby, too.'

Mariah smiled and shook her head. 'I am so spoiled that I spent twice that amount on my clothes, which is why I did not need to buy more clothes in London for my trousseau. I shall give you a draft for fifteen hundred pounds on my bank. No, do not deny me, Sylvia. I want to do this for you—and if Hubert is in trouble I would help him if I could.'

'You are always so generous,' Sylvia said and dabbed her eyes with a scrap of lace that wafted lavender water into the air. 'I feel awful for asking you, but it would be such a relief to me.'

'You did not ask, I offered. Do not concern yourself about repaying, though if it makes you easier in your mind you may do so one day.'

'I can only thank you. I am sure Hubert will be in funds again soon. When he tells me I may have what I please, I shall repay you.'

'Say no more of it,' Mariah said. 'Now, let us go and see who has arrived, for I am sure that I heard voices in the hall just now.'

Mariah was thoughtful as they went into the reception hall and discovered that several members of the duke's family had arrived. In the flurry of introductions and greetings, the slight awkwardness that had arisen with her friend was forgotten. Mariah had an uncomfortable feeling that Lord Hubert's request that his wife did not overspend related to his business dealings with Count Paolo.

She said nothing to Sylvia, but decided that as soon as she had a moment to be private with Andrew she would tell him of her suspicions, though of course she would say nothing of the loan.

* * *

There were new arrivals all day long. Lucinda was busy greeting her guests and seeing to their comfort. Mariah offered to help, but was required only to keep the other guests company, which she was happy to do. They were all well known to her and most were curious about her marriage and talked so much that she had no chance to slip away with Andrew when he arrived with his sister and her husband, who had come to spend the day with them. However, being the centre of so much attention kept her well away from Count Paolo, though she was aware of him watching her intently whenever he was in the same room.

Thankfully, Justin had been in charge of entertaining the male guests and he had taken the count off to play billiards for most of the afternoon. Mariah did not see him until she went up to change for dinner and found him loitering near her door.

'Are you looking for your room, sir?' she asked. 'I fear you have taken a wrong turning.'

'I was waiting for you, Mariah,' the count said, his eyes narrowed intently. 'You have been avoiding me since I arrived, but you know we must talk. We have unfinished business.'

'I think you mistake the matter, sir. I gave you my answer to your offer, which was obliging had I wished for an affair, but as you see I am to be married to the man I love.'

'In Milan you looked at me as if you wanted me,' the count said. 'I think that perhaps you like to tease, *madame,* but you have chosen the wrong man. I told you that when I want something I do not let go easily. I have not changed my mind, though it seems you have.'

Mariah raised her head proudly. 'Forgive me, but I do not wish to hear this. I have promised you nothing at any time. Yes, I found you attractive when we met, but that does not mean I wished to be your wife, sir. I told you in Milan that there could be nothing between us. I am to marry the man I love three weeks from now. I do not understand why you persist in this when—'

He moved towards her, and frightened by the menace in his eyes, Mariah gave a little cry of alarm as his hand reached out to catch hold of her wrist.

'Please do not touch me!'

'You belong to me, Mariah. I thought I made that clear to you when we spoke before.' His grasp tightened, hurting her so that she gasped with pain. 'If you marry Lanchester, you will be a widow within the month. You are mine and I intend to have you.'

'Let go of me or I shall scream,' Mariah hissed, anger taking away the fear. 'The duke's servants will throw you out if I complain of your behaviour. If you do not wish for a scandal, you should let go of me now.'

'I do not fear the duke, his servants or Lanchester.' Count Paolo's gaze narrowed. 'I mean to have you and when I want something I get it.'

'I do not think you can risk a scandal at this time. It would not suit your business arrangements—' Mariah gasped as he dragged her towards him, his eyes burning with such fury as he looked down at her that she was afraid of his mental state.

'What do you know of my business? If that foolish bitch has told you anything...'

'You will not speak of my friend that way.' Mariah conquered her fear, gazing up at him defiantly. 'She knows nothing—but I know that you are in debt. It is the reason you need more investment from new partners—and the reason you want me. You think to take the fortune Winston left me for your own ends, but you would be sadly disappointed, sir. My money is in trusts that even I may not break.'

'You lie,' he said, but there was shock and uncertainty in his eyes. 'Bitch. Breathe a word of this lie to anyone and I shall kill you.'

He let go of her and pushed her away so that she stumbled and fell against the wall; then he turned and walked off, disappearing round the corner of the hall. Mariah shuddered, wrenched at her door and went inside quickly, locking the door after her. She was trembling and shaken as she entered her bedchamber, so much so that her maid looked at her in concern.

'Are you ill, my lady?'

'No, no, I shall be all right in a moment,' Mariah said. She lifted her head, conquering the desire to weep. The count was without doubt an evil man. At their first meeting she had been conscious that something was very different about him. Then she had found him exciting and charming, but now she knew that his charm was merely a veneer that hid his true character.

He had threatened Andrew's life if she went ahead with the wedding. She must find the right moment to be alone with him this evening and tell him of the count's threat.

Chapter Ten

Dressing for the evening, Andrew's thoughts turned again and again to the woman he was to marry. Until recently he had not realised how much she meant to him, but that morning as they walked he had found it difficult to keep his mind on the necessary discussions about their home and future. All he had wanted was to scoop her into his arms and carry her to his room so that he could make love to her. However, he was aware that to do so might seriously impair his ability to concentrate on other things.

Count Paolo must be watched. Mariah was frightened of the man, though she had not said so in as many words. The fellow was strange; his eyes seemed almost dead at times, but at others held a bright glitter, especially when he watched Mariah—which he did whenever she was in the room. He was clearly obsessed with her—but to what limits would his passion carry him?

He would have preferred the man to stay under his roof so that he might keep an eye on him, but it would appear rude to overset Lady Avonlea's arrangements and might alert the count. It was best that he felt himself secure. Andrew was unsure of his involvement in the recent events in Milan, but it was best to keep an open mind, though he must be watchful for all their sakes.

Satisfied with his appearance, Andrew thanked his valet for his assistance and left his bedchamber. Meeting with George and Jane, he exchanged pleasantries with them as they all went outside for the short carriage drive to Avonlea.

Andrew was greeted by Justin, and glad of the chance for a few words in private with him before the ladies came down for the evening.

Andrew was waiting at the end of the landing when Mariah left her room and walked towards the main staircase. He smiled as she came towards him, feeling a glow of admiration and pride as he saw how beautiful she looked. He held out his hand to her.

'You look so lovely, Mariah,' he said as she took it. 'I wanted a moment alone with you before dinner. You will not mind if I steal you away to the library for a short time?'

'I have been wanting to speak with you all day,' she said and the urgency in her voice made him raise his brows.

'Is something wrong?'

'When we are alone. I should not wish anyone to overhear.'

'You are troubled. What is it, my darling?'

'I fear something is very wrong,' Mariah replied, but would say nothing more until the reached the library.

'I know you did not think the count a threat,' she said. 'But I am certain he is not what he seems, Andrew. I think he has cheated Lord Hubert in some way and will do the same to anyone foolish enough to invest with him.'

'What makes you say that?'

'Sylvia told me something in confidence, then, earlier this evening, the count waylaid me outside my room. He told me that we had unfinished business and threatened...' She took a deep breath, then, 'He threatened that if I married you I should be a widow within a month. I told him that I would never marry him and that I knew he was in debt. He then grew very angry and told me I should be sorry if I repeated the lie.'

'You will not do so to anyone else, Mariah.' He looked at her sternly.

'So you still think I have imagined it all? I tell you, Andrew, he is a dangerous man. I do not think he would hesitate to kill—and I feel he is mixed up in the attempt on your life, though I know it makes no sense.'

'So you have put two and two together and made five.' Andrew frowned. 'I agree that he is a dangerous man, Mariah. I am sorry he made those threats to you. Forgive me for not admitting that I suspected him before this, but I did not wish to spoil things for you. With our wedding so close it should be a happy time for you.'

'You do think him dangerous?' Relief swept over her—if he was of the same opinion, he would not be careless. She arched her right brow at him. 'What are you up to, Andrew?'

'I suspected that he was involved somewhere, though at first I could not see where an Italian count might fit into the affair. I recalled that he had lived in France for several years. It is possible that he served in Spain when I was out there with Wellington.'

'Do you think you made an enemy of him?'

'As far as I know we met for the first time in Milan, when

I enquired about importing some of his wine—but he may have known Lieutenant Grainger out there.'

Mariah stared at him in silence for a moment. 'Lieutenant Grainger? Did something happen at that time that made the lieutenant think you should know—perhaps because he was more dangerous than we could have guessed?'

'It is merely a theory,' Andrew said. 'I cannot be certain of anything—but supposing one of our men was a spy and the count was his paymaster...'

'Lieutenant Grainger?'

'Or someone else, perhaps?'

'Do you mean Lieutenant Gordon?' Mariah frowned. 'He seems to have disappeared, does he not? You said his mother and sister have not seen him for some months...'

'Yes, the mystery deepens. I have no idea where the count fits into this business, though, like you, I feel that in some way he is more involved than I first imagined.'

'Lieutenant Grainger wanted to tell us something important. What made him go off suddenly that night at the ball? Do you think the count threatened him?'

'He may have done so, though I cannot see why.' Andrew shook his head as she questioned with her eyes. 'I am as much in the dark as you, Mariah. I have spoken to Justin, because I need to stay here in this house at night so that I can keep an eye on our friend—and I do not wish him to be aware of it.'

'But Jane and Lord George are staying with you...' Mariah wrinkled her smooth brow. 'You cannot neglect them.'

'Jane will understand—and if I know George, he will want to lend a hand. We have to flush our enemy out, Mariah, and I think I may know how.'

'What do you mean?'

He refused to be drawn further on the subject. Instead, he drew her into his arms, held her close and kissed her in a way that put an end to Mariah's protests that he was keeping secrets from her again. Her body suffused with heat and desire rushed through her as her flesh melded with his and she leaned into him, feeling the burning need in him.

'This is what I brought you here for, my love,' he said, caressing the side of her face with his fingertips. 'Do you know how much I long for our wedding? I count the days off, but it seems so long.'

Mariah laughed, delighted with his lovemaking. Now he was the impatient lover she had longed for.

'Anyone would think you were in love, Andrew,' she teased. 'If you are so impatient, my dear one, we can anticipate our wedding a little.'

'Oh, how I should like to accept that sweet invitation,' he murmured, holding her close so that she could feel the burn of his need. 'However, I must make certain that you are safe, my love. If I let my guard down, that rogue would have the advantage—but when you sleep tonight, know that I shall not be far away from you.'

'Truly?' She gazed up at him, eyes glowing. The way he held her, the way he looked at her, seemed to speak of his feelings for her. She felt that she was precious to him and her heart filled with love and happiness. 'I shall sleep more soundly for it, Andrew. I confess that last evening I did not feel safe until I was in my room with the door locked.'

'Well, you shall not be alone again,' he said and kissed her nose lightly. 'I shall stay close—and should the count attempt anything, he will be sorry.'

'Thank you,' she said and pressed her face against his chest. 'I have been spoiled for most of my life, Andrew—but I never truly felt that I belonged to anyone until now. If I were to lose you, I do not know what I should do.'

He tipped her chin so that she looked up at him. 'You will not lose me, dearest. The count is a rogue, but I think him a coward. He would not kill if he could get another to do his dirty work—though if he were cornered he might strike out like a wounded beast.'

'Take care,' she whispered and then laughed as she heard the longcase clock in the hall strike the hour. 'We must go or we shall keep everyone waiting for their dinner.'

To Mariah's surprise the count was not present at dinner. When the ladies left the gentlemen to their port and went into the dining room later, Lucinda told her that he had sent word to Justin that he must leave immediately and had gone off with only a small amount of baggage, leaving an address in London for the rest of his things to be sent on.

'He apologised and said he had received news that he was urgently needed at home.'

'Needed at home?' Mariah's nape tingled. 'Did a messenger arrive with a letter for him?'

'Justin asked the butler. He said that none had arrived that he knew of—but perhaps one of the servants took it up to him without saying anything. Anyway, he has gone. I thought you might be pleased?' Lucinda looked at her questioningly.

'I certainly have no desire for the count's company,' Mariah agreed. 'I cannot pretend to be sorry he has gone.' It was as if a dark shadow had lifted, at least for the moment. Yet something did not ring true and she could not help wondering if he were planning a nasty surprise for her.

Mariah would not make her hostess anxious by telling her what she truly thought. The count must have known she would tell Andrew of their meeting. He might have thought she would warn others that he was a bad risk as a partner in business. Perhaps he had left rather than face her again.

The idea that there might be something more sinister behind the count's sudden departure was building at the back of her mind, but she resolutely pushed it away. Andrew was on his guard. He would not be careless and she was being watched over. She felt safer for knowing that the count was no longer in the house and would not linger in hallways to catch her off guard.

A feeling of relief swept through her. He was no doubt a dangerous man, but perhaps he had realised that she was a lost cause and had simply gone off to try his luck elsewhere.

She decided that she would not allow his threats to worry her and was persuaded to play some music for the company. She was still at the pianoforte when the gentlemen entered. Andrew came to her and they discussed various pieces of music they both knew, then joined together in an amusing little duet for their friends. After that another lady took Mariah's place and she was free to talk to Andrew as the last drinks were handed round.

'You know the count left suddenly?'

'Yes. I dare say he had urgent news from home.'

'Perhaps. You will feel easier now that he has left, my love.'

'Yes, of course. I imagine there is no need for you to stay here now.'

Andrew smiled oddly. 'I do not think we need to talk about that gentleman again this evening, Mariah. I have been showered with gifts by our friends—they are at home waiting for you to inspect. Shall I reply to my own particular friends or will you do it for me? I confess I am not good at such letters.'

'Tomorrow I shall visit and we will look at the gifts together—and I shall write the letters if you wish it.' She shook her head at him, a smile in her eyes. 'Shame on you, sir. People are so kind. We must thank them all properly.'

Andrew accepted the scolding with good heart and they were joined by another gentleman and then two ladies.

There had been no chance for a further private conversation that evening, though Mariah did snatch a moment to say goodnight at the foot of the stairs before she and Sylvia and most of the other ladies went up.

'Sleep well and do not worry, my love. You are safe in our care.'

'Thank you,' she said, and then in a whisper he might not hear, 'I love you so...'

She left him to make his own farewells and went upstairs, a little smile on her lips. The future seemed brighter all at once and she was anticipating all the happy times to come.

Alone in her room, Mariah accepted her maid's help to dress for bed, brushed her hair and then slipped between the sheets. She was sleepy and thought that she would rest well that night.

* * *

Mariah was not certain what had disturbed her, but she was suddenly wide awake and tingling. A trickle of fear crawled along her spine as she tensed, listening. She could hear something… The door to her dressing room was opening. No one but her maid would ever enter that way and her nerves prickled, because none of the servants would dream of disturbing her at this hour. She could feel the pounding of her heart as she caught the sound of a footstep—bare feet made only the slightest of sounds, as whoever it was approached her bed. Her eyes were closed as she waited, holding her breath, and then someone snatched away her covering.

Mariah was tensed and ready. She rolled to one side and jumped out of bed, snatching up the brass candlestick from beside the bed. Through her curtains the light was barely strong enough to see more than the dark shape of a man, but her instincts warned her that only one man would dare to do such a thing, and the sweet smell of his hair oil told her that it was indeed the man she feared.

'Stay away from me, Count,' she hissed. 'I do not know how you managed to get in here, but you have broken all the rules of society. You will never be admitted to a decent house again.'

'Witch! I care nothing for other people's opinions or your stupid rules. You English think you are so clever, but you are the fools. You thought to escape me, *madame,* but you are mine. I shall have you—and I will make you give me what belongs to me. Before I have done you will beg me to…'

Mariah lashed out as he lunged at her. Her weapon struck against his shoulder and he shouted, but more in anger than in pain. In the half-light she was hampered and he seemed to be able to see like a cat. He grabbed her wrist, twisting it so that she gave a cry of pain and the candlestick fell to the floor with a bump, rolling away. In that moment Mariah screamed. The count grabbed her by the waist, forcing her backwards towards the bed. She struggled as he thrust her down on to the mattress, hitting at him with her fists, kicking and biting, spitting in his face, and then she screamed again as his weight came on her and she could feel him pulling at her nightgown, wrenching it up, his intention to rape her clear.

Suddenly, there was light in the room. She heard a shout and then someone took hold of the count and yanked him off her. Now Mariah could see that Andrew was in the room; he was her rescuer. He grabbed the count by the throat, seeming as if he would break his neck with his bare hands, but the count brought his arms up and broke the hold. The men struggled furiously, then the two of them were on the floor, thrashing and yelling as they fought.

'This way, Mariah,' Justin cried and she fled towards the open door leading into the hall. He was holding a pistol and she could see from the look on his face that he meant business. 'Go to Lucinda and stay there until we tell you.' He flung a wrap over her shoulders and gave her a little push. 'She is in her room and awake, waiting for you.'

'Thank you,' Mariah said on a rising sob. 'You were watching for him, of course.'

'Andrew was close by, but the cunning devil came the servants' way and we did not realise he was in your room until you cried out. Go now. I promise you that this will be over very soon now.'

Mariah nodded and ran on bare feet along the landing with its soft Persian carpet to Lucinda's apartments. As she tapped the door it was opened instantly and she was drawn inside. To her dismay she was trembling and, when wrapped in her friend's arms, she found herself weeping.

'Do not cry, my love,' Lucinda said. 'It will all be over very soon now. Justin has the house surrounded and footmen are everywhere. Even if the count escapes from them he will not get far.'

'I am so stupid,' Mariah sobbed and wiped her cheeks with the back of her hand. 'I thought he had gone, given up—but… he tried to…he is mad. I am sure his obsession has turned his mind.'

'Hush, my dearest. Justin would not let me tell you what was planned. It seems they thought the only way to catch him was to allow him to try whatever he intended, but it was not fair to you. Had you known what was going on, you would not have been so frightened.'

'I was startled and shocked, but I fought him,' Mariah said. 'It is only now that I am being foolish.' She wiped her cheeks on the wrap Justin had provided. 'I came here when Justin told me to, but I should have stayed to see what happened. Andrew was fighting him, but Justin was there and he had a pistol.' She caught back a sob of fear. 'What do you think they will do to him?'

'Justin will tell us when he returns,' Lucinda told her. 'I have some wine here. Will you take a glass to soothe you?'

'Yes, perhaps a sip or two,' Mariah said. Her hand trembled as she took the glass from Lucinda, but she held it with two hands and willed herself to stop shaking. 'For a moment

I thought he would have his way, for he was so much stronger than me, but then Andrew came and…he saved me.' Tears trickled down her cheeks. 'I thought—hoped—he might be nearby, but I did not realise that he was so close.'

'He guarded your door all night—and has done since the count came here. I know you thought he went home with Jane and her husband, but each night he doubled back and stayed until you stirred.'

'Andrew did that for me?' Mariah looked at her in awe. 'Why did he not tell me before?'

'Because he did not wish you to know how concerned he was, dearest. Andrew loves you very much and he wanted you to be happy. It will soon be your wedding and he did not wish you to feel afraid.'

'He told me earlier that he might stay this evening, but when the count left so abruptly I thought he would consider the need was over.'

'Andrew suspects the count may be a murderer,' Lucinda said. 'He has had agents watching him since you were in Paris. He says the count's wife died in suspicious circumstances soon after Winston died… Oh, I wasn't supposed to tell you. Justin will be cross with me.'

'Do you think…did he have her murdered so that he could…?' Mariah sat down in a chair as her legs went weak. 'He couldn't have done such a wicked thing. Oh, Lucinda. If he killed his wife so that he would be free to marry me…that poor woman! It is true that for a brief time I did flirt with him in Milan. I feel so guilty…'

'No, Mariah. It is not your fault. How could it be? You did not even know him when his wife had the fall down stairs that killed her. She would not divorce him, because she was a Catholic, and he wanted sons. He may have other reasons for what he did. Besides, we do not know for certain that he murdered her—only that she died in a suspicious fall down some steep steps at her home. It was whispered that he had her murdered, but nothing was proven.'

'He had her murdered and it is my fault. He saw me and wanted me for his wife, so he killed her. He is evil beyond imagining. How could any man do such a terrible thing?'

'He must be insane, Mariah. No sane man would do the things he has.'

Mariah felt devastated. She had thought nothing of her brief encounter with the count in Milan and had not considered what feelings or hopes she might have aroused when she rejected him. What a selfish, careless fool she had been. She should not have let him think she might marry him even for a moment. At the time she had not wanted to cause offence, but she might have caused something much worse.

'I have caused so much upset and trouble,' Mariah said, feeling chastened. 'Andrew must blame me for all this…' She shook her head as Lucinda tried to deny it. 'No, you would exonerate me of all blame, but I was contrary and careless, Lucinda. I must bear some of the blame. Something about me seems to encourage men to wicked acts.…'

It seemed a long time before Justin came to tell her that the count had been captured and taken away.

'What will you do to him?' Mariah asked. 'Must I bear witness at his trial?'

'Do not concern yourself about the count,' Justin told her.

'He is being confined in a place away from this house. Tomorrow he will be brought before a magistrate, a friend of mine, and, depending on the sentence, confined to prison for a long time. I do not think your testimony will be necessary.'

'Thank you.' A shiver ran through Mariah. 'I should return to my room now.'

'Can you bear to?' Lucinda asked her. 'Would you not rather have a different room—or stay here with me tonight?'

'No, I shall not let that man destroy me,' Mariah said, lifting her head proudly. 'Where is Andrew? I should like to speak to him…' Her heart caught with sudden fear. 'He is not injured?'

'No. He had something to do, but he is around somewhere. Would you like me to tell him you wish to see him?'

'Yes, please. If he could come to my room.' Mariah blushed. 'It may not be quite proper, but after what happened this evening it hardly seems to matter.'

'Of course he will come,' Lucinda said. 'Shall I send a hot posset up to you, my love?'

'No, I shall be perfectly comfortable once I have seen Andrew.'

Mariah smiled and left her friends. Outside her room, she hesitated, took a deep breath and went in. She was carrying a lighted candle and she lit several others about the room before setting straight a chair and a stool that had been knocked over in the struggle. Some books had been dislodged from an occasional table and she was bending down to retrieve them when she heard a knock at the door. For a moment her heart caught, but she breathed deeply and went to answer it.

'You asked for me?' Andrew said, looking at her in concern. 'Did that devil hurt you, Mariah?'

'No, you were in time,' she said on a shaky breath, and then to her utter dismay felt the tears trickle down her cheeks. 'I am so sorry to have caused you so much trouble. This is all my fault. If I had not allowed him to think…but it would have been rude…'

Andrew moved into the room, taking her into his arms. His mouth hushed her with a kiss and she subsided against his shoulder, her tears wetting his coat as she sobbed out her anguish.

'The man was obsessed with you,' he said. 'You had no fault in this, Mariah. Besides, I think there is more than we yet know. He wanted you and your fortune and I was in the way—so the mystery of the attempts on my life are solved, but it does not end there. Where does Grainger come into it—and where is Lieutenant Gordon?'

'I am such a fool. At this moment I can think only of his obsession with me. If that poor woman met her death because of me…'

'Hush, my love,' Andrew murmured, his fingers stroking at her nape. 'If the count had his wife murdered, it was his fault and his alone. I believe that you were right when you said the balance of his mind was disturbed. You—and your fortune—obsessed him, and perhaps he was always of an unstable mind. If my agents are correct, he is deeply in debt. Your friend Lord Hubert has told me that he has lost thousands of pounds in the venture Count Paolo offered him. Fortunately, he drew back before committing himself to the last penny and he will recover, but it has made his situation awkward for the moment.'

'I knew Lord Hubert was in trouble because he told Sylvia she must be careful what she spends and he has always spoiled her. When did he speak to you?'

Mariah drew back, wiping her cheeks with the kerchief Andrew handed her. She smiled and blew her nose, her storm of emotion calming.

'Lord Hubert arrived yesterday, but stayed at my house so that the count would not suspect he had been rumbled, but he must have guessed something was wrong. That is why he pretended to leave, but actually hid in the attics and crept to your room by way of the servants' entrance. I am not sure what he hoped to achieve by his attack on you—perhaps blackmail.'

'Yes.' Mariah shuddered. 'I should not have wanted anyone to know of my humiliation.'

'Well, he will not harm you again. He is being kept under lock and key until the morning. He will be tried and I think there is enough evidence against him to have him sent to prison without using what happened here this night.'

'Justin said as much.' Mariah looked at him. 'You were right when you said I have been contrary and proud. I was spoiled and I became heedless. I know that by flirting with the count even for a short time I brought this whole business on myself.'

'I do not think that is true,' Andrew told her, reaching out to touch her cheek. 'You were not to know what kind of a man he really was. If I had spoken to you earlier at the lakes, it might not have happened. Yet, perhaps he would still have tried to kill me. Had you been grieving for my loss, he might have caught you on the rebound. I am sorry for the harsh things

I said to you, Mariah. You are neither selfish nor heedless. I know that you care for people—and your proud manner often hides uncertainty.'

Mariah smiled up at him. 'You are coming to know me, Andrew. I am not always as confident as I seem, but my pride carries me through.'

'If I hurt you by things I said in the past, please forgive me, dearest. I should never have been harsh to you.'

'It is forgotten,' she said. 'All I want is for you to care for me—and for us to be happy together.'

'You will make me the happiest of men when we marry.' Andrew ran his thumb over her bottom lip, sending a tingle of desire spiralling through her. 'It is our dance tomorrow evening, my love. You will be so tired. I should leave you to sleep now.'

'No, please...' Mariah caught his hand. 'Stay with me, Andrew. Stay with me all night—in my bed. I do not want to sleep alone tonight.'

'In your bed?' Andrew questioned as she moved closer, gazing up at him. 'What are you saying, my darling?'

'I want you to love me,' she whispered huskily. 'I want you to make me forget all the horrid things that happened with the count—love me and take away the fear and humiliation.'

'My precious love,' he said and put his arms about her. 'If you are sure, I shall stay. I want you so much, so very much.'

Mariah surrendered herself to his arms. His kiss was hungry, more possessive and sure than ever before and she melded against him, giving herself up to the pleasure of being in his arms. She felt nothing but pleasure and sweet anticipation. No thought of the count's attack on her was in her mind as she looked up at Andrew, her longing and need so plain that he must see.

'I love you, Mariah,' Andrew whispered as he joined her on the bed. 'I think I always did, even when we were young and you followed me everywhere. I just did not know my heart. I was not sure we should suit, but now I know that without you my life would be empty.'

Mariah's throat was tight with emotion. She could say nothing because her heart was too full, but she opened her arms to him, allowing him to discard her nightgown by pulling it over her head and watching with a smile as he threw off his own clothes. He had such a beautiful, strong body, though the scars on his upper arms and chest told of wounds in war. Mariah wanted to touch them, to kiss his smooth flesh.

Then he was lying beside her, the heat of his flesh against hers as they came together, bodies straining to meet in sudden need and urgency. Andrew kissed her forehead, her nose, her eyelids and her throat. His hand caressed her breast and then he bent his head to stroke delicately at the rose-tinted nipples, licking at her and taking her into his mouth to suck gently. His teeth grazed her slightly and she moaned, her back arching towards him. She could feel the moisture between her thighs as his hand sought her intimate places, stroking the nub of her femininity with one finger as she breathed deeper and a little cry escaped her.

He kissed her navel, lowering his attention to the dark blonde curls that smelled of her musk as she became wet for him. When his tongue touched her there, she cried out with pleasure, bucking and arching as the feeling intensified. The pleasure he gave her was beyond anything she had imagined.

Then, when she thought she could bear no more, she felt his weight as he lay on her, his hand parting her thighs and the heat of his pulsing manhood thrusting at her moist opening.

'Please…please…' she begged, her body arching towards him, begging for something she hardly comprehended.

As he thrust up into her she felt a sharp pain, but her cry was smothered beneath his kiss. He stilled for a moment, looking down at her as he felt the resistance, then he broke through her hymen and entered the warm silkiness of her sheath. She moaned and arched her hips to meet his thrust, giving herself up to the pleasure. There was a little pain, but Mariah wanted to enjoy the moment she had longed for and she ignored the slight soreness, panting, her hands raking at his shoulders as the intensity of their loving reached its height. Sweet and sensual, endless pleasure, and then he came in her at the moment that she felt the first wave of pleasure break over her.

She cried out and clung to him, her long legs curling over his hips as she felt his weight slump on her and heard his moan of pleasure. 'I never knew it would be so good.'

Andrew held her for a little and then rolled to one side, turning towards her, gazing into her face. 'You were a virgin,' he said in a contrite tone. 'Why did you not tell me, my love? I could have taken it slower the first time, tried not to hurt you. We might have enjoyed our pleasures without going so far.'

'You only hurt me a very little,' she said and reached up to kiss his mouth. 'Perhaps I should have told you before, but I wanted you to discover the truth for yourself.'

'All those things I said to you.' Andrew looked rueful. 'Accusing you of taking lovers. I never dreamed that you would still be a virgin, Mariah. You were married…'

'Winston kissed me, but there was nothing else. He told me before we married that he could not be a proper husband to me—but he loved me. He treated me as a little girl that he could dress up in pretty clothes and show off to his friends. I think he truly loved me, but he was never well enough to be a husband in the true sense. Yet I was faithful to him—and, afterwards, there was no one I wanted, until we met again.'

'My poor Mariah,' Andrew said and stroked her cheek. 'No wonder you flirted and thought of taking a lover. It must have been difficult for you—a wife and yet not a wife.'

'Do not pity me,' she said. 'Winston gave me all he could and while he lived I was happy enough in my way.'

'But for how long would that have lasted? You are a passionate woman, Mariah—a woman who needs physical love. You needed more than a fake marriage.'

'Yes, perhaps. I dare say I might have taken a lover had you not come back into my life. I had offers in plenty, but I could not trust anyone. It wasn't until we met again—' She broke off, suddenly shy, afraid to confess it all.

'Go on, my love,' Andrew prompted. 'I have wondered what your feelings truly were towards me. I thought you wanted a husband because you were vulnerable to the fortune hunters. I thought that any decent man might do.'

Mariah looked at him oddly, her cheeks pink. 'I let you think that, Andrew—and for a while I did consider making either a marriage of convenience or taking a lover, but only because you did not speak. I thought that when you came to Paris, while I was there with Justin and Lucinda, you would speak, but instead you seemed to withdraw. It almost broke my heart and so I went away with Sylvia and Lord Hubert rather than let you see.'

'Yes, and that was ill done of me,' Andrew confessed and touched her cheek. 'In part it was because of the business with that damned letter—and then I wondered if I might endanger you if I had an enemy—but also I was uncertain. You fascinated me, but I had feelings for Lucinda, which you knew of—and I could not see the treasure that might be mine if I had the wit to reach for it.'

Mariah hesitated, then, her finger tracing a pulse at the base of his throat, 'Do you still have feelings for Lucinda?'

'I am fond of her, as I am of Jane, and would help her should she need my help—but I never felt a half of what I feel for you, Mariah. Nor for any woman I have known. Yet still I did not know you. I remembered the spoiled brat who flew into a temper if I teased her and I wondered if you would grow bored with me, with being my wife.'

'I could never be bored with you by my side. Yes, I was spoiled and I do have a temper when roused,' Mariah said. 'Did you not realise why I was so angry when you teased me then, Andrew?' He shook his head and she laughed huskily. 'I had a terrible crush on you before you went into the army. You were my hero. I wanted you to fall in love with me, but all you ever did was tease me and tell me off.'

'Did you really have feelings for me then?' Andrew laughed and drew her near, their bodies slicked with sweat as they pressed closer. 'I never knew it. I thought of you as a spoiled brat. You were always so prickly—like a little hedgehog—when I was around, though I knew Jane was fond of you.'

'How else should I be when I was breaking my heart for you and you either ignored me or treated me as a child?'

'I saw you as a child,' he said, and his hand stroked down the satin arch of her back. 'I never truly saw you as a woman until I returned from the army. Had it not been for Lucinda's predicament I might have realised my feelings for you sooner. But you seemed so confident and you were rich—much richer than I am, Mariah. I did not think you needed me.'

'Money is both a blessing and a curse,' she said, and her finger circled his ear, her lips so close to his that her breath was a caress. 'I have given some money to Lucinda's daughter, Angela, though neither of them will know it until she is older. I shall also offer Lord Hubert help if he needs it—but after that I want you to take charge of my affairs, as we talked of, Andrew. I do not want to be bothered with such things and you will take care of our children's inheritance far better than I.'

'Yes, that is how I shall see it, as our children's inheritance,' he said and kissed her. 'I have been such a fool, Mariah.' His hand moved up to her nape, playing with her heavy, luxuriant hair, a look of desire in his eyes. 'Are you too sore… Can you bear it if…?'

'Love me again,' she whispered, moving closer. 'I have longed for this so many times, Andrew. I fear you will think me too demanding, but I want you again. I want to feel your lips and your hands touching me, to feel you inside me.'

'I can never get enough of you,' he murmured and caught her to him. 'If you still have doubts, put them from your mind. I adore you, Mariah. You are all I want in this life.'

'Then we are both content,' she said and gave herself up to his loving once more.

He was the man she had loved for most of her life. She had waited for him, refusing the lovers she might have taken and the men she might have married, because in her heart she had known that only one man could give her the love she needed. Now she had found him and she was content to be his wife and live with him at Lanchester, bearing his children and growing older together.

Chapter Eleven

'You look lovely,' Lucinda said as Mariah came down the stairs to join her on the evening of the dance at Lanchester. 'That dress is stunning. I do not think I have ever seen you look so beautiful.'

Mariah stroked the soft tulle of her ball gown. It was made of white silk, the skirt caught up with little rosebuds around the hem. The bodice was heavily encrusted with tiny crystals that sparkled and looked pink in the candlelight. Her long, thick hair was caught up in a swirl at the back of her head and dressed with more rosebuds and a string of diamonds, and she had a diamond collar with a large pearl drop.

'I ordered this gown in Paris for this evening,' Mariah told her. '*Madame* finished it just this morning. I was not certain whether it would be done in time, but it is rather lovely. I fear it cost a fortune.'

'Well, why not?' Lucinda said, looking at her with approval. 'Lady Hubert told me that you had offered to give her husband ten thousand pounds to help him weather the difficulties his business dealings with the count have caused. It was generous of you, my love.'

'He will accept the money as a temporary loan,' Mariah told her. 'Sylvia should not have said. It was a private arrangement with her husband. I do not want praise for helping my friends, Lucinda. They did a great deal for me when Winston died. Indeed, I do not know how I should have gone on had they not insisted on bringing me home. They are not to blame for the count's behaviour.'

'We shall not speak of that despicable man,' Lucinda said. 'You know, of course, that he was brought before the magistrate and remanded for trial for fraud and theft?'

'Yes, Justin told me, but I do not wish to think about him this evening,' Mariah said. 'This is our special night and I want to welcome all our friends and dance the night away.'

'That is what you must do,' Lucinda said. 'The coach is ready. If we leave now, we shall be the first to arrive at Lanchester Park and I am sure Andrew is waiting for you most eagerly. You are the hostess this evening and must be there to greet your guests.'

Mariah touched the large baroque pearl at her throat. 'This was his gift to me for this evening. Do you not think it beautiful?'

'Yes, it is very fine,' Lucinda said. 'I have not the slightest doubt that he will spoil you, Mariah.'

'Oh, no, I do not wish for it,' Mariah said and shook her head. 'If Andrew loves me he will treat me as a woman he can respect and not a spoiled child.'

Lucinda nodded and looked thoughtful, but said no more as they went out to the coach, which was drawn up outside the house.

The two ladies entered the coach, Justin following them.

He gave the order to move off and they were soon bowling down the long gravel drive.

Mariah smoothed her elbow-length white gloves as she glanced out of the window. She had noticed that six grooms were to attend them, which was more than Justin usually took, though he seldom travelled without at least three out-riders. However, she took little notice. The count was no longer a danger to her, because he had been taken off to prison to await his trial and punishment.

For a moment she recalled that Lieutenant Grainger was still at large, but then dismissed the thought. Where did he fit into the mystery—and did he have anything to do with the attempts on Andrew's life? No, she would not think of it. This was her special night, when all her friends would congratulate her on her coming marriage. She intended to enjoy every moment.

A smile touched her lips as she thought of the night she had spent in Andrew's arms. She was to stay the night at Lanchester after the ball and perhaps he would come to her again. Her wedding was but three weeks away, but it seemed too long to wait. She longed to be Andrew's wife so that she could wake up and find him by her side in the mornings. Every minute spent away from him seemed an hour and her love grew deeper with each breath she took.

When the short journey was done and the coach drew up outside Andrew's house, he was waiting to greet her. Light was spilling from all the windows and there was an air of festivity about the place, coloured lanterns in the trees.

'You are stunning,' Andrew said when he saw her, his

voice low and throbbing with desire. 'Welcome to your home, Mariah. Will you let me take you through to the ballroom? I want you to see it before the guests arrive.'

Mariah took his hand, allowing him to lead her into the house and through to the rooms that had been opened up and cleared of furniture to give them a space for dancing. She was surprised at how spacious the ballroom looked and enchanted by the banks of white carnations, roses and camellias that had been massed at the foot of the dais, where the musicians were just beginning to play. They must have come from professional hothouses and must have cost a fortune. Yards upon yards of white tulle were looped about the walls just below the frieze and silver stars hung from the chandeliers, helping to shower the room with sparkling light.

'How festive it looks,' she said. 'Do you always do this at Christmas, Andrew? And how did you manage to find such wonderful flowers?'

'No, the flowers were ordered specially for you from hot-house growers. On Christmas Eve I shall have a tree brought in and perhaps you would like to help Jane dress it—though of course you will be helping Lucinda with the arrangements for her party that night.'

'I should like to help Jane in the morning,' Mariah said and smiled up at him as he bent to kiss her cheek. 'This is wonderful, Andrew. I did not expect it to look so well.'

'I wanted it to be perfect for you.'

'And it is,' she said softly. 'Today everything is perfect. I am so happy.'

The look he gave her was so hot that she felt her cheeks

heat, knowing that he, too, was remembering their night of passion.

'Yes, I feel that, too,' he told her, taking her hand on his arm. 'I think our guests will begin to arrive very soon. We must make ourselves ready to receive them.'

Mariah glanced round the crowded ballroom. Until this moment she had not realised how many friends they had; all the reception rooms were overflowing and even the library had been brought into use as a card room for those gentlemen who did not wish to dance.

Mariah and Andrew had opened the dancing together after greeting more than one hundred and fifty guests. They had waltzed the length of the ballroom to applause from their friends, before other couples began to join them on the floor. Since then Mariah had danced with several gentlemen, friends of Andrew who seemed sincere in their good wishes. She had been showered with compliments and generally made a great fuss of by all.

She was waiting for Andrew to come to her for their next dance, which was the last before supper, but the music had already started and he had not arrived. Looking about her, she realised that she could not see him and frowned.

Walking up to Lucinda, she asked if she had seen Andrew.

'No, not for several minutes,' Lucinda replied and wrinkled her smooth brow. 'I saw him talking to Justin a while back and I thought they went out together. Perhaps they went to the card room for a while?'

'That seems odd,' Mariah replied. 'He cannot have forgotten our dance—and he ought to be here with his guests.'

'You know how gentlemen love their cards. No doubt he saw you dancing and enjoying yourself and thought you would not miss him for a moment or two.'

Mariah nodded, but she had an odd prickling sensation at the nape of her neck and something told her that the explanation was not so simple. Andrew might have gone out for a moment, but he would not have forgotten to return in time for the supper dance.

She hesitated, then turned towards the door that would lead her by way of a small parlour to the library. What was so important that Andrew had left the dance floor?

Two footmen were in the small parlour, clearing used glasses. They glanced at her, but said nothing as she passed through, pausing outside the library for a few seconds before entering. She saw at once that the tables were empty. Cards had been left lying where they were thrown down and several wineglasses were still half-filled. It was so strange, she thought, and then saw that the long, double glass doors leading out to the veranda were open.

Mariah walked slowly towards the open doors. Why would gentlemen leave the card tables in a hurry and go outside on such a night? It was cold and frosty, a full moon giving the sky a curious white light. Deciding to investigate, she went out on to the veranda and saw that a struggle of some kind was going on. Her heart raced and then she saw that the men were bringing someone back into the house. His arms were held by two of Justin's footmen and both he and Andrew and several other gentlemen were following.

Instinctively, Mariah ran to the door of the library and returned to the small sitting room. The footmen had gone and she stood behind the open door, listening as a babble of voices reached her.

'Will you listen to me?' A voice she recognised as Lieutenant Grainger's rose in desperation. 'I came here tonight to tell you the truth, Lanchester, not to cause trouble. Had I known you were entertaining, I should not have intruded.'

'He was caught sneaking into the house,' someone said. 'You should send for the military and have him arrested. He is a deserter and goodness knows what else.'

'Let him speak,' Andrew said. 'Speak out, Grainger. There are witnesses enough to hang you if you lie.'

'I swear to you that I am innocent of any crime.'

'Then why did you run away in Milan?'

'Because I know things about Count Paolo. He is a vicious man and a deadly enemy. He has already killed twice to my certain knowledge. He paid someone to kill his wife—and then he himself killed the man who carried out his vile work.'

'How do you know that?'

'Because Lieutenant Gordon told me what he'd done before he, too, was murdered.'

His words brought a deadly hush. Outside the door, Mariah's nerves tingled.

'You had best tell us the rest of it,' Andrew said. 'How came Gordon to be involved with him?'

'Lieutenant Gordon was a spy for the French in Spain,' Peter Grainger said. 'He was deeply in debt and driven to raise funds in a way that shamed him and his family. I insisted that he confess and take his punishment and he asked for a little time to settle his affairs.'

'I had guessed as much,' Andrew said. 'But there is more to it, I think?'

'Yes, I have played my part, to my shame. Gordon has a sister. Her name is Lucy and I love her. I should like to marry her, but my aunt and uncle would not allow it if they knew what her brother had done. It was enough that he was forced to leave the army in shame and disappear to Italy—but if the rest came to light I could not hope to make Lucy my wife.'

'Tell us, was Count Paolo his paymaster in Spain?'

'Yes, of course. He gained a hold over Gordon, though I know not how. He would never say, but I think it was a debt— or some misdeed. I can only think that he became more and more entangled with the rogue. When he fled to Italy in disgrace, he sought the count out and became his tool. He was involved in many evil schemes, but the murder of the count's wife played on his mind. He returned to England, but was afraid the count would come for him.' Grainger hesitated, then, 'Not only did he betray his comrades and his country, he stole the regimental silver.'

'Good grief,' Justin said. 'I knew the man was a rogue, but I should never have suspected this.'

'Why did he take the regimental silver?'

'He had some idea of going to the Americas and wanted money, but then he realised he could never sell it. He hid it and one night, when we met by chance, he became drunk and told me everything.'

'You know where the silver is now?'

'Yes. After I realised that Gordon was dead, I intended to return it, but was not sure how to do it without incriminating myself. When I saw you at the Lakes I thought perhaps you might do it for me…'

'And the letter throwing suspicion on me?'

'I fear that was Lucy. She wanted to protect her brother—it was wrong of her and she regrets what she did, but she thought only of our future.'

'How did you know Gordon was dead?' Justin asked.

'Because I found his body at his lodgings. I went there to try to get him to give himself up, but I was too late. Some-one was there before me. That someone was Count Paolo. He stood for a moment in the street, looking about him. I saw him quite clearly but I did not think he had seen me. However, I was wrong…'

'I wondered if it might be something of the sort,' Andrew said. 'Why did you not tell me this sooner, Grainger?'

'Because the count threatened me. When he saw me with you in Milan, he thought we were on to him. He was not sure how much I knew, but I must have given myself away because he had some of his bullies grab me. I was tied up and left a prisoner on the night of his masquerade, but I escaped. Since then I have been in hiding and following him, watching him. I knew that he had men following Lady Fanshawe and sus-pected that he intended her to be his next wife. He wanted her money.'

'Why were you at the inn that night—and why did you al-most knock me down in your haste to escape? Had you come to me at once, we might have saved Lady Fanshawe a deal of distress.'

'It was my intention to do so, but I hesitated because I feared that you might not believe me—that you might have me arrested for concealing what I knew about Lieutenant Gordon. I had his body buried in secret and even his mother and sister do not know that he is dead. I should have reported all this long ago. I know that, but he was my friend and I love his sister.'

'And if I had been brought before a military court for the loss of the silver—would you still have kept your silence?'

'No one believes ill of you—the charge might have been dismissed.'

'Shame on you!' several voices cried, but Andrew hushed them.

'Why have you come to us now?'

'Because the count is an evil man and he needs to be stopped—Lieutenant Gordon stole that silver and he did other unspeakable things, but he was under the influence of a monster. He was afraid of Count Paolo and in the end he paid the price.'

'Where is the silver now?'

'I found it amongst his things. I have it hidden.'

'You are little better than your friend, sir!' Justin cried.

'No, that is hardly fair,' Andrew said. 'Lieutenant Grainger has paid a heavy price for his part in this. I think you may be pardoned, sir, but you must keep your word to testify at the count's trial and give back the regiment's silver.'

Mariah moved silently from the door. She had heard enough and was slightly ashamed of eavesdropping, though much of what Lieutenant Grainger had related was as she had suspected. She left the room and so she did not hear what was said next or the uproar Lieutenant Grainger's words caused.

The revelation of just how evil the count was had shocked

Mariah, even though she had suspected that he had done terrible things. For the moment she was too overcome with distress to return to the ballroom and so she went upstairs to her room. There, she washed her face with cool water, tidied her hair and her gown, sitting on the bed for some minutes to recover her composure.

The count had had his wife murdered and then killed her murderer—and he had, according to Lieutenant Grainger, done other unspeakable things. Mariah shuddered, feeling sick as she remembered the night he had attacked her in her room.

She would not allow that man to ruin her special night! Getting to her feet, Mariah brushed the creases from her gown, left her room and started back down the hall towards the stairs. She had gone no more than a few steps when she heard something and sensed someone behind her. Her instincts were alerted and she turned, staring in disbelief as she saw the man standing just a few feet away from her. He looked dishevelled, his eyes wild, as if the madness had overtaken him.

Mariah did not stay to confront him, but ran as swiftly as she could to the head of the stairs. The count was coming after her. She screamed, knowing that he was dangerous and that her life must be in danger. If he had escaped from his captors, he had come here with one purpose in mind. As she reached the top of the staircase she screamed as he lunged at her, took a step forwards, missed her footing and went tumbling down the staircase, hitting her head against the banister.

As the darkness closed over her, she heard something that might have been a shot.

* * *

Mariah opened her eyes to find that a sea of anxious faces surrounded her. She sought the one she needed and reached feebly for his hand, her lips moving, though no sound came from them.

'Hush, my love,' Andrew said and caught her hand. 'It is over. He is dead. Justin shot him when he pushed you.'

'I lost my footing but he…' She could not continue.

'We saw what happened. Grainger told us he had escaped and come here. He has told us everything—the whole truth.'

'I heard…I know what he did,' she whispered. 'I am so sorry…'

'Count Paolo has paid the price for his wickedness. Grainger has confessed and will be dealt with leniently. I think he has decided that he will wed Lucy and take the consequences. If he is dismissed from the regiment, he will have to search for work, but if his aunt and uncle will not accept his wife, I shall find him a place on one of our estates. His testimony will clear my name and we may forget this wretched affair. Now we must all move forwards. The mystery is resolved and an evil man has paid the price for his crimes.'

Mariah nodded, closing her eyes. Her head ached where she had struck it and she felt a little faint, but she struggled to sit up.

'I should go back…our guests…'

'Our guests will understand. Lucinda and Jane will make your excuses,' Andrew said. 'Do not argue, my darling. I am going to carry you upstairs and I shall stay with you until you sleep.'

Mariah nodded, feeling too shaken to protest. When Andrew lifted her into his arms she wrapped her arms around his neck, laying her head against his chest.

'As soon as Grainger told me the count was here I went to look for you. When I realised you were not in the ballroom I thought you might be in your room and I came to look for you. I saw what happened.'

'I think his mind had gone. I told you he was unstable, but at the last I think he had gone over the edge.'

'Do not think of it,' Andrew said and kissed her hair. 'He will never hurt you again.'

'I feel safe with you,' Mariah said. 'I never want to leave you again, Andrew.'

'You shall not,' Andrew told her softly. 'We shall all visit Avonlea for Christmas, but then you will come back with me. I care not what others think. I want to be with you, to care for you until you are well again. Besides, I have a surprise for you—it is a wedding gift from Jane and George but something I think you will love.'

'I love you,' she whispered and reached for his hand.

Mariah wanted to tell him that it was just a little bang on her head and that she would soon feel better, but she was feeling too fragile to argue. It was too good to be in his arms and to feel his strength and his love protecting her.

In her room, Andrew helped her from her beautiful ball gown, then tucked her into bed. He made her pillows comfortable, then sat on the bed beside her, stroking her hair.

'Go to sleep, dearest,' he said. 'You've had a nasty shock and a fall, though I think you are not much harmed. In the morning the doctor will come to see how you are, but for now you should rest.'

Mariah smiled up at him. 'My head hurts a little, but I shall be better soon. Stay with me, Andrew. Do not leave me.'

'I have no intention of leaving you,' he said and lay down beside her on the bed, his body close to hers. 'Rest now, Mariah. I am with you and always will be.'

Mariah sighed and closed her eyes. The comfort of his body lying close to her made her feel safe and loved and very soon she drifted away into sleep.

It was late in the morning when she woke to discover that Andrew had gone and a maid was bringing in a tray with a pot of hot chocolate and some soft sweet rolls.

'His lordship told me he thought you would wake shortly, my lady. I hope I did not disturb you?'

'Oh, no,' Mariah said and stretched. She could feel a slight soreness at her right temple and touched what she knew must be a bruise. However, otherwise she felt perfectly well and welcomed the sight of her breakfast tray. 'I was ready to wake up. I think it must be quite late?'

'It is almost noon,' the maid said. 'Lord Lanchester said that the doctor would be here in an hour—and you were not to get up before he came to see you.'

'I do not think I need a doctor,' Mariah said. 'But since my lord wishes it I shall do as he asks.'

A smile touched her lips. After the previous night any lingering doubts as to the depth of Andrew's love had gone. A warm feeling of well-being was creeping through her. She felt loved and wanted, because Andrew had been so gentle and loving to her.

'Have all the guests gone, Lily?'

'No, my lady. Most have stayed on because everyone was anxious for you. They all wished to be reassured that you had suffered no lasting harm.'

'I suppose everyone in the house knows what happened?'

'Yes, my lady. That wicked man tried to harm you—and he was a murderer. The duke was very quick and brave to shoot him. Everyone is saying he is a hero.'

'I hope he will not find himself in trouble for shooting the count.'

'Oh, no, my lady. How could anyone think he did something wrong? I heard Mr Crawford say that no court in the land would convict him even if he was brought before the magistrates, which I am sure he will not be.'

Mariah nodded. She knew that Andrew had asked his sister's husband to stand up with him at the wedding. Justin was to give her away and Lucinda's daughter, Angela, and two of the Avonlea cousins were to be her attendants.

Mariah ate her breakfast, watching as the maid tidied the room and asked what she would like to wear when she got up. She went off to fetch some hot water and Mariah settled against the pillows, reading some of the notes that had been brought up to her with her breakfast.

Everyone was outraged that she had been attacked and she smiled, thinking that she had not been aware of so much love and affection towards her.

The doctor arrived soon after Mariah had washed and settled herself in a fetching wrap. He looked into her eyes and asked her to follow his finger. After examining the wound to her temple and pronouncing it slight, he told her that all was well.

'You were lucky, Lady Fanshawe. A fall like that might have resulted in far greater injuries.'

'Yes, I am very lucky,' Mariah agreed. 'Indeed, I think I am the luckiest woman alive. I take it that I may get up now?'

'You should not rush about too much for a while. If you have headaches, send for me, but otherwise I think you are perfectly well.'

Mariah thanked him. He left and she got up, retiring behind the dressing screen to change into the gown her maid had put out. She came out when she heard someone enter the room, turning her back as she struggled to fasten the hooks at the back.

'Can you fasten these for me, please? I cannot quite manage those in the middle.'

'Certainly, my love,' Andrew's voice said and she glanced over her shoulder, smiling at him. 'I think I can manage a few hooks.'

'I dare say you have had practice?' she said, a little challenge in her eyes. 'All those ladies in your past, Andrew...'

He raised his brows at her. 'I am glad to see that this last incident has not changed you, my love. You are still my contrary Mariah.'

'Would you wish me to be any different?'

'No, I do not wish to change you in the least.' He dropped a kiss on her back, making her laugh and wriggle, because his breath tickled. 'I know you now, my darling, and I want you exactly as you are.'

'I am so happy,' she said and turned to face him, lifting her face for his kiss. 'The doctor says I am perfectly well so you need not treat me as if I were made of porcelain.'

'What are you suggesting, my wicked one?' he asked and pulled her close, bending his head to kiss her lips softly. 'I hope you realise that everyone knows where I spent the night. I fear your reputation has gone, my love.' His hands were caressing her bare back, making her squirm with delight.

'From all the letters I have received, no one cares for that,' she said and smiled in her old teasing way. 'I dare say some will count the months until our first child is born, but that does not concern me.'

'Nor should it,' he said and touched her cheek. 'We shall be married within a few weeks.'

Mariah nodded, then frowned. 'Is Justin in trouble for what he did?'

'No, not at all. I witnessed the whole, as did several of our friends. Justin shot the count before he could do you further harm. Besides, he would have been hanged if he was sane enough to stand trial. Otherwise he might have been chained as a lunatic in Bedlam. I believe he might have chosen to die as he did had he a choice.'

'Yes, I think it was kinder,' Mariah said. 'I cannot feel pity for him after what he did—my concern was only for your friend.'

'Justin will stand up with us at our wedding,' Andrew said. 'We have nothing further to concern us. All the shadows are lifted and we may look forward to the future.'

'I am truly happy,' Mariah said and gazed up at him. 'You are happy, too—glad that you asked me to marry you?'

'Yes, of course. You are the love of my life and I want to spend the rest of my life making you happy, dearest Mariah.'

'I love you,' she said. 'I love you more than I ever knew was possible.'

* * * * *

Afterword

Mariah turned her head to glance at the man standing by her side before the altar. She felt the love well up in her and knew that she had found the safe haven she had sought for so long. Andrew Lanchester was handsome, strong and passionate—and he loved her. She felt so lucky that she was half-afraid her happiness would be snatched away from her. He turned his head to look at her, a smile of enquiry in his eyes, and any lingering shadow fled. Andrew had protected her when she needed him; he would be by her side for the rest of her life. As he slipped the ring onto her finger, she felt the glow of his love surround her. She was no longer a reluctant widow, but a wife. From now on she would share each day with the man she loved and all those lonely hours would fly away.

As the bells began to ring out joyfully, Mariah took her husband's arm and walked out into the bitter cold of a frosty January day to be greeted by cheers and the laughter of friends. She was not aware of the cold; held close to Andrew's body, she felt only the warmth of his nearness and the satisfaction of knowing that she was loved.

Taking her hand, Andrew hurried her to the waiting carriage, away from the scattered rose petals and rice, drawing her inside and straight into his arms. His kiss was passionate and hungry, evoking an eager response from her as she clung to him, returning his kiss.

'What were you thinking just now?' he murmured. 'I hope it wasn't that you had changed your mind?'

Mariah laughed and arched her brow at him. 'Foolish man. I could never, never think that, my love. I was just wondering how I came to be so very lucky.'

'I am the lucky one,' he murmured huskily. 'I hesitated so long and it was only when I began to think that I might lose you that I finally saw how much you meant to me.' He took her hand and kissed it. 'I never understood what was lacking in my life until I realised that I loved you. We are both fortunate, Mariah—and with God's blessing we shall have a long and fruitful life together, my love.'

'Yes, I think we shall,' she murmured. 'I believe the future will be all that either of us could hope.'

'Yes, it will.'

She moved closer, kissing him on the lips. When he allowed her to move away, she arched her brows. 'How did Jane and George know that I wanted a wolfhound? The puppy is delightful and one of my very nicest gifts.'

'Jane wanted to know what she might give you that you would like, my love. I had thought I might buy a puppy for you, but I let my sister have the honour.'

'It was a lovely surprise and I adore him already.'

'Not as much as you adore me, I hope?'

'Well...' Mariah threw him a teasing look. 'I think it will be a close-run thing...'

'You deserve that I should spank you.'

'Yes, please,' she said, laughing up at him. 'Foolish man, do you not know that I adore you?'

'And no one else will do?'

'I could never love anyone as I love you, Andrew.'

'Nor I,' he said. 'We are fortunate, Mariah. Not many people love as we do.'

His lips brushed hers gently, sending a thrill of pleasure winging through her. She arched towards him, feeling a surge of desire and knowing a fervent longing to be in his arms, his bed, as one.

'I can hardly wait to lie with you,' he murmured huskily. 'But I feel we must control our need and do our duty to our friends—a pleasant duty, I think?'

'Yes, of course. We have such good friends,' Mariah murmured her approval. They were nearly at the house. For the next few hours they must entertain and welcome their guests and would have little time for private conversation.

That night, when the lavish reception was over and their guests had all gone and she lay in his arms, warm and satiated with love, she would tell him of her suspicions. A few weeks in Spain would be sufficient for their honeymoon, because her wandering days were done and she was looking forward to the future at Lanchester with her husband and the children they would have.